Also by Roberta Rich
and Gallery Books

*The Midwife of Venice*
*The Harem Midwife*

Praise for Roberta Rich's Previous Bestselling Novel
*The Midwife of Venice*

"Rich's fascinating historical details and her warm empathy for her protagonists will capture historical fiction fans and readers who enjoyed Anita Diamant's *The Red Tent.*"

—*Library Journal*

"A cliffhanger-strewn debut . . . [A] breathless historical adventure."

—*Kirkus Reviews*

"An engrossing, well-written, and fast-paced story about a fascinating period in history. The descriptions of sixteenth-century Venice were so vivid, they were almost tangible."

—Joy Fielding, *New York Times* bestselling
author of *Now You See Her*

"Riveting and compulsively readable, *The Midwife of Venice* combines fast-paced adventure with richly evocative historical writing."

—*Fresh Fiction*

"Successfully captures the seedy side of sixteenth-century Venice."

—*Publishers Weekly*

"A compelling and engaging novel, a well-researched high-stakes drama written with elegance and compassion: fascinating!"

—Sandra Gulland, internationally bestselling
author of The Josephine B. Trilogy

"Rich skillfully incorporates a wealth of historical detail into her riveting tale of a heroine who won't give up on her marriage."

—*Chicago Tribune*

"By definition, novels set in Venice must exude atmosphere, and this one positively drips with it. . . . Rich capably depicts the strength of women and the precariousness of their lives."

—*The Globe and Mail* (Canada)

"A meticulously researched page-turner that evokes renaissance Venice with remarkable clarity, radiance, and vigor."

—William Deverell, award-winning author
of *Kill All the Lawyers*

"A suspenseful tale. . . . The book is obviously well researched, and its descriptions of Venice and Malta are both fascinating and realistic."

—*Vancouver Sun*

"One of the best novels to be written in the genre of historical fiction since *The Girl with the Pearl Earring*."

—*Blogcritics*

"Not only did Roberta Rich transport me to sixteenth century Venice with its seductive tapestry of smells, sights, textures, and beliefs—she involved me in a poignant story of seasoned love. I don't know which I admired more."

—Katherine Ashenburg, author of *The Dirt on Clean:
An Unsanitized History*

"Beautifully conceived. . . . The pages fly by."

—*Historical Novels Review*

"Enticing. . . . Exotic perfumes and foul odors almost seem to waft off the page."

—*The Toronto Star*

# THE
# JAZZ CLUB
# SPY

A Novel

## Roberta Rich

*Gallery Books*

NEW YORK  LONDON  TORONTO  SYDNEY  NEW DELHI

# G

Gallery Books

An Imprint of Simon & Schuster, Inc.

1230 Avenue of the Americas

New York, NY 10020

First Gallery Books trade paperback edition December 2023

GALLERY BOOKS and colophon are registered trademarks of Simon & Schuster, Inc.

For information about special discounts for bulk purchases, please contact Simon & Schuster Special Sales at 1-866-506-1949 or business@simonandschuster.com.

The Simon & Schuster Speakers Bureau can bring authors to your live event. For more information or to book an event, contact the Simon & Schuster Speakers Bureau at 1-866-248-3049 or visit our website at www.simonspeakers.com.

Interior design by Paul Dippolito

Manufactured in the United States of America

1   3   5   7   9   10   8   6   4   2

Library of Congress Cataloging-in-Publication Data is available.

ISBN 978-1-9821-9131-3

ISBN 978-1-9821-9132-0 (ebook)

*To my sister, Alice Rich, with all my love*

A spy in the right place is as good as 20,000 men in the field.

—*Napoleon Bonaparte*


And Moses sent them to spy out the land of Canaan, and said unto them, Get you up this way southward, and go up into the mountain:

And see the land, what it is, and the people that dwelleth therein, whether they be strong or weak, few or many;

And what the land is that they dwell in, whether it be good or bad; and what cities they be that they dwell in, whether in tents, or in strongholds;

And what the land is, whether it be fat or lean, whether there be wood therein, or not. And be ye of good courage, and bring of the fruit of the land. Now the time was the time of the first-ripe grapes.

—*Numbers 13:17–20*

# THE
# JAZZ CLUB
# SPY

# Prologue

*Stulchyn, The Ukraine*
*January 1920*

Horses do not trample children, not even dead children. That's why I wasn't afraid. Not at first.

I heard the Cossacks before I saw them. I was in the henhouse. Ma had sent me to collect eggs for breakfast. I was placing them in a rush basket lined with straw when the thunder of hooves, the snorting of horses, harsh shouts, and the metal clang of swords reached me. Soon there were other sounds—women and girls weeping, the screams of men and boys.

I ran to the window of the coop and saw a dozen soldiers in the distance. Even though I had never seen them before, I knew who they were. Ever since I was a baby, I'd heard stories of the Cossacks, the czar's special troops, and their terrifying attacks.

I couldn't stay in the chicken coop. The Cossacks would come for our plump hens and anything else they could eat or stuff in their saddlebags, including me. I was five, old enough to know that the Cossacks' taste for little children was as strong as their thirst for vodka.

But where could I go? The river was too far, the banks too steep. I would fall in and freeze. I wore my nightie with the blue and red flowers and the red hat my *bubbe* had knit for me. Running was no use. I must hide. But where? I could sprint to our cottage where Ma, my sister Bekka, and baby Yossel were, but the soldiers would catch me. I was the fastest girl my age in our *shtetl*, our village, but no girl can outrun a horse. There were no forests, no trees to conceal me. Because it was such a cold winter, Count Oshefsky, who owned our village, had ordered the woodlands chopped down for firewood: first the ash, then the pines, then the birch, then the oak.

The Cossacks were headed for our village square. I could see the hoofprints, big as dinner plates, their horses left in the snow. I smelled the stink of the pig fat they used to grease their saddles. I watched through the window of the coop as two Cossacks left their comrades and approached our cottage. One was old with rings of fat around his neck. In his hand, he held a pine torch, which he touched to the roof. Whoosh, and soon it was orange flames. I expected Ma and Bekka to run out with baby Yossel in their arms, but no one appeared. Had they escaped? Or worse, were they trapped inside? My fear turned to anger, and I wiped away the salty tears that dripped down my cheeks.

I yelled at them to go away, but they paid no attention. I straightened and, through the window, threw eggs, warm from the broody hens, at the soldiers. One hit the hindquarters of a horse, making him skitter and buck. I ducked down again. Through the window, I saw the other soldier, a young man around Bekka's age, force his horse in a circle, sawing the iron bit back and forth until its mouth was torn and bloody, and trot toward me. I made myself as small as possible. The Cossack looked more like a dybbuk from a nightmare than a man. His eyes were cold and blue. His lips curved up like a scimitar. A *papakha*, the traditional hat made of sheepskin, sat high on top of his head like a drum, and from his neck swung a leather pouch, probably filled with the bones of small children. He whirled his *nagaika*, his whip, over his head. His stallion reared up, hooves pawing the air like drunken peasants throwing punches outside the village tavern. But before he could reach me, his comrade with the torch shouted to him, and they both galloped toward the shul. I started to panic, afraid for Pa, who attended morning prayers.

I let out the breath I was holding. Desperate, I snuck a peek through the the loose boards in the back of the hen house. A few feet away, I spotted the carcass of my bubbe's cow, Laska, twenty feet away. The fawn-colored Laska with her soft brown eyes had died of old age when the ground was too frozen to bury her. The vultures and crows had picked her bones clean. An idea swooped into my head. The Cossacks would not see me curled inside Laska. I murmured a *broche*, a prayer, in thanks. She had given me her rich milk. Now she would give me the gift of her bones. God and Laska would keep me safe.

I hiked up my nightie to my knees, opened the door of the coop, and ran, crouching low. Laska's carcass was a white mound, covered in snow, straw, and chicken droppings. I tugged aside her skull. Luckily, I was small for my age. After wiggling and squirming, I jammed myself in, as snug as an egg in its shell. My head, covered in my red cap, stuck out of the opening where Laska's calves used to come from. I was safe, but what of Ma, Bekka, and Yossel? And Pa? Where were they?

I shouldn't look, but I couldn't help myself. I pried apart two ribs and peered out to see the village square, where the Cossacks were shouting and waving their swords and pine torches. Despite the cold, sweat trickled down my back.

Uncle Tubal and my cousin Saul ran past, their *peyot*, sidelocks, fluttering around their ears. Their prayer shawls flapped, the fringes whipping back and forth underneath their jackets.

Rabbi Avram sat propped against the stump of an oak. His clothes were streaked with horse dung and filth. He hugged the Sefer Torah, the Holy Scroll, to his chest. Someone had cut off his sidelocks and beard, leaving bloody slashes on his cheeks and chin. I opened my mouth to call to him. Then I noticed his guts spilling out of his belly like the measuring tape tumbling out of Ma's sewing basket.

I forced myself to look away, bile in my throat, as sparks shot into the air like giant fireflies. The timbers of the shul caught fire, smoked, smoldered, and then crashed to the ground with a thump. If I squinted, I could see inside the shul. The altar cloth my mother had embroidered with gold thread curled up in the heat. The candlesticks were gone. The silver kiddush cups were gone. My breakfast porridge turned hard in my belly.

The Cossacks fanned out, setting fire to the straw roofs of cottages, attacking our neighbors with bayonets as they rushed out of their homes. My friend Rachel had a wound on her neck and she staggered through the snow, calling for her ma, leaving a trail of blood behind her. I saw more things I didn't want to see. My cousins Betta and Zofia lay in the snow holding hands, as though they had dropped to the ground in the middle of a game of statues. The horses swerved to avoid them.

I shut my eyes and kept them closed for a long time. Laska's ribs poked into my back and legs, but I pretended they were Ma's arms hugging me tight. *It will be over soon, Giddy.* Ma always said this when bad things happened. Any minute, she would come and scoop me into her arms. Until then, I would be brave. I imagined myself snuggled in her bed, wrapped in a goose-down quilt, dreaming of a warm spring morning, golden wheat rippling in the field, and new lambs bleating for their ewes in the meadow.

When I opened my eyes again, all was still except for the *boom boom* of my heart and the odd snap of burning wood. Had the Cossacks ridden off?

The wind had stolen the heat from my body. I shivered in my

nightie and red knitted cap. I was turning into a block of ice. It was not possible to survive outside in the winter in our mountain village unless you were fat or had lots of furs to wrap yourself in. I was not fat.

No matter how I twisted, I couldn't pry apart Laska's ribs. I had slipped inside easily in the morning sun, but now the cold had frozen her solid. I tried to squirm my way out, but her bones were as hard as the iron hoops around a barrel. Maybe I hadn't been so smart to hide inside Laska. It was no use surviving the Cossacks' attack if I froze to death. I tried to get free, but my arms and legs were stiff. I gripped the little finger of my left hand in the palm of my right and squeezed. Sometimes this helped me stay calm. More time passed. I had to pee.

I craned my neck, trying to see if anyone was around to help, but there was no one.

"Ma," I called softly at first, then I cried louder, "Help me, Ma."

"Giddy?" A faint voice carried across the wind.

"Ma?" I yelled.

"Giddy! Where are you?"

"I'm here! I'm here!"

I peered out between Laska's ribs. Relief flooded me at the sight of my ma running toward me with baby Yossel tucked under her arm like a loaf of challah.

But then the air once again filled with the peaty smell of horse. The two Cossacks from before returned and galloped toward me.

"No!" Ma screamed. "Stop! Leave her alone!" But they didn't stop. She picked up a piece of smoldering timber and hurled it at the soldiers. It hit the older one in the back of the head. His face darkened and he turned his horse toward her. I watched as he bent down, seized her by her braid, and swung her onto his saddle as if she weighed no more than me. Yossel flew out of her arms like a melon falling out of a huckster's wagon, then rolled a few feet. His head came to rest with a wet thud against a rain barrel.

I strained against Laska's ribs, folding my legs under me so I could thrust my way out. It was no use. I let out a scream. I clawed at the bones, breaking my nails and bruising my cold-clumsy fingers. I flung my body against Laska's bones, but the carcass didn't give way. I gashed my arms trying to reach between the ribs, like bars of a cage. Blood soaked my nightie.

All I could see were a horse's hooves approaching. The horse didn't know there was a girl inside this heap of cow bones. He would trample me for certain. I wet myself. My pee warmed me for a second, and then everything went black.

I came to hours later. The sun was low in the smoky sky, the taste of copper was in my mouth, and Ma's arms were around me as she rocked me back and forth. Her clothes were torn and there was blood everywhere, on the snow, on Ma's skirt, and there was Pa, walking toward us, his head low, his hands splattered with blood. But the Cossacks had gone. They had galloped away with the candlesticks from the shul, our red hens, and my childhood.

# Chapter 1

*Midtown Manhattan, New York*
*January 1939*

I pushed open the door of the staff changing room at Sid's Paradise. Good, it was empty. I always got to the jazz club early so I could get ready in peace and still have time to snoop. I discarded my simple wool sheath and sweater and shimmied into my skirt and top. Glancing in the mirror, I adjusted my pillbox with the chin strap until it dipped over one eye, and then shoved my feet into the satin peep-toe pumps that made me feel as tall as the Chrysler Building.

My bodice, red with black trim, was cut low, the cups ample enough to hold dollar bills. I'm kind of chicken skinny in the chest department, so I tucked in a couple of foam pyramids to keep my bubbies company. Men like big bubbies, which is the only reliable thing I know about the opposite sex. Out of habit, I tugged down the sleeves of my costume to hide the scars that run from my elbows to my wrists. Exactly nineteen years ago today, the Cossacks rampaged through my village. The scars furrowing my arms are a reminder of how brave I had been, how I had tried to wiggle my way out of Laska's knife-sharp bones.

My ma used to say, "The same heat that melts butter hardens steel." I had experienced the worst life could throw at me and I had survived. I guess that made me steel. Now I was in America, the land of opportunity.

But being trapped in Laska's carcass had left me with more than just physical scars. I am uneasy in small spaces. In our tiny berth on the *Homeric*, the ship that brought us to America, I had screamed and cried until my ma took me to sleep on the deck under the stars, where she wrapped me in a thin blanket and held me in a tight embrace. I had the same panicky reaction in rooms without windows, cubicles in public toilets, and elevators. Everyone thinks elevators are the greatest invention since the wheel. No thanks, I'd rather march up the stairs on my two strong legs. The word for this is *claustrophobia*. *Claustrum* is Latin for "a closed-in space," and *phobia* means "fear." I like words. They help me to figure out what I feel. And they make me sound more educated than the average cigarette girl.

I twisted around to catch a glimpse of my back in the mirror. How I longed for a pair of stockings that weren't full of runs and darned holes. Someday, when the rent was paid, the groceries were bought, and the heat and light bill were up to date, I'd get a pair of silk stockings. I imagined the cool, sheer feel and the raspy sound when I crossed my legs. It was easier being broke in Russia, where everyone was poor as Job's turkey. Here in America, the rich were all around me, and at Sid's Paradise, I got a close look at how the wealthy ladies dressed so elegantly and maintained an illusion of porcelain skin and huge eyes without appearing overdone or trashy.

Now I mimicked what I had observed on my own face. I rubbed a layer of Vaseline over my eyelids and powdered them. I scraped a bit of soot from the coffee percolator on the hot plate, mixed it with a few drops of water, and applied a line of black to the base of my eyelashes with a fine brush. I was working on my own formula for real eyeliner made with beeswax, coconut oil, and charcoal, but in the meantime, it was this or nothing. The brown of my irises contrasted nicely with the black soot, making my eyes appear bigger and rounder. Next, I squeezed my lashes between the jaws of my new eyelash curler, then swept on a violet eye shadow I'd created myself. When I was done, I strapped on my tray, which was piled high with Camels, Pall Malls, Luckies, cigars, candy, Planters peanuts, matches, and yo-yos. Schlepping my wares from table to table left me with deep marks on my shoulders, but complaining I was not. I was damn lucky to have this job, especially after getting canned from Grossinger's Ladies' Wear, where I had sewed buttons on ladies' shirtwaists for twelve hours a day. Now I sold Camels to customers every Friday and Saturday and earned two bucks a night plus tips, which was more than I used to earn in a week at Grossinger's.

A final look in the mirror and I was ready for battle. Bumping open the change-room door with my hip, I entered the cocktail lounge of the jazz club. Immediately the smell of smoke, whiskey, and Shalimar perfume hit my nose. Sid's Paradise was bogus tough—not the type of joint where people got shot or knifed, but not the Persian Room at the Plaza Hotel either. It was just sketchy enough that the uptown types could brag about rubbing shoulders with mobsters, crooked building inspectors from city hall with wads of cash, and girls like me who wore red skirts that barely covered their behinds. The patrons also loved the bartender Sam, his vodka gimlets, American jazz, and us cigarette girls.

It was still early, only 9:00 p.m. The maintenance man was scattering shavings from candle stubs on the floor. This made the hardwood floor smooth for the fast dances like the foxtrot, the Lindy, or the Black Bottom, but it was tricky navigating that surface in high-heeled red pumps while carrying a heavy tray.

On the stage, the band was warming up, and when the pianist spotted me, he launched into my favorite, "Puttin' On the Ritz." I gave him a wink and swayed in time to the song.

From his usual seat near the stage, Sid Kravitz, the boss, lifted his index finger like a buyer at a diamond auction on 47th Street. That's all he needed to do to summon any of us girls. "Going to be a full house tonight, sir," I said, plucking a Cohiba cigar from my tray as I sauntered over. I knew exactly what he wanted and exactly how he wanted it done.

Looks are deceiving. Sid is the toughest Jew on the Lower East Side, but you'd never guess that to look at him in his black frock coat, which hit him midthigh—not quite long enough to conceal the *tzitzit*, the strings, that hung from his prayer shawl, but short enough to reveal the bony knees outlined by his gabardine trousers. He could be as cold as a mackerel if someone crossed him, but he took care of me. And once in a while, I took care of him behind the locked door of his office. Nothing that took too long, just the Buffalo handshake. You'd think he had all the action he could handle in that department, but Sid was under a lot of pressure. It wasn't easy running a business. He had to worry about keeping the customers fed and lubricated, the cops off his back, and the staff from stealing too much. For him, it was just a way to unwind, no more sexual than Ma rubbing my feet after hours of standing in these goddamned high heels.

"Hattie sure knows how to bring in the crowds." His voice was quiet and educated. To hear him speak, anyone would assume he was a college professor instead of the owner of a nightclub that had started out as a speakeasy in a one-room apartment in a brownstone on 52nd Street. Now he owned the entire building, and this block of 52nd had become the mecca of jazz and was affectionately called Swing Street.

"She sure does, Mr. Kravitz."

Hattie Feldmar was our headliner and my best friend. She had put in a good word for me with Sid, told him I could speak fluent Russian and converse with all the well-heeled émigrés who sashayed in on the weekend in their black sable and gold cigarette holders. She was the reason I got this job, but I made it up to her in my own special way.

After sniffing the cigar to make sure it was fresh, I slipped off the band and twirled it back and forth next to my ear to check for soundness. When I offered it to Sid, a kitchen match was already in his hand. I turned so my tuchus was ten inches from his hand and waited until he struck the match along the back zipper of my skirt. He waved me away as he touched the flame to his cigar, then puffed to get it going. I started to circulate with my wares.

The hard-drinking regulars and the single men looking for action—sometimes girls, sometimes gambling in the back room—had already begun drifting in. We also got our share of the rougher types—stevedores, truckers, bricklayers, and garbage workers from the city—but they never lingered for longer than a beer or two. Sid made sure of that.

Couples settled at the little round tables and smooched discreetly between sips of gin fizzes. These people in their mink stoles, waltz-length crepe de chine dresses, and dinner jackets didn't worry about the hollow-eyed kids lined up at the curb at closing time, hoping for a few pennies for performing somersaults, juggling, or spinning cartwheels. They just wanted to get a spot near the stage so they could hear every word Hattie the clairvoyant received from the spirit world.

While my friend had a natural gift for second sight, she supplemented her act by using information I gathered. Like Hattie, I had a special talent: my eyes were my third ear. I got my practice at Grossinger's, where dozens of immigrant men and women sat hunched over sewing machines. The room thumped with the vibration of the foot treadles and the whir of the Singers. To make ourselves heard, we all learned to lip-read—in Russian, Hungarian,

Armenian, Polish, Yiddish, and once in a blue moon, English. A regular League of Nations, that place was, may it burn to ashes. For my snooping, Hattie gave me 30 percent of her tips.

As I floated from table to table with my cigarette tray, the band struck up a ragtime tune, and the singer, a slim girl wearing chandelier earrings and a black strapless so tight her ma must have powdered her like a baby to get her zippered in, belted out, "I'll be down to get you in a taxi, honey." What a set of pipes. She drew out the word *honey* like it had ten syllables. Soon the dance floor was full.

After a round of applause, she launched into "My Baby Just Cares for Me" and more people squeezed onto the floor. One couple twirled into a dim corner, and the fellow cupped his hands around the girl's behind as they shuffled to the beat. *It must be a wonderful thing to have such easy familiarity with another person's body,* I thought, glancing at the bar where Mr. Van der Zalm, one of the club regulars, was lounging, a foot on the brass rail.

Me and every other girl at Sid's, and maybe even a couple of the fellows who did the stage lights, had a crush on Mr. V. He had a rich man's confidence, long legs, and teeth as white as a politician's. I made a habit of flirting with the guests—Sid liked us to be friendly—but I could never work up the nerve to approach Mr. V. He was a mystery to me.

He always came in alone and left alone, though there was no shortage of willing girls in the club or at the Hotel Taft across the street. He wasn't a boozer—never drank more than two or three martinis. Nor was he a music lover. He listened to Sid's bands with a neutral expression, and I never saw him dance. He seemed so composed, so self-contained. The only thing he seemed interested in was Hattie's readings—and he often paid for a private session, which she offered to her patrons at the end of her performance. Who, I wondered, might he need to contact in the afterlife?

I had to stop mooning over Mr. V.'s blue eyes. Time to go on the snoop for Hattie. After all, that was the reason I was here. For the next hour, I worked the room, selling cigarettes, matches, breath mints, and gum, and eavesdropping on conversations until Caterina, the Italian girl who worked the hatcheck counter, waved me over.

"Giddy, gotta minute? I need a smoke so bad."

"Sure I do." Her booth was a gold mine of secrets. I often covered for her when she went to use the can or duck outside in the alley for a ciggy—Sid didn't allow staff to drink or smoke on duty.

With a grateful look, Caterina lifted the hinged counter and floated off, letting the men get a good long look at her big caboose. I stowed my tray and turned to the line of waiting customers with a smile, showing my good, straight teeth.

I took mink stoles, Persian lamb jackets, and camel-hair double-breasteds, giving Bakelite tokens in exchange, and as I slipped the luxurious garments onto wooden hangers, I frisked the cool taffeta pockets as expertly as a precinct cop. Tsk, tsk, the things women leave in their coats: hastily scribbled phone numbers on the backs of receipts, lace panties, addresses of unlicensed doctors in Brooklyn, old dance programs, love letters.

Once I found an item that looked like an oversized ladies' compact, but when I opened it, there was no mirror, no powder, no puff, just a dome-shaped device made of flesh-colored rubber. It took a minute before it dawned on me—it was a Dutch cervical cap, designed to prevent a girl from getting knocked up. Another time I came across a pearl-handled revolver. The men were just as bad. They squirreled away bills from seedy hotels, French ticklers, rolls of cash as thick as potato blintzes, and photographs of girls wearing net stockings and not much else. When Caterina returned reeking of a Lucky Strike, I'd gathered enough scuttlebutt for a dozen shows. Time to deliver my report to Hattie.

I snuck backstage to her dressing room and, after a quick knock, let myself in.

"Hi, Giddy, how's by you?" Hattie was sitting in front of her vanity—what she called her rickety table with the cracked mirror from Wosk's Used Furniture—reading a book with a butterfly on the cover. I squinted, trying to make out the title: *Beyond Death* by Edith Pansy Fairweather.

"Some light reading?" I teased.

Hattie met my eyes in the mirror. "You look like Theda Bara in *The Unchastened Woman*. Your eyes are big and round and smoky. I look like something the cats dragged in."

"Not once I get through with you," I said, taking the book from her hand and fishing my makeup kit out of my bag. As always, she started to fidget. "Sit still, for the love of Mike. You'd think I was about to cut you open with a rusty kitchen knife and yank out your appendix."

I could talk to her like this because we'd know each other since we were kids and I'd rescued her from the clutches of Pavel, the school bully. He had been pointing at her leg brace and calling her a cripple and a "three-legged freak." I've always had a soft spot for underdogs, and Hattie was a scrawny Jewish girl from Russia like me. The only difference was she got polio the year after her family arrived in America. Anyway, I felt bad for her, so I screamed at Pavel, shoved him into the drinking fountain, then took out my hanky.

As I was wiping off Hattie's snot and tears, she said in a sad little voice, "Sometimes I wonder if I would have got polio if we'd stayed in Russia. One thing is for sure, they never would have admitted me to America the way I am now."

I said, "God took away your leg, but perhaps he will give you something in exchange."

"That's an optimistic way to look at it," she'd replied, in an unconvincing tone of voice.

We'd been pals ever since. Later she told me she had given Pavel's girlfriend a reading and predicted he would end up behind bars before he was old enough to shave his pimply face, which hadn't sat well with him. Think what you want about clairvoyants, but Pavel did get arrested for robbing a dry cleaner on Broome Street.

Since grade school, I'd filled out everywhere except in the chest department, but Hattie still looked like an underfed child. The starving-seer look, combined with her deep brassy voice, gave her stage presence, though, and for tonight's performance, she was dressed to kill in a bombazine dress with a graceful scoop neck and a full skirt that hid her leg brace. Around a graceful scoop neckline hung a string of pearls that, who knew, might have been the real McCoy. Hattie had been doing her clairvoyant act at Sid's for four years. She also gave private readings. In hard times, like now, everybody wanted Hattie's advice, from hotshot financiers to cutters and pressers in the garment district. While she never named names, she hinted that a few were very generous.

The dodge the two of us had going at Sid's was working well, but I wanted to open my own store selling beauty products. Faces—all faces, not just beautiful ones—interested me. When we came to America, Pa bought me a set of pastel oil crayons and I drew portraits of everyone in shul. I got pretty good. Catholic neighbors who couldn't afford a photographer to take pictures at funerals sometimes hired me to sketch a likeness of the corpse. But my passion was makeup, and I was tip-top at mixing creams, lotions, and cosmetics—everything a girl needed to look more like Marlene Dietrich and less like a JOTB, or in other words, a greenhorn just off the boat. Face paint, Ma called it. To me, it was war paint.

But I was just an immigrant girl with no education, money, or connections. My family depended on me, and if I failed, we would be out on the street, going to Jewish charities where those hotsy-totsy German Jews looked down their noses at us Ashkenazi Jews from the shtetls of eastern Europe. They curled their lips at us Ostjuden. The tiny nest egg I'd managed to amass would melt away faster than a hot fudge sundae in August. The thought occurred to me: Maybe Mr. V. in his fancy suits was a banker. Maybe he could be my backup plan.

As I began to cleanse Hattie's face with my special lanolin cold cream, I asked, "Are those real pearls you got on? The mitt-reading business must be booming."

Her hand flew to her neck. "Private sessions. This Russian from God knows where. Doesn't speak a lick of English."

"Oh, I thought they might be from Mr. V. What does he ask you about anyway?"

Hattie shook her head. The river of information flowed in one direction. From me to her.

"He's here again tonight. Is he a banker? He looks like one."

"What's your fascination with him? Did you see him in the gents' or something?"

My cheeks grew warm. I had. On nights when I didn't get behind the hatcheck counter, I would rifle through handbags in the ladies' washroom. I couldn't sneak into the men's, but if I went upstairs, there was a knothole in the floor right over the urinals. I could hear everything pretty well and see the men standing there, schlongs out, chatting to each other or Winston, the Jamaican fellow who handed out towels and soap.

Winston and I were pals. Last week when I lost my key to my locker in the staff dressing room, he gave me a lesson on how to pick a lock using a hairpin. A useful skill in my profession. I practiced on the vestibule door of my tenement building until I had it down pat.

I could get that door open faster with a hairpin than I could fish the key out of my pocketbook.

Winston did more than hand out toiletries. He also asked the men if they were looking for company after the club closed. If I ever got desperate for money, I could count on him to direct men my way. May it not come to that.

Hattie interrupted my thoughts. "From the way you're blushing, you have. Toque or baldy?" she asked.

"I didn't notice," I lied, busying myself by squeezing a tiny amount of mascara onto a brush.

"Like hell. I'm guessing baldy."

"Lucky guess."

This was a game we played. *Toque* was a word I'd picked up from a French Canadian customer that meant a knitted cap for winter. *Baldy*, well, that's self-explanatory. Hattie kept score on the back of an old playbill from when Josephine Baker appeared at the club; so far it was toques seven, baldies twenty-four. Most men were circumcised, even Gentiles.

"Now look up at the ceiling," I commanded. Hattie's eyes were her best feature—round and luminous but fringed with pale lashes. Hattie acquiesced, and I applied the mascara with light strokes, making her lashes appear long and thick. "For the *pièce de résistance*, which means the best part, I got something I want to try." I presented my latest creation, a box about the size of a Lucky's cigarette package, containing the essential components—rouge, eye shadow, and foundation—all neatly arranged. I had designed this to be small so girls could slip it into their pockets or evening purses. "I made this last week."

"Very nice." Nothing in her voice made me think she was either impressed or interested in my invention. Hattie could be such a pill sometimes.

As I dabbed foundation on her face with a small sponge, I asked, "So, you never answered my question. Is Mr. V. a banker?"

Hattie blinked, making the mascara smear. "No, he's a big cheese on Ellis Island, director of immigration or something like that. He pretty much runs the whole show. Satisfied? Now, let's have the snoop report, Sherlock."

I was disappointed but tried not to show it, and then launched in. "A Russian woman, high-class, with a gorgeous amber necklace and a rock the size of a monkey's testicle—"

Hattie shot me an irritated look. She didn't like me to kid around during our briefings. "Get on with it."

"Then stop interrupting. As I was saying, this woman, who's sitting at table fifteen near the stage, was upset. I heard her whisper to her companion that she couldn't stand another loss, that Irina's death had made her feel so guilty."

"And Irina is . . . ?"

"A French poodle? A baby? An aunt? Who knows?" Hattie just needed a few vague facts to start her reading, then she got the customer to fill in the details. It was uncanny to see her in action. "She's wearing a black strapless shantung sheath cut on the bias, kick pleat. Gardenia corsage."

"What else?"

"Wait till I tell you. I got gold—pure gold."

"Gold, I need."

I mixed some white pigment with the pink on the back of my hand and added a drop of water. "Hold still." As I applied it to her cheeks, I told her about the older woman from Hoboken who'd checked her coat. "Inside the pocket was a photo of a smiling family on a sunny beach, and on the back, in smeared ink, were the words 'Teddy, nine years RIP.'"

Hattie's eyes lit up. "Good work. What's she wearing?"

"One of those tulle skirts with a dozen crinolines underneath that rustle with every movement. Know the kind I mean? The older ladies wear them." I don't know why I bothered to ask. Hattie had as much interest in fashion as I have in playing first base for the Yankees.

For the next few minutes, I fussed and painted and powdered as I fed Hattie nuggets of information. Sometimes I felt guilty snooping through people's personal effects, but then I reminded myself that Hattie was like a priest or a rabbi, soothing customers' grief by delivering messages from loved ones. Sometimes I wondered if Hattie could be a comfort to Ma. Maybe put her in touch with Bekka or baby Yossel.

Pushing the thought from my mind, I snapped the lid of my kit closed and stood back to admire my handiwork.

"How do I look?" Hattie asked, twisting to catch her reflection in the cracked mirror. With her Dutch-boy haircut and solemn expression, she looked like the figure on the Quaker Oats can, assuming there was such a thing as a Jewish Quaker.

"You look every bit the mysterious psychic." In fact, she looked not too bad. Her skin had some luster, the dark circles had disappeared, and her eyes were brighter. "Break a leg out there, Hattie," I said like I always did before she went onstage. Hattie was superstitious about me wishing her good luck.

"Thanks for your help," she said.

There was a knock at the door. I picked up my tray and headed to the lounge.

It was showtime.

# Chapter 2

———◇———

*Midtown Manhattan, New York*

Hattie was at her best. Like most psychics, she started slow and teased details from the customers, or made shrewd guesses from their reactions, like whether they nodded or shifted in their chairs. At first, she stuck to vague comments that could apply to any Tom, Dick, or Helen—"I sense you're the type of person who others like and admire." Who isn't likely to puff out their chests and agree? Or "I sense that someone close to you passed away recently." And for older patrons, "I think you've had a health scare." As she worked the crowd, wowing them with her extraordinary powers, I stood in the wings, open-mouthed. Me, who had fed her information. When she got to the story of Irina, the Russian woman leaned forward in her seat. Apparently, Irina was her daughter back home who had died of pneumonia. It made me think of Bekka and wonder, as I often did, how she had died. Her body had never been recovered after the pogrom. Had she died in the fire that had destroyed our village? Been slaughtered by a Cossack, her body left for the wolves to devour? Had it been a quick and painless death? I didn't know. Pa would never speak of it. Ma told me once, when she was in her cups, that as soon as she heard the Cossacks, she ran with Yossel to the cemetery and crouched behind a tombstone. But when I asked about Bekka, she clammed up.

After the show, Hattie had her private sessions. Cunning little

Hattie. This was where the real lettuce was. I imagine it was at these times she was at her most convincing and the customer was most relaxed and willing to part with lots of cash. What she earned in these sessions was all hers. I didn't get my usual cut, more's the pity.

Her stream of private customers took longer than usual, and by the time I got to her dressing room, it was 2:00 a.m. Her mascara had run again, and she looked like a photo I'd once seen of a baby raccoon. If I could invent waterproof mascara, I'd be rich as John D. Rockefeller. I took a paper napkin, spit on a corner, and wiped away the smears under her eyes.

"God, nobody knows how strenuous it is being a clairvoyant," she said.

"Or being a cigarette girl," I added.

"And how it works up an appetite. Fancy a bowl of soup?"

"You're not waiting for Mr. V. to come in for a reading?"

"Mr. V. again?" Hattie threw me an eye roll. "Not tonight. I think he slipped out after my show. Shall we then?"

I nodded and we left the club and made our way along the garbage-strewn pavement, past clusters of unemployed men huddled on the corners, Heinz's famous fifty-foot pickle sign, and the Flatiron Building on Fifth Avenue. At last, we reached the Horn & Hardart's Automat on Eighth Avenue.

"The miracle of the Automat," said Hattie, leaning on her crutch. "The feeding of the multitude one nickel at a time, twenty-four hours a day."

Hattie was always quoting the New Testament, which was an odd thing for a Jewish girl to do, but then Hattie was an odd girl. It was one of the reasons I loved her.

"You can't argue with their prices or their food," I said.

Inside, the brightly lit restaurant was filled with shiny Formica tables and matching metal seats. Tiny glass windows like miniature aquarium's covered three walls. Behind every window was something mouthwatering. A tuna fish sandwich on white, a bowl of tapioca with a maraschino cherry on top. For the hot food, there were steam tables filled with macaroni and cheese, Salisbury steak with mashed potatoes, beef stew, maybe fish chowder if you were lucky. If you weren't so lucky—creamed spinach. Genuine American food, not a knish or a piece of *helzel*, stuffed chicken neck, in sight.

I steered Hattie to a table, then went to fetch us some food.

In front of a grilled cheese sandwich, I did like the sign instructed: "First drop your nickels in the slot. Then turn the knob. The glass door clicks open. Lift the door and help yourself."

I also got a bowl of vegetable soup for Hattie and a piece of apple pie à la mode for me, then carried the tray to our table and placed the sandwich and soup in front of Hattie, waving away her offer of a dime. Hattie nodded her thanks and dug in. Between mouthfuls, she rummaged around in her purse and slid several bills across the table to me, 30 percent of her tips. I counted them before I tucked them away. Six bucks. Not bad for a night's work.

"So, Helena Rubinstein, how are the plans coming along for your shop?" she asked.

"I've got my eye on a storefront. My plan is to start small, then expand as more customers come in. Great Depression or not, I'm going to do it. I'll call my creams 'skin food' and cater to sweatshop girls."

Hattie smiled. "Poor girls got the right to look nice, too. So are you leaving me without a partner at Sid's?"

"I've got to take a chance or I'll get nowhere. But you won't be rid of me yet. I'll hang on to my job at the club."

"You should work two jobs?"

"At first."

"No," Hattie said. "If you've only got one tuchus, you can only dance at one wedding."

I laughed. "My bubbe used to say that." I took a bite of pie. The apples were tart and tasty, and the crust was just right. "If all goes well, I can take better care of my family. We could move out of the tenements, maybe get a flat in the Bronx. A better place to live would cheer Ma up. Ma's never gotten over Yossel's and Bekka's deaths. She shouldn't have to sew police uniforms for Mr. Portnoy, Arnold could go to City College . . ."

"You're a good daughter, Giddy. And as for Bekka and Yossel? There was nothing you could have done."

"So many died in the pogrom. It haunts me. Older people, kids like me, even the rabbi. Why did God spare me of all people? He must have had a reason. I figure that reason was to succeed in America. To become a somebody."

"And you will. I feel that." Hattie placed her hand over mine. "As tight as things are here, it's nothing compared to the old country. When I was a kid, a schmear of schmaltz on a piece of stale bread was a treat. My bubbe sewed a secret pocket in the underside of my apron and then sent me out to roam the countryside. When I came across something on the road, or in someone's yard, I asked myself, Can I eat it, burn it, or wear it? And if the answer was yes, I stuffed it in my apron. My father, God bless him, sold a few sacks of wheat every fall to save for our passage money. I'll never forget standing on the deck of our ship, watching the Statue of Liberty as we pulled into New York Harbor. Welcome to America. The land of the free, the home of the brave and infantile paralysis. Still, if not for my father, we'd still be in Russia living on our knees like peasants, instead of here in America where a working girl can hold her head up high."

Hattie didn't want anyone's sympathy, especially mine. Not that I would say this, but it was her mother's fault Hattie got polio. I probably would have caught it, too, except Ma hung a fresh bulb of garlic around my neck every day before I left for school. In the summer, she never allowed me to go to movies or parks or play with other kids. Since losing Bekka and Yossel in the pogrom, she fussed over me like I was a baby, even after Arnold came along.

I looked down at my empty pie plate. Hattie's speech got me thinking of my own pa, who had left us two years ago. Because of him, I had to work doubly hard to keep the three of us afloat. As resentful as I was of him, I would forever be thankful that he somehow found the money to bring us to America, especially with what was happening in Europe now.

Just four years ago, Germany passed the Nuremberg Laws, which declared that Jews were no longer considered German citizens and prohibited them from marrying Gentiles and working in certain professions. There were rumors of Jews being resettled by shipping them off in trains headed east into Poland and Czechoslovakia. Photos of Nazi soldiers goose-stepping through the streets of Munich filled the newspapers. At the Tivoli Theatre, I watched Pathé newsreels of Hitler spewing his hatred in every speech.

Fascism was spreading faster through Europe than diphtheria and whooping cough through the tenements. In England, the Blackshirts, a fascist group, demonstrated by marching through Jewish neighborhoods, provoking violence. Even here in America, we had the German American Bund, who just last week held a rally in Jersey lead by the criminal Fritz Kuhn, who referred to President Roosevelt as Franklin Rosenfeld and the New Deal as the "Jew Deal."

By the time Hattie and I left the Automat, it was dawn. The sun was trying to shine through the gray sky and an icy gale was coming off the East River, sharp as a knife.

We shivered like we had Saint Vitus' dance as we waited for the number 56 streetcar. A small group was huddled around the stop. At first glance, they appeared to be well-dressed businessmen until their worn shoes, threadbare suits, and thin faces gave them away.

These men were unemployed but putting up a brave front by going out every morning to look for nonexistent jobs. They reminded me of my pa, at least before he abandoned us.

The streetcar lumbered to a stop in front of us. I offered my arm to Hattie, but she brushed me away and hopped up the first stair of the platform with her good leg. Gripping the railing, she half threw, half lifted her other leg with its heavy iron brace onto the step, then repeated the process until she reached the top.

She ignored the look of pity in the driver's eyes and we shuffled along to find seats. It was a much later streetcar than we usually caught, but it held a crush of passengers. The lucky few with jobs were returning from the graveyard shift. The unlucky many rode the streetcar all day to dodge the January wind and enjoy the steamy warmth of the heat vents.

We squeezed into a seat, the bell rang, and off we went. Out of habit, I began scrutinizing the faces around me. My eyes moved over an old woman wearing a babushka with a shopping bag full of cleaning supplies between her ankles and a distraught young mother holding a whimpering baby, and landed on a man who took a seat on the opposite bench. He looked so familiar I almost nodded hello. He was brawny and wore a hat of sheepskin patched together with leftover bits of rabbit fur and mink for the crown.

The effect was comically old country. I was about to nudge Hattie, but something made me pause. I remembered such hats—some with earflaps—from my old village Stulchyn. His overcoat, too, marked him as Russian, maybe a *kulak*, a wealthy peasant, from near where my family was from. I tried to think where I had seen him before. In the neighborhood? From Sid's Paradise? A peddler from Hester Street Market?

The streets were filled with men who dressed just like him, yet he had an interesting face—all planes and angles and shadows, like one of those Stalinist posters for farm collectivization reprinted in *Life* magazine. There was a coarseness to his mouth. My fingers itched to draw him. If only I had a paper and pencil with me.

He must have felt my gaze because he looked up, and when his cold blue eyes met mine, my hands went to my arms and the old scars there. My body remembered before my mind caught up. I looked away. Was it even possible to recognize someone from so many years ago? I snuck another peek at him. He was older now by nineteen years, his beard flecked with gray, his eyelids droopy, and his jowls like loose chicken skin. But the eyes and flat cheekbones had not changed. If I could hear him speak, listen to his accent, find out if he spoke in the same harsh, guttural Russian of our region, I could at least figure out if he was from around my village.

The ticket collector came down the aisle and stopped in front of the man, waiting for him to cough up his fare. I leaned forward, hoping he would say something, but he just tugged off his glove, reached in his coat pocket, and handed over a coin. Then the ticket collector moved on to the next passenger. The tip of the man's little finger was missing. A scrap of memory surfaced. It was hazy at first, then it took form and shape—the taste of blood and cartilage and bone and the scent of fear and the sounds of heart-stopping screams.

I had bitten off that finger. It was the Cossack.

# Chapter 3

The Cossack exited the tram a few stops before me. Hattie had already disembarked, so I hopped off, planning to follow him, but he melted into the crowd of passengers waiting to get on. Frustrated, I headed home. Perhaps I could sketch his likeness before his face disappeared from my mind. I raced the rest of the way. When I reached our tenement on Cherry Street, I took the stairs two at a time all the way to the third floor. Our apartment was just three rooms—a front parlor facing the street; a kitchen, where Arnold slept on a cot; and a small windowless bedroom, which didn't help my claustrophobia, for me and Ma.

In the parlor, Ma's sewing work cluttered the space. Pieces of garments were draped everywhere, and the ironing board occupied a permanent position in the middle of the room, but the place was *heymish*, homey, thanks to me. I'd cut and pasted pictures from the Sunday *Post* on the walls. There were photos of children on shiny bikes eating ice cream cones, and even one of President Roosevelt waving his long cigarette holder from the back seat of his limousine.

It was still early, but my brother Arnold was already up, his school bag slung over his shoulder.

"Giddy? You look like you've seen a ghost."

"It's nothing. I'm fine." He was always able to read me like a book. "Is Ma awake?"

"Still sleeping," he replied. "She had a couple belts of schnapps last night."

I sighed. Drinking isn't a Jewish thing. All the gossips in the neighborhood carped, commented, and condemned. In our tenement, privacy didn't exist. We knew when Mrs. Shapiro—the Yenta of Cherry Street—made matzo ball soup; when Mr. Berkovitz in 3C farted, which was often; when Mrs. O'Riley's waters broke; and when poor sixteen-year-old Ruth Pokorny died from a back-alley abortion. And *they* all heard when Ma had too much to drink, because she sang sentimental songs and burst into tears over the words of her favorites. Privacy is a luxury only the rich can afford.

"Don't worry. I got her to bed before she started warbling 'My Yiddishe Momme.'"

"No mention of life in the old country?"

"I headed her off."

"Good."

Arnold didn't know the circumstances that caused us to leave our homeland and he didn't need to. He was a real American, born the year we arrived in the States. All he knew about our life in Russia was that it had been difficult and that Ma had had a baby, Yossel, who died. But he wasn't aware of Bekka. Bekka's death was a forbidden topic in the house. It was better for him that way. He had to focus on the future because I had big dreams for him. Not only was he an excellent student but he had a part-time job at the Tivoli sweeping up after the Saturday matinee. A few more months of high school and then, may God be listening, City College of New York.

I stepped back, taking in his smart black jacket and trousers. He had grown up to be as handsome as the movie star Errol Flynn. I used to drop him off at the boys' entrance to his grammar school, one chubby hand clutching mine, the other his lunch bucket filled with schmaltz sandwiches on rye. Now he was a somber eighteen-year-old who attended the free lectures down by Cooper Union and railed on about the Spanish Civil War, Bolsheviks, and the perfidy of union busters. Fortunately, Arnold was an armchair anarchist, not a bomb thrower.

He studied my face for a moment. "You sure you're fine?"

"Yes, it was just a long night."

"All right." He adjusted his bag. "I'm off to the library to study. Then a lecture by Emma Goldman."

I raised my eyebrow. Goldman was a firebrand—a radical and a supporter of women's rights and free love. "Forget about being an anarchist. There's no money in it. Anarchy is just a stage you're going through, like teething, or throwing tantrums, or stealing penny candy from the corner store. Instead of getting up on a soapbox, go to law school. There's no shortage of underdogs to defend: tenants being gouged by landlords, deserted mothers stealing food for their kids, union organizers arrested for disturbing the peace. With a law degree you can make the world a better place."

"I'm already halfway there. No judge would give me as hard a time as you and Ma."

"You could be the first one in the family to go to college. I'm serious. You could be a somebody."

"You should go, too, Giddy."

"Fat chance. City College may be free, but I still have to support you and pay for your books. No, you are our future." I gave him a hug, then pushed him out the door. "Go to the library. Study. Such a genius you are. I'm so proud of you."

Arnold turned back, an amused expression on his face. "Thanks, Giddy," he said before bounding down the stairs.

Someone in the family had to *kvell*, gush, over him. Ma certainly didn't. When Ma looked at Arnold, I knew she wished she was looking at Yossel. I closed the door.

After Arnold was born, Ma often had dark moods. When one struck her, she would stay in bed, face turned to the wall. On those days, I would take Arnold to Mrs. O'Riley to nurse. If she wasn't home, I'd just prop a bottle on a pillow next to him and shove the nipple in his mouth. I would leave small pieces of bread and jam on the rail of his crib before I left for school so he would have something to nosh on when he woke up. They say that in America the children bring up the parents, but that's only half-true. The children also bring up each other.

Then for a while, things were good. Ma got a well-paying job uptown at an exclusive ladies' lingerie shop where she sewed dainty French seams on silk, satin, and fine chambray negligees. Pa was still working as a fur cutter at Goldstein's then. We were happy. There's a photo of the four of us in Seward Park. In the picture, Ma is sitting on a bench holding Arnold on her knee, looking a bit stiff, but I'm nuzzled next to her and Pa is standing behind us, his hand on Ma's shoulder. That was before the Depression put him out of work.

But Ma and Arnold's relationship was always strained. I remembered a conversation I'd overheard years ago—one of many I tried to forget. Ma had been frying eggs. Arnold, who must have been about ten years old, sat in the kitchen, elbows on the table, blowing on his glass of hot milky tea. "You don't seem to like me as much as you like Giddy," he'd said. "Is it because I'm a boy? Or because I don't look like you? Or because I sassed you when I was little or skipped school? Is there something about myself I can change? Or is it the way I am?" Ma had said nothing, just grabbed the spatula and flipped his eggs. It had broken my heart to listen.

With Arnold out the door, I tiptoed into the bedroom I shared with Ma. She was snoring, her mouth agape. The room stank of booze. It embarrassed me, Ma's drinking. For that I was ashamed. And then I was ashamed of being ashamed. With everything she'd been through, she was entitled to a nip occasionally.

As quietly as I could, I retrieved my sketch pad and colored pencils and retreated to the parlor. The window was about the size of an eviction notice and grimy with coal dust, but there was enough light to draw. I focused my mind on the man on the tram—the hat, the heavy slab of a face, the jowls and downturned mouth, the graying stubble on chin and cheeks, the buttons of his gray overcoat.

My memory of the pogrom was full of gaps. The Cossacks setting fire to our home. The pouch of bones dangling from the Cossack's neck. The burning shul. Smoke stinging my eyes. The screams of women and children. Hooves galloping toward me. The taste of blood in my mouth. Ma's ripped, bloodstained clothes. Pa's hands.

And then there was baby Yossel. When we found him next to the rain barrel, his skull was crushed, his body as lifeless as a rag doll tossed aside by a careless child. The village carpenter couldn't keep up with the need for coffins, so Ma washed Yossi's body, wrapped him in a linen cloth, and placed him in an apple box. But the earth would not receive him. The ground was frozen solid. We had to bury him like the pagans did, above the ground, mounding branches, pebbles, and ashes over him. At least Yossi was not alone. In the cemetery were many fresh corpses to keep him company, but not Bekka's.

This haunted me—the question of what became of her poor body. It was as if she had never existed, as if she had never braided my hair or made me a crown of daisies in the spring, or in the winter stuffed my boots with old newspapers when they leaked. Once I was sick with pleurisy and having trouble breathing. Bekka knew *hasa bhankus*, or cupping, to draw the poisons out of my lungs. She heated a dozen special round glasses with a candle and gently applied them to my back. The heat created suction and made them stay in place. I must have looked like a porcupine with all those glasses clinging to me. Every time I took a breath, they jiggled together, creating a tinkling, merry sound.

My last memory of my sister was a week before the pogrom. She was walking toward the communal oven, a wooden trough holding unbaked bread dough balanced on her hip. Her brown hair was twisted into a thick single braid, shiny as a loaf of challah.

Before the Cossacks attacked, in my child's imagination, our shtetl had been a safe and golden place with its thatched roofs, chickens, cows in the pasture, a few shops, the market on Friday, and fields of winter rye. In summer, wheat waved in the fields; in the fall, our root cellar overflowed with apples; and in winter, the whole village was white with snow. After the pogrom, it was a smoldering ghost village. We had to leave. Even though our apartment here in New York was cramped and drafty, we were better off. In America if you worked hard, you could make something of yourself. And that was exactly what I intended to do. But first, I had to deal with the past.

I turned my drawing this way and that, adding light to the low brow and shadows under the flat cheekbones. It took several attempts until I was satisfied, then I made another copy.

I studied the portrait. I had been so sure on the tram, but I started to second-guess myself. Did I just think this Russian was the same Cossack because I had been remembering Stulchyn and that terrible day? Many men had missing fingers. It could have been a coincidence. What were the odds that the same man who had attacked us was here on the Lower East Side? The only way to know for sure was to ask Ma, but she was fragile as a chick. Me, Arnold, and Pa, when he was still living with us, avoided subjects that would upset her. But now I needed the truth. If this was the man, I had to find him.

My sketch complete, I yawned, the long night catching up to me. I needed sleep. I tucked the drawing between the pages of a newspaper, then stumbled toward Arnold's cot in the corner of the kitchen and curled up.

# Chapter 4

———◆———

*Lower East Side, New York*

When I awoke, it was to the sound of Ma's favorite soap opera playing on the old Philco radio. "Once again, we present *Our Gal Sunday,* the story of an orphan girl named Sunday from a small mining town of Silver Creek, Colorado, who married England's richest, most handsome lord, Lord Henry Brinthrope."

I blinked and rubbed my eyes. It was late afternoon. Ma was sewing at the kitchen table. Draped over her shoulder, like a baby she was about to burp, was a blue police shirt, the sleeves attached but the collar not yet set in.

"Good, I was just about to wake you, *tsikele,*" she said. *Tsikele* means "little goat," which sounds silly in English, but warm and funny in Yiddish.

Ma had attended night school classes in English at the Henry Street Settlement House "like a *bocher* boy"—a yeshiva student—as she put it. A scholar she was not. Yiddish was her first language. Russian her second. The only English word she used was *aggravation.* As in, "Gitel, don't give me aggravation." As a child, I had assumed it was Yiddish until my third-grade teacher explained it was a perfectly good American word.

"I let you sleep because you work so late at Sid's," she said, taking the dressmaker's pins out of her mouth and sticking them into the cushion on her wrist. She wore her old cardigan, a moth-eaten number buttoned over her thin chest.

Ma didn't like me working at Sid's, but she didn't argue about it even though arguing was a reflex in my family. Like when the doctor hits your knee with a tiny hammer. If your leg is normal, it jumps; otherwise, it just dangles there over the edge of the examination table. The only reason Ma didn't say anything was because we needed the money.

With so many people—even skilled men like watchmakers, cigar makers, and operators with their own Singers—out of work, and me getting fired from Grossinger's, I had to earn every dime I could. Ma's job wasn't enough to cover our rent and bills. I pretended that because Sid and nearly everyone who worked for him was Jewish, his club was respectable—a place for fancy uptown goyim to drink Manhattans, listen to jazz, and experience something they couldn't get on Park Avenue. Ma pretended to believe me. That was our deal.

"Look what I have for you from last night," I said, fishing two dollars out of my purse. This would buy our groceries for the week. There was another six bucks tucked between my bubbies from Hattie, but that was for my nest egg. I was saving for emergencies, Arnold's books for college, and of course, the lease for the storefront on Broome Street I had my eye on.

Ma took the money, squirrelling it away into the empty Maxwell House coffee can over the sink.

"How about some chicken soup? And I got some of that bread you like."

I nodded, suddenly famished. "Thanks, Ma."

"You can't work on an empty stomach. You don't eat enough."

"You're right."

"Are there at least some eligible men at that club?" Ma asked as she heated up the soup.

"Don't start," I said, too sleepy to argue.

Ma had threatened to enlist Mrs. Lowenstein, the *shadkin*, match-maker, to find me a husband. I looked forward to this with as much enthusiasm as I looked forward to *helzel*, stuffed chicken neck, for Shabbat dinner. Ma meant well, but I had bigger plans. Once my family was taken care of, I wanted to be a career gal. I loved that expression—career gal. It had such a carefree, modern ring. In *Stage Door*, Katharine Hepburn played a young actress trying to break onto the stage and become a star. She was my ideal woman. I'd seen the movie four times.

"Do you flash your dimples? Smile? Let them see your nice, straight American teeth?" Ma was saying. "You worked hard to get them, pressing that wooden ruler against your teeth to force them to line up in the fifth grade."

"I was scared of having buckteeth like what's-her-name," I replied. Once I had pushed so hard the corners of my lips bled, but I kept on until the ruler broke and I had to steal another one from school. "And I'm still young—"

"Twenty-four is not so young."

"Ma, stop with the pressure."

"I want what's best for you, Gitel. A house, a family. This is what life is all about. Here in America everything is possible."

Like *Our Gal Sunday*, that was baloney, but seductive baloney—except maybe it was possible to meet a decent man with some dough who would share the burden of supporting my family.

Ma set down a bowl of soup in front of me and handed me a spoon.

I took a big spoonful of the tasty broth, then tackled the pieces of chicken at the bottom of the bowl. "You make the best chicken soup in New York, possibly the world."

Ignoring the compliment, she kept on at me. "So many men

would marry you in a second. Not just because you're pretty. What girl isn't pretty at your age? You have a goal. Men respect that. They don't want some hothouse orchid with nothing on her mind beyond Saturday night and bubkes in the bank, whatever they may say. What about that nice man who owns the bakery on Houston Street?"

I sighed. She pretended not to notice.

"Bagels, bialys, rye, hamantaschen, rugelach. You name it, he bakes it. War, famine, pestilence, death, depression—bakeries prosper, believe you me. When a bakery goes bust, it means the end of the world, and then we all might as well hold hands and leap into the East River."

"You make it sound like he owns Macy's." This wasn't her first lecture on the sterling qualities of the baker. "Besides, he sweats all the time."

"You make him nervous."

"He sweats because he's fat and he wears that scarf around his neck."

"It makes him look stylish. And it's called a cravat."

"It makes him look like he's covering up a goiter."

"He's not fat. Beefy, maybe, muscular, maybe, but not fat." Ma lowered her voice. "It's not a bad thing to be with a fella who likes you more than you like him."

I realized she wasn't talking about the baker anymore. She was talking about Pa.

Two years ago, I was drinking a glass of tea with him at this very kitchen table. He got up, combed his beard with his fingers, put on his coat, and told me he was popping out to buy the *Jewish Daily Forward* from the newsboy on the corner. He kissed me goodbye and never came back. I didn't know why he left us. Maybe he'd found a new American wife or jumped in front of a streetcar, unable to face another winter of breadlines.

At first, I was glad he was gone. We were poorer, but life was calmer, at least for Arnold and me. My brother was more relaxed. He stopped biting his nails. I was free to come and go without having to listen to lectures on the need for a Jewish state and the glories of Palestine and how the Bolsheviks and Stalin were transforming Russia into a workers' paradise. It's not a nice thing to say about your own father, but no one could deny Pa was a ranter and a raver, given to unpredictable fits of anger. Mostly he was filled with hatred for himself.

But Ma got worse. Her fits of depression came back. She began sleeping with her purse under her pillow, and she packed her old trunk from Russia with underwear and a cake of lye soap. She became reclusive, refusing to leave the house. I did all the errands now, including picking up Mr. Portnoy's cut pieces for her to assemble and schlepping them back once they were completed. Her drinking started then, too. And one day, she did something stupid that I don't like to think about it. Let's just say it was lucky I got home in time to turn off the hissing gas of the oven and fling open the windows. A lot of women in the tenements took this way out when life got too much. Clean, cheap, easy, painless, fast.

After that, I took her to a doctor who told me Ma suffered from a disease called neurasthenia. The symptoms were self-doubt, paralysis of will, insomnia, and some other things I can't remember. In time she improved. Little by little, she seemed to accept that Pa was gone for good. She no longer raced to the door when she heard footsteps in the hall, but she still had her moments of sadness.

So when, to my surprise, I spotted Pa sleeping in the reading room of the New York Public Library last winter, I'd tried to reason with him, get him to return home for Ma's sake, but he refused. I didn't understand how he could be so selfish.

I looked at my mother now. "I don't have time for your matchmaking," I said. "I need to experiment with an idea before I go to Sid's." I took my bowl to the sink and washed it out.

Then I set out my supplies—beeswax, coconut oil, and charcoal— as Ma went back to her sewing. I was trying to perfect my formula for eyeliner. In a small saucepan, I melted the beeswax, careful not to let it smoke, then mixed in the oil and a pinch of charcoal. I let it cool on the window ledge so the wax would harden. I took out a small brush and tried to stroke it over the mixture. I groaned. Too hard, way too hard. "Damn it," I swore. "I can't seem to get the right consistency."

Ma came over and took a long look. "Melt it down, add more coconut oil, about two teaspoons," she suggested.

I re-melted the mess, then did as she recommended.

She stirred the mixture and let a bit drip off the spoon. "Now add a tiny bit of cocoa powder to soften that harsh black of the charcoal."

I did as I was told. Again, I let the mixture cool. I picked up a smidgen with the brush and stroked it onto my eyelids. To my delight, it worked. I quickly filled several small jars and packed them in my purse to distribute to the other girls at work. I always gave away free samples of new products in exchange for honest reviews. Hattie would be so impressed with the results—not that she gave a hoot about makeup, but she would admire my perseverance. I had had many failures.

"Ma, you're a genius. Thank you so much."

It was now dark. I had to be at Sid's soon, so I retreated to the bedroom and changed out of yesterday's crumpled clothes. I washed my essential parts with a damp washrag, then wrapped my ratty housecoat around me and ran a comb through my hair. I kept it trimmed in a bob, the bangs cut straight, the rest at jaw level, even like a helmet. I pulled on fresh undergarments and my wool sheath. I never put on my costume at home the way some of the cigarette girls did. Ma wouldn't have let me out of the house. But I had a problem I needed her help with. My last pair of stockings was a mess of runs and holes and covered with mud. I went to Ma in the kitchen, my Maybelline eyebrow pencil in hand.

"Ma, I need you should help me," I said in English. When she pretended to ignore me—quite a feat since she was right in front of me—I said in Yiddish, "*Plez*, Ma, *itst*."

"What? I got to finish this." Ma flipped her braid, streaked with gray, onto one shoulder.

"I don't have a pair of stockings. Draw seams on my legs."

"With what should I draw?"

I handed her my eyebrow pencil. She wasn't too happy about aiding and abetting my job at Sid's, but what could she do? I climbed onto the kitchen table, bunched my wool sheath up to my waist, then stood, a hip cocked to take the weight off my left foot, which had sprouted a bunion from the sky-high heels of my costume.

Ma tapped my right heel. "Together." She could make me feel about twelve years old when she barked in that tone of hers. She put a hand on my kneecap to steady my leg and drew a line starting from the back of my thigh to midcalf, then to my ankle. It tickled like an ant crawling down my leg.

I craned my neck, trying to see over my shoulder. "Did you get the line in the middle? It doesn't feel like you got it centered."

"Don't worry, with such a face, who's gonna be looking at your legs?"

"But they're such nice legs." Putting my hands on my hips, I flung up my leg like one of the Rockettes at Radio City Music Hall. I kicked higher than my head, narrowly missing the clothesline strung across the kitchen where Ma's housedress was drying. I wasn't too bad.

"Such a wiggle worm. Stand still."

It was a cheap pencil and required a lot of pressure and a steadier hand than Ma's to make a crisp line, but she did her best. As she began on my other leg, I thought of the sketch wedged between the pages of the *Jewish Forward*.

"There's something I gotta talk to you about, Ma."

She glanced up, suspicious of my change in tone. "*Vas tut zikh?*" What's going on?

"Remember that fairy tale you used to read me, *Vasilisa the Beautiful?* Our shtetl was like that . . . until the Cossacks came—"

She held up a hand. "About this, I do not wish to discuss." She turned away, leaving my second leg half-done. "I need to finish this for Mr. Portnoy."

She slipped on her thimble and picked out a needle from her precious bullock's horn filled with beeswax, which kept the needles from rusting and made them easier to slide through fabric. It was a gift from her grandfather who had been a sailmaker in Odessa and one of the few things that had survived the raid on our village. She considered it a lucky piece.

I stilled her hands. "Work is not a wolf. It won't run off into the forest." It was an old Russian proverb I'd heard a million times. "This is important. I saw one of the Cossacks in Midtown." It was a small fib, but I didn't want her to guess he lived nearby. "Still dressed like in the old country. He wore a fur hat and one of those double-breasted overcoats."

"They all wore those ugly hats."

My mother had never spoken about what had happened after I blacked out, but the memory of her torn, bloody clothes haunted me. As I got older, I suspected that when the Cossacks spotted me, she provoked them in order to draw their attention away from me. Then they attacked her. The price of my salvation was Ma's rape. On my shoulders, that guilt weighed heavily.

"But this man's face—it was familiar. I bit off his finger. I think he's the one who . . ." I trailed off.

Ma froze. "How could you recognize the man? You were asleep the whole time, thank God. Half frozen to death. It's a miracle you survived. Not like our Yossel of blessed memory."

"And Bekka."

"And Bekka." She blinked hard, her voice a whisper. "It was as though the angel of death had come to live in our village."

I hopped down from the table. "What if he's here in America? I need to know."

"Giddy, you saw a ghost. About the Cossack, I will not speak."

If Ma hadn't been terrified to leave the apartment, she would have stormed out. Instead, she focused on basting two panels of pants together. The loose trail of stitches, like white rice on a blue background, held the seams until they could be stitched on her Singer. One snip of the shears, and how quickly the whole garment would fall apart. Kind of like our life.

"At least look at my sketch," I said, fishing it out. "I did this quick, before I forgot what he looked like." Ma wouldn't glance at it, even though it was six inches from her nose. "You're not looking."

"Enough!" she shouted, shoving the drawing aside. It fluttered to the floor, where it rested face down. "They all looked the same with their Tartar eyes black as the bottom of a well."

"We used to be a happy family. I am sure of that. Then it all came to an end when the Cossacks thundered into our village."

"Stop with the past. I'm dying of the past. The past makes me want to kill myself."

She scared me when she talked like that. "Don't say that, Ma."

"Don't tell me what I can or cannot say in my own house. Did President Roosevelt just repeal the First Amendment?"

What was I doing, pressuring her like this? I went to give her a hug and she tried to push me away, but I put my arms around her waist and held her so tight she couldn't get free. I could feel her heart thumping against mine, her shoulders shaking with sobs.

"I'm sorry, Mamaleh. Sometimes I don't know when to stop." To call her "little mother" often calmed her. But not this time. Stronger measures were called for. I guided her to a chair, then retrieved the bottle of schnapps from under the sink and tipped a healthy splash into two teacups.

"*L'chaim.*"

"To life." We clinked and sipped.

After a moment, Ma spoke. "Giddy, because I have nightmares, you should, too? You were smart and so brave. God in his mercy told you where to hide."

"I wanted to save you." I rubbed my arms, the scars rough under my hands. It was an old habit, and she took my hands in hers to stop me. It wasn't exactly true. I was five years old. Rationally, I couldn't have saved her. What made me feel so guilty was that Ma had sacrificed herself to save me. If she had simply stayed hidden in the cemetery with Yossel, she would have been safe and Yossi would still be alive. But she heard my screams and she came to me. I couldn't say this to Ma because she would not talk about what had happened. And for years I had pretended I had seen nothing.

"You stayed alive. That was the best gift you could have given me." Her eyes brimmed with fresh tears, but she blinked them back. "Come, now." She picked up the eyebrow pencil. "You've got half a seam on your one leg."

I climbed back up on the kitchen table and she finished my leg, a little off-center, but I didn't complain. I had put her through enough today. When she was done, I scooped up the sketch and tucked it away. I threw on my coat, checked my pocketbook to make sure I had tram fare, and set off for Sid's Paradise.

I didn't have my answer, but I wasn't giving up. My gut told me I had seen the Cossack. All I had to do now was find him. When I did, I was going to make him pay for what he did to my family, to my ma.

# Chapter 5

———— ◈ ————

*Midtown, New York*

My mind was still on the Cossack as I rubbed Hattie's feet with my special lavender cream in her dressing room. She was slumped in her chair, her mascara smudged, her face slack with fatigue. From the club came the sounds of the band and the crowd hooting and hollering as they danced.

It had been another busy night. Hattie had held the audience captive with her readings as usual, but I'd been distracted thinking of how I was going to track down the Cossack. I'd walked through the streets by his tram stop on my way into work, dawdling as long as I could without being late. No luck. I resigned myself to the fact that I needed Hattie's help.

"Hattie . . . ," I began, feeling my way. "There's a man I need to find. A man from the past." I felt like a chump. Me, who'd been helping her hoodwink customers for months. But I had to start somewhere.

Hattie sat up, suddenly alert. "A man from the past? From Russia?"

"Yes, one of the Cossacks who raided my village. I think I saw him on the tram on our ride home."

She nodded. "I knew something was bothering you. You were as stiff as a poker next to me. I was going to ask why, but then my stop came up." Hattie was observant. In our business we had to be.

"I want you to do a reading on him. I need his name and where he lives or works. Something that will lead me to him."

"You expect me to close my eyes, snap my fingers, and his address will appear on my forehead? Who do you think I am? The New York Telephone Company operator?"

"Don't get so excited." Hattie's a high-strung girl but I keep her calm. A cousin of mine runs a couple of Thoroughbreds at Aqueduct. He has an old Labrador retriever that sleeps in the stall with his most skittish mare. I'm the human equivalent for Hattie. "I want you to try."

"And then what're you going to do once you get your lunch hooks into him?"

I didn't answer. "The first step is to find him." I reached into my bra and pulled out a dollar that a customer, a building inspector from Staten Island, of all places, had tucked between my bubbies. I held it out.

She waved it away. "Save it for your store."

"Thanks, Hattie."

"But I'm going to need a little more to go on. Describe this tram rider," she said, straightening the orange-and-black afghan in her lap. "I didn't get a close look."

"He was in his late thirties, tall—taller than me anyway—dark hair. I drew a likeness of him." I dug around in my pocketbook and handed her the sketch.

She smoothed the portrait over her knee, closed her eyes, then sat so still I thought she had fallen asleep.

"He's showing himself to me," she began. "He's secretive, obsessive, and ruthless. I see him in a stable with a currycomb in his hand. Grooming a horse. Over and over, long, smooth strokes. The man's shoulders are heaving. His face is pressed into the horse's flank. I think he's crying." Hattie started to rock like an old man davening in shul. "I see him in a privy covered in . . ." She held the afghan to her nose. "He's hiding but I can't tell from who."

*Whom*, I wanted to correct, but I kept quiet. Concentration was the key to Hattie's success.

"Now there's the rocking of a steamship, the stink of vomit, the sound of a foghorn, the smell of cabbage and pigs' knuckles, of diapers. Now that typical tenement smell of sewer gas, moldy plaster walls, and rat droppings." Silence. "I see a woman with a baby on her hip. Blond hair. Pale."

A lot of details that didn't give me any clues to finding him. I waited, the cracked seat on her old wooden chair pinching my backside. After another minute, I ventured, "Hattie?"

But there was nothing more. She opened her eyes. I tried to conceal my disappointment.

"Hattie, level with me. Do you have second sight or not?"

"Sometimes the power is not there to guide me," she said. "Sometimes I fail. Sometimes, I don't blab about everything I see. Which may be wrong of me, but once in a while it's too frightening and I have to break free of the nightmare and improvise instead."

"Did you improvise just now about the man on the streetcar?"

"No, I wouldn't do that to you. I just didn't see what you wanted me to. But I did smell those things, which is unusual. Usually, in a séance, I don't smell odors. One thing I do know, though. This isn't a fella you want to fool with. He's strong; he has a way about him. Very determined. A kind of coiled-up rage, like an animal. He's fierce. I see him as a man who gets an idea and sticks with it, no matter what."

I believed her. She was wound tighter than a *dreidel*, a top, her shoulders so high they were practically touching her pearl drop earrings. "Hattie, thank you for trying."

She reached for my hand. "I know you, Giddy; perseverance is your middle name. But I'm serious. Be careful."

She was right. I wasn't about to give up, but I patted her good leg as if I was heeding her advice. "I'll wait for you outside."

I rose and went to the door, but when I opened it, I nearly collided with Mr. Van der Zalm, his hand raised to knock. He was even more handsome up close, and I wished I had powdered my nose and applied a fresh coat of Noir Red lipstick.

"I was hoping Hattie was still here," he said, peering over my shoulder.

He hadn't been around the club tonight—I would have noticed—but clearly his need for otherworldly communication had called him here at the last hour. I glanced back. Hattie signaled to me she needed five minutes to change her clothes. I flashed my hundred-watt smile, showing my pearly whites but not too much gum. "She'll be ready in a moment. Perhaps I can entertain you in the meantime," I said, shutting the door behind me.

I wanted to ask him about the nature of his visits with Hattie, but she would be furious if I did. Hattie regarded customer confidentiality as sacred. You'd think she was a fancy-pants psychoanalyst on the Upper East Side instead of a girl with an occult act in a nightclub run by a Jewish mobster.

I extended my hand. "Allow me to introduce myself." I was proud of that sentence, because it made me sound like a dignified career woman, not some bimbo whose ass every fellow pinched until it was as bruised as a peach from the Hester Street Market. "My name is Giddy Brodsky."

Miss Post's etiquette book says it's the lady's task to take the initiative in the hand-shaking department. The goyim are keen on shaking hands. I thrust out my paw and he clasped it, using just the right amount of pressure, not a bone cracker like some, but not a limp fish either. His skin was smooth as butter. This was not a hand that had ever touched anything coarser than the tiller of a sailboat, or maybe a tennis racket, or polo mallet. No wedding ring, but he wouldn't be the first married man in the world not to wear one.

"My name is Carter Van der Zalm." He looked me square in the eye, unlike most other men at the club, who focused their attention farther down.

"A pleasure to make your acquaintance."

"I believe you've sold me cigarettes. You work a long night, Miss Vronsky," he remarked. His speech was so educated sounding—a series of beautifully rounded vowels, each word as rich as a mouthful of chocolate fudge.

"It's Brodsky, with a B, but you can call me Giddy."

"Giddy," he repeated.

A pause stretched between us. Was he going to tell me his first name? Or was Carter his first name? "I understand you work on Ellis Island," I said. "Must be interesting work. All those immigrants passing through." It sounded so trite, but I couldn't think of anything else to say.

"It's absolutely fascinating."

I wasn't sure if he was kidding—it's hard to tell with Gentiles—so I smiled, just in case. "I hear you run the whole megillah." When he lifted an eyebrow, I added, "The whole shebang."

"I am the director of the Board of Special Inquiry, which reviews cases in which immigrants have been denied entry."

Carter? What kind of a name was that? I would be the first to admit that Jewish men have terrible names—Schlomo, Nissim, Pinchas, Schmuel, Nuchem. The list goes on. But any one is a better name than Carter. And yet, I kind of liked it. It suited him.

I wouldn't know from a Board of Special Inquiry if it bit me in the keister, except it must involve meetings and paperwork and sounded boring, but an idea was forming in my mind. "Do you keep track of everyone who arrives?"

"Of course we do, but our records are not open to the public," he said.

He shifted his weight from one long leg to the other. The creases in his worsted-wool trousers were so sharp I could have used them to slice pumpernickel. "But I'm not the public," I said.

"You certainly aren't." He seemed amused then, which made me wonder what monkey business he got up to when he wasn't at Sid's. Then I remembered seeing him in the gents' and blushed.

"Hattie's probably ready for you now," I said, stepping aside from the door. "I'll see you around."

He lifted his hand to knock, his blue eyes still on mine. "It was a pleasure talking to you."

When Hattie answered, he entered and closed the door behind him, taking with him a whiff of tobacco and pricey aftershave— Knize Ten, if I wasn't mistaken, judging by the leather, citrus, cinnamon, and clove smell.

Curious, I stood there for a minute listening, but all I could hear were murmurs. That was fine. I had more important fish to fry: the Cossack. And if Hattie couldn't help me, maybe Mr. Van der Zalm could.

# Chapter 6

<><>

*Ellis Island, New York*

My conversation with Mr. Van der Zalm got me thinking that the Cossack might be new to the country. After all, I'd been taking the number 56 streetcar for years and I'd never seen him before. Also Hattie had mentioned a steamship during her reading, so I took the ferry to Ellis Island in hopes of confirming my suspicions. It was probably a fool's errand—if I were a horse at Aqueduct, the bookies would put my odds of getting any information out of Mr. Van der Zalm at one thousand to one—but I wasn't ready to accept his no as a final answer. I had ways of wearing people down. It's both a good and a bad quality.

The salt-laden air stung my face as I clutched the railing, bringing back memories of our arrival in New York on the *Homeric* all those years ago. When the Statue of Liberty had come into view with her stern expression and excellent posture, I'd assumed it was a statue of Ma, and I'd marveled how the Americans had captured her likeness and displayed her in time for us. I'd thought America was the greatest country on the face of the earth. I still think so.

My bravado wavered as I entered the red-and-white-brick immigration building, which was as huge and scary as I remembered. Before I wrenched open the heavy metal doors of the main hall, I peered in and realized the entire Lower East Side, including Seward Park, would fit into the main floor with space to spare. I wanted to race the hell back home. Large spaces, like this building with its high ceilings and mammoth windows, made me feel like a mouse in a lion's cage. *Be brave,* I told myself, *be bold.*

In the reception hall, a long line of immigrants waited to be examined like cattle at a weighing station. Some people wore three or four layers of clothing, probably every stitch they owned. *Vey,* the things people schlepped from the old country. An ancient woman slumped on a bench with an enormous brass samovar between her bowed legs. Next to her was a man with a lumpy bindle and a knotted-up tablecloth stuffed with pots and pans slung over his shoulder. His little girl wore a scarf wound around her head and jaw like she had a toothache. She stood staring, snot dripping from her nose, gripping her pa's hand.

All at once, I remembered the doctors in white coats with stethoscopes dangling around their necks, the smell of rubbing alcohol and iodine, and the dreaded "buttonhook man," as he was called, a doctor who checked my eyes, looking for infection.

I still recalled the pain when he rolled back my eyelids with the buttonhook, then waved me through. I later learned he was looking for yellow pus, a symptom of trachoma. Only passengers in steerage were subjected to this torture. Second-class passengers were waved through without a medical exam. "God damn the rich capitalist bloodsuckers," Pa had muttered under his breath as we watched the girl in front of me being examined. She wasn't as lucky as me. The eye doctor drew an X with a circle around it in blue chalk on the lapel of her green coat. Her parents sobbed as she was taken away and, I assume, sent back to Russia.

*You're a naturalized American citizen,* I told myself. *They can't deport you.* I took a deep breath and moved forward, looking up at the tall ceilings. The metal grillwork on the huge windows shone. The marble floors glistened from being burnished by the soles of thousands of feet. Even the guards gleamed in their blue uniforms, their glasses reflecting light from windows set high up on the walls—windows like you might see in a cathedral, should you frequent such places. A shiny brass spittoon sat in the corner, half-concealed behind a screen.

So many reflective surfaces, so few places to hide. One thing was apparent: unlike my former sweatshop, where the workers were mostly female, here the staff was male. The inspectors and guards—all fair-skinned and clean-shaven—were a far cry from the men in my neighborhood with their bushy beards, jutting eyebrows, and wiry chest hair sprouting over the top button of their shirtfronts. The air smelled of nervous sweat, salami, garlic, old clothes, unwashed bodies, vomit, and hope. It made me want to sneeze.

But then I saw the kissing post, the big white pillar smack-dab in the middle, where families reunited with their New York relatives who came to meet them. More than just a post of mortar and brick, it was the symbol of a new beginning, the promise of a fresh start in America. I didn't want to appear a JOTB, but I kissed my fingertips, then touched the post, just for luck.

There was a steely-eyed guard five feet away, scrutinizing the immigrants in a way that made me think he wished the whole crowd would get deported and the sooner the better.

Despite my stocking problem—my bare legs were covered in turkey flesh—I looked smart in my navy skirt, white ruffled shirtwaist that Ma had ironed just so, red felt cloche hat, and makeup applied with a light touch. Much as I wanted to, I couldn't turn tail and run. I hadn't spent five cents on the tram and another dime on the ferry—money I should have been saving for my new store—to run home to Ma. Getting answers about the Cossack was just as important to me as my business. Besides, what was the worst that could happen? I get the bum's rush? Hustled out by that guard? From that, I wouldn't die. Not even close.

Above my head a clock struck eleven o'clock. I gripped the little finger of my left hand in the palm of my right and squeezed, my trick for calming myself; then I approached the guard, and in my best accent, I inquired if I might see Mr. Van der Zalm.

The guard opened and closed his mouth like a grouper fish at the Fulton Fish Market. I didn't need to be clairvoyant to know he was thinking I had no business talking to a man like Mr. V. and he should toss me out. "Do you have an appointment?" he asked.

I smiled—a practice smile for Mr. Van der Zalm—making my dimples deepen. "Just tell Mr. Van der Zalm that Miss Giddy Brodsky is here to see him. We're old friends," I lied.

"I'll see if he's available," the guard said after a long moment. "Wait here."

Thirty minutes passed, and I was about to give up hope when the guard returned and to my surprise—and maybe his, too—led me upstairs to the mezzanine, where I had a view of the people milling on the floor below.

I wasn't proud of it, but these greenhorns, so optimistic, so naive, made me feel superior. Soon they would discover that the streets weren't paved with gold. Some of them weren't paved at all. And if they were Irish or Italian, they would be expected to do the paving. It wasn't what they'd hoped for, it wasn't what the White Star Line promised in their fancy-colored advertising posters, but it would be a hell of an improvement over where they had come from, assuming they were allowed to remain. I was once one of them.

The guard ushered me into a large office where, behind a mahogany desk the size of Rhode Island, Mr. Van der Zalm sat writing in a black ledger with a gold fountain pen. He looked as regal as King George of England on a ruby-encrusted throne. I cleared my throat.

He looked up and frowned, as if trying to figure out why I looked familiar.

"Giddy Brodsky," I said. "Your favorite cigarette girl from Sid's Paradise." I grinned and shook my behind, pretending to swish a little skirt.

"Of course," he said, rising. He came around the desk. "I didn't recognize you without your cigarette tray and cheeky pillbox, Miss Brodsky."

I know a custom-made suit when I see one. It was all I could do not to grab Mr. V.'s lapel between my index finger and thumb. What a lovely piece of goods. British tailors considered zippers and belts vulgar, or so I read in *Women's Wear Daily*. They preferred button fastenings and suspenders, which did not ruin the drape of a well-cut pair of trousers. This suit had buttons and suspenders all right. The trouser cuffs bisected the top of his brogues in two. The shirt? Hilditch & Key of London or I'd eat it. The whole megillah screamed Savile Row. Maybe even Scholte, the Duke of Windsor's tailor. Fifty dollars if it cost a dime. Mr. V.'d never worn it to Sid's, of that I was certain. For us nightclub hoi polloi, his double-breasted pinstripe was plenty good enough.

In my cheap shoes and patched coat, I suddenly felt like a mutt. I thrust out my hand, trying to act confident. "Just Giddy is fine," I said.

He took a seat behind his desk, then gestured to a chair. "Please, have a seat. How are you?"

I'll say this about the goyim: nothing fazes them. If he was mystified by my visit, he concealed it well.

Smoothing my skirt behind my knees, I lowered myself gracefully as if I sat in a genuine leather chair with brass studs every day of the week. "Not too bad. And how's by you?" As soon as the words were out of my mouth, I wanted to kick myself. I sounded like an ignoramus. This was not the way Gentiles talked. "And how are you?" I corrected myself.

"Very well, thank you," he replied, the perfectly modulated words falling from his lips like droplets of honey.

He was handsome in that goyish way: eyes as blue as the sky, a shock of blond hair, poreless skin tanned the color of chestnuts. But in the middle of a New York winter? Where should such a tan come from? I imagined he would be right at home in a Norfolk jacket and plus fours, drinking scotch from a thick-bottomed crystal glass. Maybe at his feet would be a hunting dog with a dead duck sandwiched between its jaws.

I scolded myself. I had to stop thinking in terms of Jew and goy. Mr. V. was a person, same as me. He put his pants on one leg at a time. He burped, farted, peed, and wheezed same as everyone. Still, it was hard to imagine him doing any of those things. Except for the peeing, of course, which I had witnessed firsthand.

"Tell me, what can I do for you?" he asked.

"I require information about an individual who entered the country from Russia about three or four years ago." I had rehearsed this line on the ferry. Three or four years was a stab in the dark. Of course, I had no idea.

His smile wavered. "I am sorry. As I mentioned at Sid's—"

I pretended not to hear him. "I would estimate his age to be late thirties. I have a sketch." I pried open the clasp of my pocketbook. The purse had looked classy when I bought it off a pushcart by the Hester Street Market, but now under Mr. V.'s gaze, it seemed shabby and cut-rate. I placed the drawing on his desk, but Mr. V. didn't glance at it. His eyes were fixed on mine.

"I know you are a friend of Hattie's," he said, his voice kind but firm. "She has been helpful to me. Any friend of hers is a friend of mine, but I'm afraid you've wasted a trip. Our records are confidential."

"There must be something you can do. I gotta find this man."

"Is this man a relative?"

The question startled me. Related to a Cossack? He might as well have asked if I was related to Bruno Hauptmann, the man who kidnapped and murdered the Lindbergh baby. "No, but I have to find him and need your help."

"I wish you the best, Miss Brodsky, but I can't help you. I am so sorry." He started to get to his feet.

He hadn't even looked at the sketch. I got a thick skin. I'm used to men flirting with me, insulting me, lying to me, belittling me—all water off a duck's back, the cost of being a woman in a man's world. I don't waste time being offended by the occasional schmuck. But the brush-off? I couldn't take it. I stood, my cheeks warm.

"Doesn't being a public servant mean it's your job to assist the public?" I asked. There was a tone in my voice I didn't much like. "Such a man as this should never have been allowed into America." To my embarrassment, I began to tear up. "I came through these halls with my family in 1920. We had to leave Russia because of the Cossacks. They attacked our village, burned our homes. America was our promised land and then last week, I see him. The man who brutalized my family." I tapped the sketch. "He was on the tram. We fled our home because of him, and now he's here." I hadn't intended to go into all this. It just popped out.

Mr. V. handed me his hanky. "Sit, please." As I blew my nose, he picked up my sketch and scrutinized it. "You're a talented artist."

"Thank you."

"Did you say this man is a Cossack?"

I sniffed. "Yes."

"And you saw him on the streetcar?"

"The fifty-six."

"Do you know his name?"

I looked down. "No."

"Neither first nor last?"

I shook my head. Mr. V. was being so gracious, maybe more gracious than I deserved.

"And you said he came here three or four years ago?"

I was beginning to feel like a dunce. "That's a guess."

"And why is it so important that you locate him?"

There was no point in telling this nice man my real intention, which was gradually taking shape. If I did, he would refuse to help me.

"I just want to talk to him." Then I told a big whopper. "I'm not a keeper of grievances." My nose should grow a yard long. I remembered every slight, slur, and insult ever directed at me.

Mr. V. raised his eyebrows. "I see." Then he sat back in his chair and folded his hands together.

"I realize I'm asking a lot. I was hoping you could look at your records or show my sketch to your inspectors."

"Do you have any idea how many people pass through these halls every day? Without a name or date of arrival it's a—"

"I know. A needle in a haystack. But there must be something you can do."

He was quiet for a moment. "I can't share the immigration records with you. That would violate the Ellis Island protocol."

My dander began to rise again and I opened my mouth, but he held up a hand.

"There is another way I might be able to help. I have other sources. Certain members of my staff keep a list of undesirable aliens—men we have, to our regret, admitted into America and who have shown their gratitude by committing crimes here. Communists, socialists, anarchists, bomb throwers, and fugitives from justice. In short, anyone who has been a menace abroad and who we have reason to believe will cause trouble here."

This information knocked me off my perch. I had no idea the immigration service kept track of people after they entered the country. But it made sense, especially now with war brewing in Europe.

"Cossacks, in particular, seem to have—how shall I put it? A difficult time adjusting to America. Their life in Russia has inured them to cruelty and lawlessness. They miss the horse cavalry, and the camaraderie of the military—"

"By *camaraderie* you mean burning innocent villages, terrorizing women and children, and stealing firewood and livestock?"

"That is one way of expressing it." Mr. V. tapped his fingers on the desk. "This Cossack of yours might well be on that list of undesirables if he has committed a crime in America. You said he was likely late thirties."

I nodded and he made a note.

"What was the name of your village?"

"Stulchyn. It's in the Ukraine."

He wrote it down, then took the sketch. "I can keep this?"

"Yes," I replied. I had another copy at home.

"I'll look at the list, narrow it down by age and region, and see what names come up. It will take time."

I had misjudged Mr. V. He was a fine man. I had flown off the handle, like always, and not given him a fair shake. "So, you'll help me?"

"If he has acted with violence on American soil, I might be able . . . " He trailed off. "Leave this with me so I can investigate. For the moment, I can't promise anything."

"You're a prince. I don't know how to thank you enough, Mr. Van der Zalm," I said.

His eyes appraised me from head to toe. The fellow at the Fool the Guesser's booth by Coney Island had scrutinized me less closely when trying to guess my weight—which, should anyone be interested, was 110 pounds—than Mr. Van der Zalm looked at me now.

"I admire your tenacity," he said. "Not many girls would have walked in here and demanded what you did." He paused. "But if I go to all this trouble for you, Miss Brodsky, there is something I want in return."

He was doing me such a kindness, I would have said yes to just about anything. Part of me hoped my quid pro quo would involve having more contact with him. "What can I do for you?" I asked.

"Keep this a secret between us. I am putting my reputation on the line by agreeing to disclose confidential information. At Sid's we must continue as we've been—patron and cigarette girl."

I had a lot to learn from Mr. V. Confidentiality was a small price to pay. I pantomimed locking my lips and tossing the key over my shoulder

"Mum's the word."

# Chapter 7

◇

*Upper East Side, New York*

Mr. Van der Zalm came into Sid's the following Friday and Saturday nights as usual, but he didn't so much as buy a pack of Pall Malls from me. He just sat by himself at the bar drinking martinis—two olives, extra dry. I reminded myself of his request for secrecy and kept my distance, waiting as patiently as I was capable. To distract myself, I thought about the containers for my new eyeliner formula. I settled on miniature apothecary jars. For the labels I would draw a sketch in black and white of the Egyptian Eye of Horus. Simple but classy.

Patience, though, is not my middle name, and the hope I had felt on Ellis Island dwindled as the second weekend passed without news. He'd mentioned it would take time to go through his records, but had he just said those things to get me out of his office? I had Mr. V. pegged as a man who was sincerely trying. Whenever I began to lose faith, I smelled the lemon scent of the monogrammed handkerchief he had given me at Ellis Island and remembered his promise.

And then, on the third Saturday, Mr. V. caught my eye as I was making change for a lady in a mink stole who'd just bought a package of Camels, and I took that as a sign and ambled over to the bar.

"Might I trouble you for a light?" he asked loud enough for Sam, the bartender, to hear.

"Certainly," I replied, selecting a book of matches from my tray.

Our fingers grazed when I handed it to him, and I swear I felt a spark. "Shall I light it for you?"

He held a cigarette between his fingers. I took a book of matches from my tray, struck it, and leaned in, cupping the flame, he whispered, "We need to talk in private. I have some information for you. Let me buy you lunch tomorrow."

Information and a meal. I was elated.

Sam hovered nearby, and Mr. V. pretended to peruse the mints in my tray. While Sam made the cocktail shaker dance a jiggety jig, Mr. V. used the cover of the rattling ice to suggest a restaurant. "Shall we say Cholly's Chop House on East Eighty-Seventh and Park at noon? They serve excellent prime rib. And it's rarely crowded."

I noticed he didn't suggest the University Club, where Hattie had accidently let slip that he was a member. I would not be allowed in. Most private joints didn't admit Jews, except through the delivery entrance and then—only then—if they were dropping off hooch, cigars, or hookers.

And what he meant by "rarely crowded" was he wasn't likely to run into anyone he knew who might think it odd that he, such a high-class gentleman, was lunching with a Jewish cigarette girl. No hard feelings. Mr. V. didn't make the rules. That's the way the world worked.

Mr. Van der Zalm took a puff on his cigarette, martini glass in one hand, waiting for an answer. *This is business,* I told myself, *not pleasure.* But who was to say that one could not lead to the other? "Cholly's at noon," I said, then turned back to the room.

It took all my self-control to finish my shift without sneaking glances at Mr. V. It was only when he left that I realized I didn't know the Upper East Side that well. I considered asking Hattie for directions, but I didn't want her to know I was meeting Mr. V. Hattie had a jealous way about her private clients, like they were precious vases and she didn't want me getting my grubby fingers on them. I settled on Arnold. He was a kid who knew how to keep a secret—one of the many traits that would someday make him an excellent lawyer.

The next morning, I told Ma I was going window-shopping at Macy's and tagged along with Arnold, who was on his way to the public library on Fifth and 42nd to research an essay on the assassination of Archduke Franz Ferdinand of Austria for his history class. He threw me a superior look at my ignorance when I told him I needed directions to Cholly's, but he obliged.

As we trudged through the slush and dirty snow, we saw a couple of drunken bums slugging each other outside a tavern. I recognized them as off-duty cops from our police precinct. "What a disgrace," I said. "They loaf around the saloons, guzzling cheap beer, then brawl."

"And they get to *schtup* the prostitutes for free," Arnold said, pushing a strand of hair off his forehead. He was as fair and blond as I was dark.

I looked at him, startled. "I can't remember the last time I heard you use a Yiddish word. And such a word. Don't let Ma catch you saying that." *Schtup* means "to press" in Yiddish but it also has another meaning.

"I'm just as Jewish as you, Giddy."

I saw the wounded look on his face. He was my brother. Nothing could change that. I put my arm through his. "Of course you are."

Arnold didn't resemble me or Pa. He had broad, flat cheekbones; blond hair, blue eyes; and a schnoz the size of a thimble. Our Jewish neighbors used to tease him by saying, "Arnie, how do you breathe through such a nose?" I had an idea why he didn't look like the rest of the family, but Ma was right. Certain things should not be spoken of. I suspected Arnold wasn't Pa's son. The timing of his birth, less than a year after the pogrom; Ma's indifference to him. But as much as I hated the Cossack, I loved Arnold.

On Broome Street, I pointed out the nice little storefront I wanted for my shop. The FOR RENT sign still hung in the window. I peered in, shading my eyes.

"I could help you fix this place up, Giddy."

I gave his arm a squeeze. "You're a good brother. I've got enough for the deposit, but the landlord wants six months' rent in advance."

"If anyone can do it, you can."

We walked on, leaving the Lower East Side. The streets were better paved, the buildings newer, and the trash picked up. Even the air was fresher.

Arnold stopped at a newsstand. The headline on the *New York Post* blared "Kaganovich to Visit New York."

"Kaganovich," I said. "That's a Jewish name. Who is he?"

"Lazar Kaganovich is Stalin's right-hand man. His nickname is Iron Lazar. Remember the famine about five years ago in the Ukraine after the farm collectivization program failed? Millions died. I read that Kaganovich was responsible for that."

"A hell of a fella." I snorted in an unladylike way. "He must love Stalin as much as Pa. What did Pa used to say? 'Papa Joe and the Bolsheviks are transforming Russia into a workers' paradise.'"

"Stalin is a tyrant, but Hitler poses a bigger threat to America. Tensions between the two leaders are high. Until this unrest in Europe is over, the French and British need Stalin on their side. So do we."

"The enemy of my enemy is my friend," I said, stamping my feet against the cold. "Let's go. We're only halfway there."

He tossed down a nickel for the paper and read the article as we headed uptown. "Looks like Kaganovich is coming to America this spring for a meeting. So far the State Department has managed to keep the reason for his visit quiet, but I got my suspicions."

"Which are?"

"I think Kaganovich wants to persuade us to sell Russia guns and munitions. That way the Red Army can defend the country against Germany."

"Fat chance of that. There's too much anti-communist feeling here in America."

Just when I thought I would die of exhaustion, we reached 87th Street, and Arnold pointed to the sign that read Cholly's Chop House. "I won't ask what you're up to, Giddy, but good luck."

"Thanks, Arnold. I didn't expect you to escort me the whole way uptown. Now you have to double back."

"Anything for my big sister." He gave me a two-finger salute. I waved goodbye and watched as he headed south to the library.

I gripped the little finger of my left hand in the palm of my right and squeezed to steady myself. My heart was going like a snare drum as I entered the restaurant. I checked my coat but kept my scarf. I was cold from the walk. A solemn-looking man in a dark suit greeted me with the words "Welcome to Cholly's" and escorted me to a banquette facing a large stone fireplace. Mr. V. was already seated.

He rose as I approached the table. "Thank you for meeting me," he said. He was wearing the same gorgeous suit he'd worn at Ellis Island. This time, however, there was a note in the pocket of his jacket.

"Of course," I said, as nonchalant as if I ate breakfast, lunch, and dinner here every day.

The back and sides of the booth were so high it reminded me of the pictures of duck blinds I'd seen in the Sunday rotogravure. In front of me on the linen-draped table was a confusing array of forks, knives, and spoons covered with lots of curlicues, and china plates so translucent I could have held one up to the light and read a newspaper through it, had I, for some strange reason, wished to do so. Above us, a chandelier cast a spotlight, making it seem like we were the only two people in the joint.

The fire crackled in the fireplace, and for the first time all day, I was warm. I unwound my scarf and discreetly slid my damp shoes off under the table. Mr. V.'s fingers rested on the damask tablecloth, tapered and smooth as candles. If he were Jewish, I would have said they were the hands of a violinist, but I'd never heard of a Gentile playing the violin, although, no doubt, many did.

"I took the liberty of ordering us some wine," he said, flashing a grin so warm that it could melt the elastic in a girl's bloomers.

I wanted to ask about the note but a waiter with a long, baggy face and a towel over his arm brought two glasses of red wine.

Once the waiter left, Mr. V. reached for his glass. "Before we dive into business, it might be nice to get to know each other a little better. Why don't you tell me about yourself? You said your family came to America in 1920. Where in New York did they settle?"

He spoke in a way I found disarming, a word I knew from the *Reader's Digest* column. But I didn't want to talk about our dingy tenement with its coal soot–covered windows and dusty stoop, where ragamuffin boys played stickball in the street, their heads shaved in summer to keep down the lice and ringworm.

Then I chided myself. To be born shirtless poor was just plain bad luck, nothing to be ashamed of. Besides, I didn't think of myself as poor, just broke. There's a world of difference. Broke is temporary. Poor is forever.

"I grew up on Cherry Street, on the Lower East Side," I said, omitting the fact that I still lived there. "You're probably not familiar with the area."

"This might surprise you, but I am. I drove through the neighborhood with some city hall officials who have plans to replace the worst of the tenements with new, low-rent apartment buildings."

"It's about time the government built decent housing," I said.

"What was it that President Roosevelt said in his inaugural

address? 'The test of our country's progress is not whether we add more to the abundance of those who have much; it is whether we provide enough for those who have too little.' I believe that, too."

I was a little skeptical to hear Mr. V. praise FDR. Most rich folks considered him a friend of the working man and a traitor to his patrician class, but nonetheless Mr. V.'s words made me like him more. I took a sip of wine as he went on.

"While I was there, I watched as a peddler threw plums and apples to a mob of children waving their hands in the air. They looked like daisies in a field."

"That was Salvatore, the fruit huckster," I said.

I had been one of those so-called daisies. As a girl, I would jostle for a position on the stoop as Salvatore tossed day-old apples, bananas, and cantaloupes. He pitched deliberately low and wide so we had to bend down to pick up the bruised fruit and reveal our torn bloomers.

Mr. V. smiled, nostalgic. "Now I can hardly go to the ballet and see the upraised arms of the dancers without thinking of those cheeky mites. Ah, the messy vitality of the slums."

Mr. V. and I had something in common: He romanticized poverty. I romanticized wealth. I imagined his world filled with grand mansions, champagne flutes, sizzling steaks, caviar, silk dresses, polite laughter, ivory cigarette holders, yellow roses in cut-glass vases, and the quiet rustle of power and money.

"May I interest you in some bread?" he asked, tipping the basket in my direction.

I demurred. I wanted to like American white bread, but to me, it tasted like wood shavings. Mr. V. had no such qualms. He placed his roll on his side plate, tore it in half, then cut a pat of butter from the block stamped with the letter C. There's a lot you can learn about a man from the way he butters his bread. Pa slathered it on in great yellow globs without regard for evenly spreading it or covering the whole piece. Mr. V. spread his butter in small daubs, coaxing it into each corner. A careful man with an eye for detail.

The waiter reappeared to take our order. I hadn't even opened the menu at my plate.

"Asparagus soup followed by prime rib and mashed potatoes?" Mr. Van der Zalm suggested. I nodded. Anything was fine by me, but I wondered where they grew asparagus in the middle of a New York winter.

With the task of ordering completed, he turned the conversation back to me. "Tell me about your family."

"Pa, I mean, my father, was a fur cutter in the garment district—Persian lamb. He died two years ago." It was a lie, but my scoundrel of a father—a passionate Zionist, a dreamer, and an all-around difficult human being—was as good as dead.

"I'm sorry to hear that. And your mother?"

"She sews uniforms for the police."

"Siblings?"

"I had a sister and brother in Russia, but they died."

"That's tragic."

And I was sorry I'd mentioned it. I didn't want to dwell on those memories. "But I have a brother Arnold who was born here."

"What does he do?"

No need to mention that Arnold fancied himself an anarchist. "He graduates from Washington Irving High this year, and then, may God be listening, will go to City College." A note of pride crept into my voice. "Arnold hardly speaks Yiddish; that's how much of a Yankee he is."

"And you? What languages do you speak?" He tilted his head, attentive, and I got the impression we had moved on from small talk. He was measuring me up for something—I couldn't tell what, but it made me feel important.

"With my mother, I speak Yiddish. Her English is not tip-top." I should blush from such an understatement.

"What about Russian?"

"Yes, I speak Russian, and I've picked up a smattering of Italian and Polish." I've always liked the word *smattering*, but it was a tough one to shoehorn into a sentence. I gave myself a mental pat on the back. Mr. V. brought out the best in me.

He looked pleased with my answer. "Are you interested in school, like your brother?"

"No, I'm a career gal. I have my own beauty business."

"Oh, really?"

"I make creams and powders. So far, I've been selling them out of our apartment and to the girls at Sid's, but I'm opening a store for customers soon." On impulse, I dug into my purse and took out a jar of La Crème du Eiffel Tower. The label was a beaut—an india ink drawing of the Paris landmark cupped between a pair of exquisite hands, sketched by yours truly. "You should try." I unscrewed the lid, and the fragrance of French lavender drifted up. "Give me your paw."

A lot of men might hesitate, but not Mr. V. When I put a dime-sized dab of cream on his palm, a little shock went up my arm at his touch. He rubbed his hands together.

"You see how fast it absorbs into your skin without a trace of greasiness? That's why it's called vanishing cream."

"I like it," he said, sniffing with appreciation. He didn't look amused and superior like some men do about female things. Then he picked up the jar. "Just one thing, Giddy. I believe the word *Eiffel* is spelled with two *f*'s."

I tucked the cream back in my purse, pretending I hadn't heard him. A hundred labels were already printed and paid for. Not a big whoop-de-do. I probably wasn't the only one on the Lower East Side who couldn't spell *Eiffel*. Maybe no one would notice. I held up my glass and took a healthy sip of my red wine. Through the glass, Mr. V. seemed bathed in a rosy glow.

"What you're doing is very admirable, Giddy," he was saying. "The American dream. You'll be another Helena Rubinstein."

"She caters to the Fifth Avenue rich ladies. My products are for working-class girls," I said as our waiter placed two bowls of what looked like green pond scum in front of us.

Mr. V. picked up the round spoon to the right of the teaspoon. I selected my corresponding utensil, but I waited for him to eat. He didn't gag, clutch his throat, or die, so I tasted a spoonful. To my surprise, it was terrific, and why wouldn't it be, with all that cream and butter? I ate it rapidly and even considered wiping the bowl clean with a piece of the lousy bread, but when Mr. V. placed his spoon on the plate under the bowl, I nixed the idea.

Within moments, the dishes were whisked away, and I saw my opportunity to turn the tables on him, find out if he had a family he spent time with between his important job on Ellis Island and his weekends at Sid's.

"So what about your family? Van der Zalm is a Dutch name, isn't it?" Of course, what I wanted to ask was whether he was married.

"My family came from the Netherlands in the seventeenth century. They were one of the first settlers in New Amsterdam, as New York was then called."

"So they were immigrants, too?" Another thing we had in common.

"In a manner of speaking."

"What business were they in?"

"Buying and exporting furs to Europe."

"And your wife's family? Also Dutch?" I was fishing shamelessly but I couldn't help myself.

A shadow passed over his handsome face. "She died last year after a long illness. We were never fortunate enough to have children."

I put my hand on his to show my sympathy, hoping he wouldn't think me too bold. "We have both suffered losses."

"Now, I just bury myself in my work."

"And Sid's? What brings you in every week? Forgive me for saying so, I've always seen you as rather straitlaced. For instance, I've never even seen you dancing."

"I have two left feet, but I like the ambience and Sam's martinis. And, of course, there is Hattie. She's terrific. I regard Sid's as my home away from home."

It was an answer, but it didn't quite explain his *constant* presence. My guess was he was lonely and at Sid's he had discovered a community, a family. My other guess was that Hattie was communicating with his dead wife. That would explain all their private sessions.

"Hattie has a remarkable connection to the spirit world, as I'm sure you know," I ventured.

"Indeed, I marvel at her abilities."

But I could tell by his tone he wasn't going to contribute anything more on that topic. Such a recent loss must be still painful, poor man.

To lighten the atmosphere, I said, "And the music? Remember the night Josephine Baker sang 'You're Driving Me Crazy'? What a voice, what a looker."

"She was a sensation," he said without much oomph in his voice.

Time for me to brag a little. "It's because of me that Miss Baker agreed to perform at Sid's."

"How so?"

"Miss Baker won't sing for an all-white audience. Of course, most clubs are segregated, including Sid's. So with Sid's blessing, I went up by Harlem to pay a visit to the New Corinthian Baptist Church.

I told their preacher if he brought ten of his churchgoers the night Miss Baker performed, Sid would make a generous contribution to the soup kitchen the church runs. I also promised to give everyone a drink on the house."

"How resourceful you are."

I preened. "That I am, but instead I should have offered a free Royal Crown Cola. Who knew the Baptists are teetotalers?"

"I hope Sid appreciates you. Cigarette girls are the backbone of his business."

I blushed. "Thank you, Mr. Van der Zalm, I think he does."

"You must call me Carter."

Just then, the waiter brought the prime rib. Although I had been famished, when I looked down at my plate, my appetite went south. The meat appeared more wounded than cooked. I started in on the mashed potatoes. They tasted strangely of horseradish but I choked them down.

Mr. V. ate like a European—his fork in the left hand, tines pointing down, and his knife in the right—and after cutting his meat, he didn't switch hands but simply speared the food and ate it. A small detail but another thing we had in common.

After a few minutes, he said, "Sorry, I am being rude. Here I am eating, and you haven't touched your meat. You don't care for prime rib?"

How could I be honest without giving offence? "It's a little rare for my liking."

He snapped his fingers, summoning the waiter. "Take this back and bring the lady a veal chop, well done."

I appreciated his thoughtfulness and being referred to as a lady. He made me feel as if there was no one else in the world he would rather be sitting across the table from than me. So charming he was. I was keeping my eye on this fellow. Maybe charm could be learned like accounting or dentistry, or Renaissance art? But I couldn't forget the real reason I was here.

I gestured to the slip of paper sticking out of his pocket. "You said at Sid's that you had information for me."

He wiped his mouth with his napkin. "The man in your sketch was indeed a Cossack in the old country. A soldier in the czar's private army." He hesitated. "But there's something else."

"Tell me," I said, on the edge of my seat.

"You're not the only person looking for him."

# Chapter 8

"What do you mean I'm not the only one? Who else is looking for him?"

"This is sensitive information, Giddy. Can I trust your discretion?"

"Absolutely."

Carter lowered his voice. "I'm not telling tales if I say that we at Immigration and Naturalization often work on security issues with the US Secret Service. My contact there, Agent Miller, is also interested in finding this Cossack."

My mouth gaped. The Secret Service was involved? "Wait, how do you know we're looking for the same man?"

"Elementary, my dear Watson," he said in a mock English accent. "Oh, great, here's your chop."

The waiter put the veal chop, hot and cooked properly, in front of me. I took a bite and let the juice run around my mouth and the meat play handball against my tonsils. The Gentiles were onto something. I had never tasted such tender, succulent meat. I finally swallowed, reluctant to let the morsel go.

"How is it?"

"Perfect, thank you."

"Good." He smiled. "When I promised to look for your Cossack, I honestly did not think I would find him. Since Congress passed the

Immigration Act of 1924, we have limited the number of immigrants permitted to enter this country through a national-origins quota. Each country, including Russia, was granted a quota based on how many of their people were already living in America. According to the 1930 census, the existing proportion of Russians is less than three percent of the population."

Usually, I hate being lectured to, but I was fascinated. This Cossack entered America because of the Russian quota, just like my family.

"Over the past three years, approximately thousands of Russians have entered the US, the majority through Ellis Island. After checking the list of undesirables, my clerk came up with several hundred names. I reviewed the list and narrowed it down based on gender, age, and town of origin. I came across a Cossack from Slavostok who came here in 1936 and fits your description." He paused to take a sip.

I couldn't quite believe what I was hearing. Slavostok, a small town, was about ten miles north of Stulchyn. This man, who didn't know me from a bump on a log, had gone to bat for me and might have found my needle in the haystack. I was grateful, but the ever-present cynical part of me wondered why Carter had put himself to so much trouble.

"If he had passed through the admission process without incident, I might not have caught him, but this Cossack was detained for two weeks at the quarantine hospital on North Brother Island on suspicion of tuberculosis."

I held up my hand. "I thought the sick weren't allowed in the country." I told him about the little girl in the line in front of me at Ellis Island who was deported.

Carter cleared his throat. "Our goal at immigration is to admit as many sound, healthy people as we can. If they have treatable medical problems, we permit them to stay. But there are exceptions.

About one percent of the people who arrive at our shores are indeed deported back to their country of origin. It is regrettable, but we need to exclude those suffering from both mental and physical defects as well as infectious diseases. As for that girl? It sounds like she had a contagious eye disease, a common reason for rejection. Trachoma, for example, causes blindness, and that can lead to an LPC designation."

"LPC?"

"Likely to become a public charge."

While I understood the reason for the policy, I still found it harsh. Many families sacrificed everything they had to come here, only to be separated upon arrival. What happened to those sent back alone?

Carter went on. "As I was saying, last week, I paid the staff at the quarantine hospital a visit and showed them your sketch. As luck would have it, one of the orderlies recognized him from three years ago. Turns out the Cossack did not have TB."

"So my sketch wasn't a bad likeness after all."

"That's right, plus the orderly had good reason to remember him."

"Why was that?"

"Your Cossack was ranting about the Red Army. As I'm sure you know, after the Bolsheviks defeated the czar in the civil war, Stalin declared the Cossacks enemies of the state because of their"—he curled his fingers into quotation marks—"'counterrevolutionary behavior.' Thousands of Cossack men, women, and children were persecuted and killed by Red Army troops. Stalin was exacting his revenge on those who had opposed him."

I nodded. We were in America when the civil war ended, and Pa had danced around our tiny apartment, delighted by the Bolsheviks' victory. I wasn't a fan of Stalin, but I hated the Cossacks even more. They had gotten what they deserved. At least that's what Pa had said. I didn't often agree with him, but this time, I did.

"Anyway," Carter said. "Another patient, a Jewish tailor from Kiev, said persecuting the Cossacks was the only good thing Stalin had ever done. Finally they got what was coming to them. Your Cossack 'pasted him one in the kisser,' as the orderly phrased it, breaking the poor tailor's jaw in three places." Carter paused to wipe his mouth with his napkin.

I did the same. "Go on."

"The Cossack was charged with 'grievous bodily assault,' but before he could be tried, convicted, and deported, he slipped out of the hospital in the middle of the night and vanished." Carter looked rueful. "According to Agent Miller at the Secret Service, this man is wanted for another serious assault and is a suspect in a murder investigation. You were unquestionably correct when you said we made a mistake when we allowed him into our country. He left a trail of violence and brutality in Russia, and now he's repeating the pattern in America."

It felt good to have my suspicions acknowledged. "This man must be brought to justice."

"Yes, and there's more." He signaled the waiter to take our plates. When he was gone, Carter continued. "We have reason to believe that he might be involved in an espionage plot."

"To do what?"

"I'm not at liberty to say. But the situation between Russia and America is very sensitive."

I remembered what Arnold had said that morning about Russia needing support against Germany. "The Cossack must hate Stalin for what he did to his people. But how does he pose a threat to America?" I asked.

"All I'll say is that he could upset diplomatic relations. Most Americans are opposed to joining a struggle taking place halfway around the world. Everyone remembers shipping our boys overseas during the Great War. President Roosevelt is trying his best to keep us out of the conflict between Russia and Germany and the rest of Europe. A Russian incident on American soil could bring us into the fray."

I shook my head, trying to make sense of all the information Carter had shared. I'd gone to Carter to find the man responsible for my mother's rape, and now I was being told he was an international threat. "What has that to do with me? Why are you telling me this?"

"Because we need to find him. And you've given us our first lead in months. A Pinkerton detective tailed him for weeks, then he lost him." Carter withdrew the white square from his pocket. "I have here the name of your Cossack and the address on his immigration paperwork."

I reached for it, but Carter held it back. "When you came to my office, you said you wanted to find this man because you wanted to talk to him, but I have a feeling that's not entirely true. You want to hold him responsible for what he's done to your family."

I rubbed my arms. The truth was I wanted to nail the Cossack's balls to the wall. I wanted to watch him die a slow, painful death. "I want him to find no peace, either in this life or the next."

Carter's eyes softened. "I do not blame you. But you must understand that there's more at stake here. I want to offer you an opportunity to serve your country and bring justice for your family."

"What are you saying?"

"I'd like to hire you to find the Cossack."

"Pardon?"

"As Napoleon once said, 'A spy in the right place is as good as twenty thousand men in the field.'"

I was so surprised I burst out laughing. "You mean cloak and dagger stuff?"

"More cloak than dagger." There wasn't the hint of a smile.

The only thing I knew about spies was what I'd seen in movies. "Do I get to wear a backless dress, diamond earrings, and strap a gun to my thigh?" I joked.

But Carter was dead serious. "You've got the brains, a sharp tongue, and a keen eye. That's more useful than a gun. You speak Russian. You can find out his haunts. Talk to his acquaintances."

I did know how to snoop. I could read lips and I knew the Lower East Side like the back of my hand.

"Spying is all about gaining other people's trust and, sometimes, persuading them to do things against their better judgment. I've watched you at the club. You're a natural. You have a way of making people of all classes and walks of life trust you. Everyone loves you, from Hattie to Sam to Winston to Sid. And as a girl, you won't arouse suspicion. You will blend in. He probably spotted our detective from a mile away."

"That's very flattering but—"

"And you have the best motive in the world for finding him."

I paused to think. He was right. I was going to keep looking for the Cossack with or without his help. But now the US government was asking me to put my personal vendetta on hold for the greater good. How could I say no? "All right, I'll do it."

He smiled. "Wonderful."

I hesitated a moment. Carter had said he wanted to hire me, which implied there would be a pay packet. I couldn't afford not to ask. "And my wages?"

"I can give you fifty dollars now and a stipend for any expenses you incur during your investigation. How would you feel about ten dollars per week?"

The amount Carter was suggesting would bring me within spitting distance of leasing the storefront, but I wasn't about to settle for the first offer. "I'd feel better about twelve."

"You've got a deal."

Carter pulled out his billfold and counted out fifty dollars in fives. I wanted to rip off my clothes and roll naked in the cash, but I refrained and instead swept the crisp Lincolns off the table and into my pocketbook before he could change his mind.

Then he slid the paper toward me. "His name and last known address."

I unfolded the paper. On it was written in neat, sloping penmanship "Yuri Ivanov, 544 Worth Street, Five Points."

Finally, I had a name for the man who haunted my nightmares: Yuri Ivanov. "Thank you," I said, tucking the paper into my purse.

Carter nodded. "We don't believe that address is current, so your first step will be locating Yuri. Then shadowing him. We need to find out what organizations he belongs to, who his associates are, who goes to his apartment, whether he has large amounts of cash, whether he has weapons, and anything else you can discover."

"How will I report what I find out? At the club?"

He shook his head. "We'll need a quiet place to talk." He hesitated a minute, thinking.

I was an old hand at making snoop reports. "I usually tilt my hat to the left at the club. If I have information for you, I'll tilt it to the right."

"Yes, excellent. Then we'll meet somewhere private—the Anchor Bar, for example."

The Anchor Bar was a booze can around the corner from Sid's. "Of course, we won't meet there every time. We will change to other venues—different bars, a park, coffee shops, the Marquis Hotel. We'll need to move the location from time to time for safety reasons."

It seemed extreme, his insistence on secrecy, but fine, I was happy to go along with it. I needed the money, and the more time I spent with Carter, the more I liked him.

"I must caution you, Giddy, if you find Ivanov, tread carefully. Do not approach him. Whatever your personal feelings, you must put them aside and focus on helping your country. We need Ivanov alive so we can interrogate him, find out what he is plotting."

Carter could interrogate him—after I did. But I kept that thought to myself. "Cross my heart and hope to die."

"I'm serious. Promise me you won't do anything rash. Ivanov is dangerous, likely armed. I couldn't forgive myself if something happened to you." He placed his hand over mine and I was moved by the warm touch.

"I promise," I said solemnly.

I was nosy by nature, which had landed me my role as snoop for Hattie, and now I was a snoop for the US Secret Service and Department of Immigration.

It seemed like a promotion.

# Chapter 9

---◈---

*Five Points, New York*

Five Points was the kind of neighborhood where girls vanish into thin air like steam over a kettle of soup. The *Post* claimed it was the most dangerous slum in the world, but I didn't need a newspaper to tell me that. It was right there in front of my schnoz. Everything about the place horrified me—trash cans overflowing with moldy vegetables, buckets brimming with night soil waiting to be collected by the honey-dipper truck, and rickety-legged children sleeping in doorways. And the manure! The peaty smell of the livery stables enveloped the neighborhood. Dried, pulverized dung turned the air a thick, gritty brown that clung to everything like a cheap hairnet. It was three o'clock in the afternoon, but it could have been dusk.

This was Five Points and today it was my hunting ground. I walked along Baxter until I got to Park Row, where it intersected with Worth, creating five points and giving the neighborhood its name. I didn't need to look at Carter's paper to remember Ivanov's last known address: 544 Worth.

I turned down Worth, scanning the buildings for a street number. I peered into tenement entrances. There was no one to ask, just a tough-looking group of Poles on the corner, and I didn't want to approach them. A couple of Irish beat cops sometimes patrolled the district, but this afternoon there wasn't a blue uniform in sight. I was putting myself in danger, but I wasn't an idiot. So when I was covering for Caterina at hatcheck last Saturday and discovered a revolver in a lady's mink coat, I nabbed it. I'd never held a gun, let alone shot one—I figured it couldn't be that hard to aim and pull the trigger. I felt better with it in my pocket, banging against my thigh.

I knew these tenements because they were like mine except worse—four apartments to a floor, each with one bedroom, a kitchen, and a front parlor, and one toilet down the hall for all four families. I wouldn't be surprised if there were ten people to a flat, plus a couple of boarders, everyone living cheek by jowl. If the tenants were lucky, maybe there was a see-through between the kitchen and front room to let in light. The air shaft in the back would broadcast everyone's fights, love cries, birthing screams, and the smell of cooking. I could have found my way around any one of these lousy apartments in the pitch-dark.

From one of the windows came the sound of a radio playing my Cole Porter favorite, "Let's Do It, Let's Fall in Love," and I did a few side steps, imagining how Carter might whirl me around the dance floor once I'd found Ivanov for him. I came back to earth when a housewife leaned out a window and hurled down the contents of a chamber pot, missing me by inches.

I wasn't surprised Ivanov had slipped through the Pinkerton detective's fingers. Five Points was the type of place you moved to when you didn't want to be found. Come to think of it, Pa probably lived somewhere around here, which would serve him right. Pray God, I didn't bump into him by accident today.

There were no numbers on most of the buildings, just signs with missing digits or, in some cases, smeared chalk marks. No wonder the Pinkerton detective hadn't been able to find Ivanov's home. I spotted one sign that was legible, number 512, and then counted up the block until I got to where logically number 544 ought to be, but it turned out to be a kosher slaughterhouse. STEINFELD'S MEATS, the sign over the door announced in both English and Yiddish. I put a hanky to my nose. The stench was enough to turn me into a vegetarian. Judging by the crumbling brick and sagging doors, the place had been there for many years. This was the address Ivanov had given the immigration folks at Ellis Island. Was this his idea of a joke? Was he saying that anyone looking for him would end up swinging from the wrong end of a meat hook?

I continued down the street, looking for someone to show my sketch. Odds were Ivanov had lived somewhere in this vicinity in a cold-water flat. If anyone asked why I was looking for him, my cover story was that I was his cousin and just arrived from Russia. I had dressed the part, borrowing Ma's old gray coat and tying a scarf around my head. I asked in the corner candy stores, checked the breweries, tanneries, and cheap diners. Everywhere, I flashed a smile and my sketch, even a quarter here and there where it might do some good. But nobody knew anything, or if they did, they weren't saying.

I passed a wall where scrawled in white paint was the slogan "America first. Only the Jew bankers want war." This was the German American Bund at work, spreading their antisemitism and gathering support for the Nazis in Germany. I'd like to see the whole bunch of them drawn, quartered, koshered, and crucified. The Nazis had to be stopped, but the idea of America joining a war made me apprehensive. Arnold was nearly nineteen years old. He would enlist if America went to war. He might be an anarchist, but he loved America as much as I did.

I tried the Russian settlement house where émigrés congregated, but that was a dead end, too. I was losing hope when I spotted an old woman wearing a babushka and a thin wool coat that had seen better days at the corner of Mulberry and Bayard. She was struggling with her bags of groceries. She dropped one and a tomato rolled out into the street. I lunged after it and returned it to her.

She thanked me in Russian. "*Spasibo.*"

"*Pozhaluysta,*" I replied and she smiled, giving me a glimpse of a gap where her front teeth should have been.

She had the manner of an inquisitive bird, of a gossip, a busybody, a buttinsky. In other words, just the ticket. I offered to carry her groceries. As we walked, we chatted about the high cost of bread and whether they would ever find Amelia Earhart, who hadn't been heard from since her twin-engine Lockheed disappeared over the Pacific on her way around the world nearly two years ago. I learned the old woman's name was Manka and she had emigrated from Kiev, the capital of the Ukraine. I teased her about being a big-city sophisticate.

At her building, she gave me the dirt on every one of her neighbors except the one I was interested in. I took out my sketch. "I'm looking for a Russian. Perhaps you've seen him around here? His name is Yuri Ivanov."

She held it two inches from her eyes. Her face changed and she gave me a frosty stare. "This man is a friend of yours? You seem like such a nice *devochka.*"

"Not a friend, just a man I need to find. Do you know him?"

"*Da,* how I wish I did not."

A ray of hope. I was on the right track. "Can you tell me where to find him?"

"We cannot talk in the street. Come up to my apartment."

She was my only lead—I had no choice. What couldn't she tell me in public? I wondered as I schlepped her shopping up five flights of stairs. I was panting by the time we reached her door. *This better be good.*

Manka's apartment was cold and miserable. Just what you'd expect in a run-down dump like this building. A geranium in a cracked pot teetered on the windowsill. The poor thing struggled, bending horizontally, seeking the nonexistent sun. I looked around for a heat radiator and saw she didn't have one.

Manka removed her babushka, revealing a coronet of thick gray braids held in place with a crochet hook, then set about making tea. She gestured for me to sit at the table and brought me a cup, which warmed my hands, though from the color of the tea, she'd used an old tea bag, it was so weak.

"You said you knew Yuri," I prompted once she sat down.

"I did not know his name, but I recognize his face from your drawing. The crazy hat." She paused. "I will tell you this for free. You are Russian. I am Russian. I like you. This Yuri is not for you."

I waited for her to say more.

"This man, a Cossack, no?" she began, her breath forming misty clouds in the freezing room. "He used to come here. He and his Free Russia pals—louts and ruffians but also some decent-looking workingmen—met at the apartment next door, 5B. They made such a ruckus—drinking vodka, arguing about politics. I couldn't sleep. The walls are so thin I heard every time one of them farted. Why couldn't they play chess like normal men?"

Thank God for the Mankas of the world. I'd never heard of a group called Free Russia, but if Ivanov was involved, I needed to know more. "What did they argue about?"

"What do all Cossacks talk about? How much they hate the Bolsheviks. They blame them for everything bad, from their hemorrhoids to their ugly girlfriends to Hitler. They want to topple Stalin from power so they can return to Russia and make their own government." She lowered her voice. "Sometimes I hear them talk about making homemade bombs and blowing up railroads and shipyards, then blaming it on Russia."

I leaned forward. Free Russia's mission was absurd, a fantasy—the Cossacks could never overthrow Stalin—but in the process of trying, they could do a lot of damage. Roosevelt wanted to keep America out of the war. If there was an incident here . . . "Manka, what specifically did you hear them say? This is important. If they are planning to hurt people, I need to know."

She gave me a look that said the meter on free information just ran out. I slapped a dollar on the table between us. "Courtesy of the US government."

She slid the money into the pocket of her housedress. "I never heard any details," she said. "You know men. They like to hear themselves talk. It is all the shit of the horse. But still, you would do best to leave this Yuri alone."

"When's the next meeting?"

"They haven't been here for a few weeks now. They must meet somewhere else."

"But I'm guessing you know where they went," I pressed.

"No, and I don't care to, and neither should you."

"Thank you," I said. "You've been very helpful."

I left Manka's apartment, trying to figure out what Ivanov was up to. On a hunch, I sought out the nearest hardware store. If Yuri was planning an explosion, he would need supplies.

The middle-aged woman behind the counter took a long moment with my sketch, then nodded. "Yes, he came in last week."

Bingo. "Do you remember what he bought?"

"Chicken wire, wood boards, nails, plaster of paris, and cheesecloth. I remember because I tried to make conversation with him, like I do with all customers. I asked if he was making a cage and nest-ing boxes for racing pigeons. He told me to mind my own—pardon my French—fucking business. I wanted to knock his block off."

I puzzled over the list—nothing seemed like components of a bomb—but he'd been here just last week, so he was still in the area. I thanked her profusely, then left, a new spring in my step. I had a full report for Carter. I was closing in on the Cossack.

# Chapter 10

———◈———

*Central Park, New York*

As my bubbe would have said, "It's so cold, the milk cows give icicles." But here I was marching through Central Park on my way to meet Carter at the Metropolitan Museum of Art. When he had suggested the Met last night at Sid's, I was excited. This was what spies did—rendezvous in public places where they could exchange secrets without attracting attention—and here I was headed to Fifth Avenue no less.

I couldn't wait to tell him what I'd found out. And if I was being honest, I wanted to see him again. Our lunch at Cholly's had revealed he was more than just a handsome face; he had another side to him, a softer, caring side. He was an attentive man who valued my opinion, maybe even admired me a little, and not just on account of my looks.

A skift of snow on the ground is fine if you're wearing a fur coat and heavy boots, which I was not. The sun shone, but there was a stiff breeze that lashed at my face until I wanted to weep. I didn't, though, because the tears would freeze on my face and make things worse. Once my business took flight—like Charles Lindbergh soaring through the clouds in the *Spirit of St. Louis* on his transatlantic journey—I would hit the spring sale at Goldstein's Furs and buy a jacket on the layaway plan, maybe Persian lamb, maybe even red fox.

I'd never been off the island of Manhattan unless you count

Ellis Island or Russia, but Central Park was what I imagined the real American countryside must look like. It had a lake and meadows, if that was the right word for these open fields where you'd expect to see sheep and cows grazing. Snow patched the ground. The in-between bits were green, such a pale green it wasn't actually green, just the promise of the spring to come. Trees grew everywhere. Some had needles. Some should have had leaves but didn't because it was winter. There were a few lonely Canada geese, which must have forgotten to check the calendar and fly south. It should have been peaceful, but frankly, nature made me nervous. I never knew what was lurking under the bushes waiting to leap out at me.

I barreled along past Belvedere Castle, conveniently marked with black metal signs outlined in red for dummkopfs like me who didn't know a castle from a pregnant buffalo. But when I heard the clip-clop of horses on the bridle path, I jumped to one side, my heart in my throat. So many years later, the sound of horses' hooves sent me right back to the pogrom. I relaxed when I saw two society girls on matching bay horses come around the bend. It was hard to tell which of the four were better groomed, the girls in their jodhpurs and derby riding hats or their horses with braided manes and tails. The riders grimaced at the sight of tents up ahead, which were clustered together like covered wagons in a Western movie. Up close there was nothing romantic about the scene. It was a Hooverville—a shantytown with hovels constructed out of scrap lumber, cinder bricks, spit, and whatever else came to hand, each thing somehow holding the other thing up. I felt sorry for the hoboes who lived there, especially this winter, which had been so cold the pipes in the tenement next to ours froze and burst.

By the time I reached the museum, my feet were like Popsicles. I skipped up the stairs, through the main entrance, and out of the cold. Inside the warmth of the museum, I looked around, my mouth agape at the sheer gorgeousness of my surroundings. I had never been in a cathedral, but this enormous building of graceful arches, fluted columns, and marble floors was like a church, only dedicated to art. How had I lived all my life in New York and never visited this place?

I put a nickel in the donations box and asked the guard in a blue uniform with gold braid if he could please direct me to the American Wing. He examined me like I was there to steal the paintings, not just gawk at them.

"I want to see the American impressionists," I added.

In a voice that could have frozen a hot knish, he replied, "Impressionism, twentieth century, second floor, Galleries 770 and 771, miss."

I climbed the wide staircase, hoping he didn't hear the squelching of my leaky shoes on every step or notice the wet footprints I left on the marble stairs.

The first thing I glimpsed in Gallery 771 was Carter's broad back filling out the shoulders of his camel coat and his blond hair curling over the collar. He sat on the only bench in the vast room, in front of a seven-foot painting of a lady with an hourglass figure. She was wearing a lot of mascara and a black dress with jeweled straps. From the lady's schnozzola, I guessed she was Jewish, maybe one of the snooty-pants Weimar Jews from the Upper West Side.

I slid onto the bench next to Carter and gently poked him with my elbow. He smiled and stood, paw extended. He couldn't help himself. Such a handshaker, he was.

"Sorry, my fingers are cold," I said, standing as well.

"You know what they say, 'Cold hands, warm heart.'"

I didn't know how to reply to that, so I approached the painting for a closer look, not so close to make the guard in the corner nervous, but close enough to see the brushwork. The dress was satin, the kind that shows every stitch even if you use the finest-gauge needle.

"A lot of labor went into sewing that getup," I said to Carter. "It looks like a simple, elegant dress, like one of Elsa Schiaparelli's designs in *Women's Wear Daily*," I added. "But there's nothing simple about it, not with that plunging neckline and draped skirt."

"Good observation."

I acknowledged the compliment with a polite nod, as I imagined Katharine Hepburn would if she was playing a career-gal role. "She's a beauty," I said of the portrait. "Who is she?"

"The painting is called *Madame X*, but her real name was Madame Pierre Gautreau. She was a Parisian socialite originally from New Orleans. This was a scandalous portrait. The artist, John Singer Sargent, initially painted her with one strap falling off her shoulder."

I dared not ask what he thought of my cigarette-girl outfit. Now *that* was scandalous. Instead, I asked, "Any relation to Singer sewing machine?"

"On his mother's side. Tell me what you think of the painting."

"Mr. Sargent can paint like a son of a gun. Madame X is regal. She's glamorous, but she needs some color in her face. Her skin is the color of pea soup with too much cream." She looked like the pale kids in the tenements who lacked spinach or meat—you didn't need to be a doctor to figure that out. Slum kids I could understand being anemic, but a socialite?

Carter peered at the painting. "You are right. She does have a slight greenish cast to her skin."

"A little red in the paint would take care of that. They're complementary colors, red and green. But you probably know that already."

"You have a good eye. I have seen this painting dozens of times and that never occurred to me." He smiled. "Not only a spy, but an art critic as well."

The only thing I knew about art was from sketching faces in charcoal and colored pencils, but I liked that Carter thought I was smart. If I had to choose between being smart or educated, I would choose smart. "So, I gave my opinion. What's yours?"

"Technically masterful, no doubt about it, and undeniably skillful. You could almost reach out and touch the sheen of the satin."

"So do you like it or not?"

He cleared his throat. "*Madame* X is erotic, sensual, and lovely, but I find overall the depiction of loose morals displeasing. There was an art exhibit in Munich called *Degenerate Art*. This painting would have fit in nicely. I prefer more wholesome scenes. Landscapes, military battles, peasants laboring in the fields gathering wheat—that type of subject."

I knew from the word *degenerate*, of course. Degenerate was like Mr. Berkovitz from 3C following me down our unlit hall, trying to catch up to me on the landing and peer inside my shirtwaist, or the O'Toole twins stealing ladies' brassieres off the clothesline, but the expression *degenerate art* was a new one on me.

I wondered if he was being honest with himself. After all, he dropped into Sid's every week without fail. What did that tell me about his morals? Was he so upright and proper? And why was it only us girls who got accused of having loose morals? As to whether Mr. Sargent was a degenerate artist or not, I didn't know, but his brushwork was firm and decisive. No floundering, no second-guessing himself.

Carter turned away from Madame X and her beautiful, haughty face. "Shall we walk around? You can give me the full report."

I followed his gaze and saw the guard in the corner observing us. "Sure," I said, looping my arm through Carter's, like we were a couple, and catching a whiff of his aftershave.

As we walked toward French impressionism, I brought him up to date on my investigation in Five Points, leaving out the detail about carrying a gun. I didn't want him to think I was going to break my promise and shoot Ivanov.

"I went by the address you gave me, but it was a slaughterhouse. So I canvassed the area with my sketch, asking the neighbors if they knew him, but no dice. No one remembered him, or if they did, they weren't talking."

"Maybe they thought you were a former girlfriend or a bill collector."

"I had a cover story." I waited a second for him to be impressed by the expression, which I'd heard in a spy movie. When he didn't react, I added, "Which was that I was Ivanov's cousin from Russia just off the boat. Whether anyone believed me, I don't know, but I dressed the part. I found out a bunch of stuff." An exaggeration, but I wanted his full attention.

"You're already a better investigator than the Pinkerton detective. He couldn't even find the address on Worth Street."

I glowed with his compliment. "Oh, I found out much more than your detective."

Carter waited for me to continue, but instead I approached a painting of a wooden footbridge over a pond filled with pink water lilies and grassy foliage. The landscape was so peaceful I wanted to step inside it, sit on that bridge, and dangle my toes in the water. The plaque read CLAUDE MONET.

"So," Carter prompted. "What did you learn?"

"I had a lucky break." I described meeting Manka, carrying her shopping, being invited up to her fifth-floor apartment. "What a hike. The rents are cheaper the higher up you go." Carter, in his fancy duds and millionaire accent, wasn't renting a railway flat in the slums of Five Points anytime soon, but he'd seemed interested in the plight of the tenement dwellers at our lunch, so I elaborated. "She wore this tatty housedress with missing buttons, carpet slippers with holes cut out for her bunions. She invited me into her place, which you would not believe—"

"I do not need to know the woman's history or what her apartment looked like. Just the essentials without the digressions."

Carter hadn't met the old girl, hadn't felt how cold her home was, how our breath came out of our mouths in plumes as we talked.

"Digression is my natural way of telling a story," I said in a dignified voice, but I complied and cut to the chase. I told him what Manka had said about Yuri's Free Russia meetings in her building. "Have you heard of them?" I lowered my voice. "They're anti-Bolsheviks determined to topple Stalin."

"We've had our eye on the Free Russia group for a while," he said quietly, glancing behind us. The guard from the previous gallery had followed us into the exhibit. Carter took my elbow and steered me into the next room, where a huge statue of a naked man stood front and center.

"Giddy, I can trust you, can't I?" Carter asked.

I nodded, though I was a bit distracted by the statute, as the fellow's schlong was right at eye level and he—*Perseus with the Head of Medusa*, according to the plaque—was definitely a toque.

I pulled my eyes away. "Yes, you can trust me."

Carter leaned in close. "We have reason to believe that Free Russia plans to assassinate Lazar Kaganovich when he arrives this spring."

"Stalin's right-hand man?" I stared at Carter, no longer interested in Perseus.

"You read the newspapers."

"When I get the chance," I said. "What makes you think Free Russia is targeting him?"

"Agent Miller, my contact in the Secret Service, had an agent working undercover in the group."

"Had?"

"He's now missing," Carter replied. "But he did discover they were tracking Kaganovich's forthcoming visit to America. Stalin claims he needs Roosevelt's arms and equipment to head off any possibility, however remote, of an invasion from Hitler."

"Hitler invade Russia? But that's so far-fetched."

"Not to Stalin. I trust you have heard how paranoid the man is? Stalin's argument is, of course, that America and Russia should unite against a common enemy—Hitler. The Free Russia group, just as paranoid, wants Kaganovich to fail."

I couldn't imagine even a man like Hitler being nuts enough to invade Russia.

Carter continued, "What better way to sabotage an arms deal than by assassinating Stalin's deputy on American soil? What would Stalin's response be? It would be grist for his most rabid paranoid fantasies. He already thinks he's surrounded by 'two-facers' and 'spies,' as he calls them."

"He would see the murder of Kaganovich as an American plot to sabotage his efforts to defend Russia," I said, the gravity of Carter's words sinking in. "An international incident like this would seriously jeopardize Russia-America relations. And if there is a war, and we all hope there won't be, drag us into it."

"Exactly. And now it sounds like your Cossack is involved. We know Ivanov is violently anti-Bolshevik. I wouldn't be surprised if he volunteered to pull the trigger." Carter sounded distracted. "Splendid work, Giddy. This information helps our case against Ivanov. If only we knew where he was . . ."

If Carter believed Ivanov was the triggerman for Free Russia, all the more reason to catch him, bring him to justice, and stop an assassination. I didn't have to think twice. "I'll learn where Free Russia meets now. I'll infiltrate the group and find Ivanov before it's too late."

"No," Carter protested. "That's much too risky. Didn't you hear me say the Secret Service agent went missing?"

"Being a woman gives me an advantage. Like you said, I'm al-

ready a better investigator than your detective. I'll be a better undercover than your agent, too."

"No, I really must insist. What if something happened to you?
First let me confer with Agent Miller on next steps."

I held my ground. "You forget I've got a personal stake in seeing
Ivanov apprehended. Remember, I came to you with his sketch. You
can't stop me from searching for him."

He studied me. "You're stubborn, aren't you?" But there was admiration in his voice.

"My ma's word is *aggravating*."

He chuckled. "Well, I know when I've been bested. If you're going
to take such risks, you deserve to be compensated." Carter made sure
we were alone, then reached into the inner pocket of his suit jacket
for his billfold and counted out a stack of five-dollar bills. "Go ahead.
It's for you. A bonus for a job well done."

The money was crisp in my hands. With this, I could sign the
lease for my storefront. The thought nearly made me *plotz*, collapse,
with joy. I was making my dream happen at the expense of Ivanov's.
"You're a prince. I can't thank you enough."

"You are most welcome. You deserve it. Maybe you can use some
of this to buy a pair of stockings. A hardworking spy needs a decent
pair of silk stockings."

I flushed with mortification. If anyone else had noticed my bare
legs, it wouldn't have bothered me—I was a girl who knew her
worth—but Carter was different. Bare legs. Bare shoulders. I didn't
want him to see me as one of those women with loose morals, like
Madame X. "Good idea," I murmured.

"And, Giddy?"

"Yes?"

"Be careful. I mean it. I would never forgive myself if something
happened to you. The men in Free Russia are a bunch of extremists."

"Don't worry. I've already thought up a cover story. I'll say I'm the widow of a man who was killed by the Bolsheviks and his dying words were . . ."

I trailed off because Carter was vigorously shaking his head.

"Right, keep it simple."

"That's my girl," he said, his hand on my waist as he ushered us out of the exhibit.

# Chapter 11

———◇———

*Lower East Side, New York*

My plan to infiltrate the Free Russia group hit a snag. Despite my efforts, I hadn't managed to locate their meeting site. I think best when my hands are busy, so I turned over the problem in my mind as I applied canary-yellow paint to the walls inside the shop on Broome Street. Much to Ma's and Arnold's delight, I had leased the storefront and I was turning it into the business of my dreams. I'd already cleaned the years of smoke and nicotine from the windows and was planning on painting the wainscoting a classy black to contrast the cheery yellow walls. Outside in the cold February air, Arnold, armed with a putty knife, scratched the lettering of the old sign, FELD-MAN'S SODAS, from the windows. If he and Ma wondered where I got the money, they didn't ask, and I didn't volunteer.

The premises on Broome Street were mine, at least for now. After forking over six months' rent in advance and buying paint, my savings had taken a big hit. The money from Carter wouldn't last forever. I needed to make a success of this business or get in line at the soup kitchen. There was no third option. No one in the garment district would hire a wisenheimer like me. My old boss had made sure of that.

There was a tap on the window. I looked up to see Little Hattie Faultfinder giving Arnold instructions on how to properly remove the old lettering. I waved her in. Arnold mouthed a thank-you.

Hattie limped in, surprisingly well dressed this morning—pleated silk blouse, feathered hat, brown jacket with a short peplum skirt, string of pearls, lipstick. She looked like a little squirrel on the track of a whole new supply of nuts. Something was up.

I found a chair for her. "What brings you to my humble store today, Hattie?"

"I had to see what's been keeping you so busy these last weeks," she said. "You've dashed out of Sid's most nights without so much as a goodbye."

Leave it to Hattie to get straight to the point. After our museum tryst, Carter and I had been meeting more frequently, sometimes at Horn & Hardart's Automat, since it was open all hours—he found it quaint to feed nickels into the slot for my tuna on rye—and once at the Anchor Bar around the corner from Sid's. Carter told me Agent Miller had reluctantly approved my operation. The Secret Service was also trying to track down Free Russia, but Carter had sung my praises and Agent Miller agreed they could use me, especially as Kaganovich's arrival was set for April. I had little by way of updates, but Carter seemed to enjoy my company and always asked after my family and my beauty business. As much as I wanted to nab Ivanov and stop him from killing Kaganovich, I would miss my precious tête-à-têtes with Carter.

Hattie inspected the room with a critical eye. "You haven't made that much headway yet. So what have you been up to? Not looking for that Cossack, I hope," she said.

I concentrated on painting the wall. "No," I lied. "You told me to stay away."

"Then it's gotta be a man. You're glowing—like you swallowed a light bulb."

"That's just a new cream I'm experimenting with. I'll whip you up some."

"How do you explain your legs? I always notice everyone's legs—you've been wearing silk stockings, not the ones your ma crayons on for you."

I couldn't reveal the government's secrets to Hattie. I needed a cover story, but I had to choose my words with care. How did that proverb go? "A bird that you set free may be caught again, but a word that escapes your lips will never return." I had to think of something close to the truth—otherwise, Hattie would know I was lying.

I set down my brush, wiped my hands on an oily rag. "There is a man," I admitted.

"It's Mr. V., isn't it?" Hattie said this so matter-of-factly, like "Mount Everest is twenty-nine thousand feet high" or "More than twenty workers died in the construction of the Brooklyn Bridge."

"How did you guess?" Her know-it-all tone irritated me.

"I'm clairvoyant. Remember? Plus, I see you making googly eyes at him at the club."

I let out a big breath. "Hattie, I'm an idiot. Carter's wrong for me but I can't help myself."

"You're right on both counts." Hattie's face was as stern as Ma's would be if I ever had the courage to confide in her.

"He's so handsome. So clean in that goyish way they have. Nails smooth and pink. Thick blond hair." I was filled with self-loathing as I gushed like an overwrought schoolgirl. "I have developed a reckless passion for him." It was a line I'd read in *Photoplay* about the scandalous love affair between Jean Harlow and the married boxer Max Baer. The phrase rolled easily off my tongue, perhaps because it was true. I was starting to fall for Carter. Not only was he the image of a sophisticated, charming, martini-drinking Adonis, but he was helping me come to terms with my past. For so long, I'd been haunted by what had happened in Russia, and now I was finally able to do something about it—all because of Carter.

"He's a doozy all right," Hattie said. "But he looks like one of those Aryan pretty boys you see in the Pathé newsreels of Nazi storm troopers."

"That's a hell of a thing to say," I replied.

"Isn't he married?"

"No, widowed. But you mustn't tell anyone we're seeing each other. It's got to remain a secret."

"Giddy, life is difficult enough. You don't have to search out grief. It will find you all on its own. I look at you, I see a girl on the A train to heartbreak."

I started to protest but Hattie wasn't through with me. She tugged at the pearls at her throat until I was afraid she'd break the string. "Can I be blunt?" she asked.

"When have you been anything else?"

"You're nothing but a diversion."

The remark stung. Sure, I knew Carter and I were from two different worlds. Whatever spark there was between us probably wouldn't last—I couldn't picture bringing him home to Ma—but what was the harm in a mild flirtation? Didn't I deserve that much?

"Rich men think us poor girls are there for the taking," Hattie was saying. "That sex is just one of many services lower-class girls provide along with ironing their shirts, washing their socks, and cleaning their toilets."

"He's not like that. We haven't even had sex." Though I had dreamed about it, thought about it, wanted it.

Hattie tapped at her brace like she did when she was nervous. "Look, Giddy, I see the man in my sessions. There are things about him you don't know. I can't tell you any details. It's confidential, but you should stop—"

"I don't believe you," I said, cutting her off. "If it was so bad, you'd tell me. Maybe you're just jealous that a handsome man is interested in me." It was a cruel thing to say, but Hattie's refusal to believe that Carter might actually be fond of me was a blow to my pride. He had said himself that he couldn't bear if anything happened to me while searching out Free Russia. He had feelings for me. I knew it.

"I'm just looking out for you, Giddy. If Mr. V. liked you, he wouldn't be hiding you away."

I couldn't tell her the real reason for our secrecy, so I pretended to concede. "I know you just want what's best for me, Hattie. You're a good friend. I'll think about what you said."

Just then, the door banged open, and Arnold came in, bringing with him a gust of cold wind. In one hand he carried a bucket of soapy water, and in the other, a razor blade for scraping off the old sign. "Looks like there's more chitchat than painting going on in here."

"Join the discussion," said Hattie. "We're just talking about love and politics."

"You'd be better sticking to politics," Arnold said, unwinding his scarf. "Take it from Bessie Abramowitz. She spoke last week down by Union Square about women organizing and joining unions, exercising their right to vote. Not wasting their time on marriage and babies."

Hattie nodded in agreement. "Like the man says, 'Women should raise more hell and fewer dahlias.'"

Arnold smiled. "Exactly!"

I sighed. Arnold read Karl Marx and hung around with frizzy-haired girls who didn't wear makeup, and intense-eyed boys with pimples and sweaty palms. I returned to painting as he launched into a lecture on women's suffrage, trade unions, free love, and socialism. I suppose I should be thankful he was obsessed with politics. Most boys his age were only interested in getting into a girl's bloomers and shooting pool down at Mooney's Billiards—at least I had him thinking about law school. But then he started into the civil war in Spain and how Franco's fascists were besieging Madrid with the help of Mussolini in Italy. His eyes were bright as he described Ernest Hemingway and Martha Gellhorn working as war correspondents. "They make me want to run off to Europe and fight the fascists. I could drive an ambulance in Spain."

When Arnold was on one of his rants, I wanted to shove a burning rag in his mouth.

"First, graduate," I interjected. "The fascists will wait for you to write your calculus exam." Arnold was intelligent in all the ways I wasn't, but I was intelligent in all the ways he wasn't. Melt us together in a big pot and we would make a rational person.

Arnold and Hattie ignored me.

"Why go to Spain?" she asked as if I hadn't spoken. "We have plenty of the homegrown variety shooting their yaps off right here in New York. Just take the tens of thousands in the German American Bund."

"Did you see the newspaper article about their rally in New Jersey?" Arnold replied. "The sons of bitches. There was a photo of a fellow in a Nazi armband carrying a banner that said 'Stop Jewish domination of Christian America.'"

"They make me want to puke. The American Nazis are always spouting their mouths off about removing 'degenerate influences.' By which they mean us Jews."

There was that word again. Carter had used it at the Met to describe the painting of Madame X, but Hattie seemed to suggest that it had to do with politics. Or were she and Arnold just getting worked up? They were both a little red in the face.

"They're gathering strength," Arnold was saying. "It's not just in America. Look at Britain and Oswald Mosley, and his Blackshirts spouting Nazi propaganda about Aryan racial purity and burning books. He leads his followers through Jewish neighborhoods in London, provoking attacks so they can get in the newspapers." Arnold's voice grew louder. "Just two years ago the Duke and Duchess of Windsor visited Hitler in Germany. King George's own brother, for Christ's sake."

I held up my paintbrush. "All right, that's enough politics for now. Arnold, why don't you grab a brush and give me a hand?"

"Whatever you say, Giddy."

But Hattie, as usual, had to have the last word. "All I'm saying is that we have our own fascists to deal with here before we worry about Spain." With that, she levered herself off the chair. "It's been nice catching up. I'll be back for the grand opening. See you tomorrow at Sid's, Giddy. And remember what I said about you-know-who."

Arnold held the door open for her. Once she was gone, I breathed easier. It had been hard to lie to her face, but it couldn't be helped. There was a lot at stake. But as I turned back to the canary-yellow wall, I realized I had a new worry. In protecting government secrets, I had revealed that Carter and I were connected. The very thing he told me not to do, but Hattie would keep our secret. I was sure of it.

# Chapter 12

*Midtown, New York*

What some folks call luck, I call flinging open the door when opportunity knocks. It was going to knock any minute. I could feel it.

It was Friday night at the jazz club. Sid had just introduced Hattie and was stepping off the stage when the red velvet curtains parted and the lights illuminated her on her stool, her long black skirt concealing her legs, her makeup perfect—thanks to me—and her pearl necklace luminescent in the footlights. Fresh applause erupted. Sid took a seat at a round table near the front where a glass of ginger beer with a maraschino cherry awaited him. Never had I seen him drink anything stronger. Hattie, calm as custard, waited for the crowd to quiet. Waiters finished serving martinis, gin rickeys, and Manhattans; ladies ceased clicking the clasps on their evening bags and powdering their noses; and finally, people were shushing each other, eyes riveted on the stage.

"I am sensing someone who needs information," intoned Hattie.

*Me,* I wanted to shout. *I want your* farkakte *guiding spirit to tell me where the hell the Free Russia group meets.* But Hattie, of course, had a paying customer in mind—I'd fed her information about a portly gent in a double-breasted suit and a Teddy Roosevelt mustache an hour ago.

So as she pressed her fingers to her forehead and launched into her schtick, I surveyed the room.

Tonight, there were enough people in the club to give the fire marshal a conniption fit. I spotted Carter at the bar sipping a martini. I was crossing toward him when two fellows entered the club and brushed by me.

One wore worker's overalls and heavy steel-toed boots, and the other, a scuffed brown leather jacket—not Paradise attire. They didn't seem interested in Hattie's reading, just stationed themselves at the far end of the bar and ordered drinks. We got the occasional customer that moseyed in thinking it was a pickup joint for prostitutes or a place for offtrack betting, but Sid ran a tight ship. The state could revoke his liquor license if there was any hanky-panky. Dubious customers soon got the bum's rush, but he hadn't noticed these two enter, so I decided to find out what I could. I smiled at Carter as I passed him, and he gave me the kind of extravagant wink only a man as handsome as Carter could get away with.

I sidled over to the two clowns, close enough to hear them speaking Russian. Some people think I've got second sight, as good as Hattie's, but really I'm just a keen observer. What I observed about these two was they were louts and rabble-rousers. They sat close together at the bar, muttering in low tones. Their accents placed them from the Ukraine. With a little lip-reading, I was able to get the gist of what they were talking about. They were pro-German, praising Hitler's policies against the Jews. Given their military bearing—spines straight, shoes shined—I figured they might be former Cossacks. It was a long shot, but I had to try.

They dropped their voices and kept darting glances at me to admire my legs and foam bubbies. "Hello, boys," I said in English. "How about a pack of ciggies or some mints to settle those beers?" They were drinking Ballantine ale, our cheapest draft.

"Nyet," they said in unison, like they were joined at the hip.

Then they turned away, but not before I noticed one of them was wearing a lapel pin in the shape of crossed sabers, a traditional Cossack symbol.

"Are you sure?" I gave my best smile. The bald one just pulled his jacket tighter around his chest and leaned as far away from me as he could get, eyes fixed on the stage. They weren't going to say anything more while I was around. Hattie had their full attention now and they didn't want to miss a word.

There was a piece of paper sticking out of the bald one's hip pocket. I bent down, pretending to adjust my stockings. The note was written in Russian. The Cyrillic alphabet is hell to read but I caught a glimpse of the word *Free* before his jacket fell back into place, concealing the paper. It was worth a try.

I had an idea. When Sam moved to the other end of the bar to pour a beefy customer his fourth double scotch, I wandered down, too.

"Sam, see those two jokers at the far side of the bar?"

He nodded.

"Keep the beer flowing. I'll cover their tab."

Sam didn't ask questions, and soon those two were tossing back glass after glass of draft like it was lemonade. I wouldn't have long to wait. I scampered upstairs and got into position on all fours at my knothole over the gents' washroom. Below me, Winston, ever the gentleman, stood handing out towels, filling the soap dispenser, accepting tips, giving recommendations on restaurants, and steering a few men in the direction of the pros who worked out of the Hotel Taft across the street.

In one of the cubicles, the beefy man from the bar was puking up what sounded like ten bucks' worth of Johnnie Walker. Squinting through my peephole, I could see the tops of men's heads—brown, red, blond, even one glistening, bald and shiny as a cue ball. With its green mosaic floor, the gents' looked like a larger-than-life billiard table.

Several minutes went by. I was beginning to think I should get back to the floor, that I was wasting my time. Those Russians were probably just stevedores down by the docks, and Sid would be furious I wasn't out front selling cigarettes.

I was about to leave. Patience, as I've mentioned, isn't my strong suit. But after thirty minutes of leaning on my elbows, belly pressed to the floor commando-style and eye glued to the knothole, the door opened and in they strolled. They spoke fairly loud, assuming—rightly—that Winston, being Jamaican, didn't speak Russian. Both were pretty drunk, judging by how long it took them to unzip, fumble their schlongs out of their trousers, and get them pointed in the right direction. Both toques. It figured.

The man in overalls gave a moan of relief. "God, I had to piss," he said in Russian. He'd taken off his ugly worker's cap, revealing a head of curly dark hair.

"You get a look at the girl with the tray of cigarettes?" asked the other one, a bald man with a ring of blond hair like a monk's tonsure.

Curly grunted. "Nice tits."

"If you like foam." This crack from Baldy.

"Get out of here."

"I bumped into her, accidently on purpose."

Curly shook himself off and put it away. So did Baldy. "You going tomorrow night?" Curly asked. "I hear Krietetsy is speaking."

"That lily-livered pacifist pussy."

"Come on, we can go for a drink after. Meet me there."

"The old lady won't like me being out two nights in a row," Baldy said.

"Who's the pussy now?"

"The baby's keeping her up. She's exhausted," said Baldy.

I wanted to yell from my perch above their heads, *Enough chit-chat. How about spitting out an address?*

"What did you name him?"

"Felix. He cries nonstop. It would be nice to have a break," Baldy said.

*I'm sure your wife is thinking the same thing*, I wanted to call down.

"Is the meeting at that same dump on Worth Street?" asked Baldy.

"Nah, they're expecting a lot of people this time. It's across from where that old pawnshop used to be. The one they tore down about three years ago."

"All right, I'll be there."

"Good man." Curly slapped him on the back as they left the washroom. "Let's go. We saw what we came to see. That little Hattie is good. Your pal was right."

Baldy gave a drunken laugh. "Maybe she can tell us how to sabotage—"

The door slammed behind them, cutting off the rest of their conversation.

I sat up, my neck stiff from lying on the floor, but it was worth it. To anyone else, that conversation would seem fruitless. It was just like a JOTB not to mention a street name, only some obscure landmark such as a long-demolished building. But the thing was, I knew where he meant. I'd once pawned Pa's watch at Moishe's on Walker Street.

From the club, I heard the applause for Hattie, a standing ovation, it sounded like. The show was over. I got up from my position on the floor and hurried down. The Russians were already gone, and if Sid had noticed my absence, he didn't say anything. I sold a few packs of smokes, Necco Wafers, and Juicy Fruit gum, then made my way to the bar, where Carter was finishing up his martini. I paused midstride and tilted my pillbox to the right. From the grin on his face, I could tell he couldn't wait to see me. He definitely had feelings for me. For once in her life, Hattie was wrong.

# Chapter 13

*Five Points, New York*

I've got no physical bravery. Moxie? Sure. I'll sass anyone, just ask my Ma, but walking down the deserted streets of Five Points at night? No. I was quaking. Even though I had the ladies' pistol I had stolen in my pocket, I didn't know if I could actually use it. And so, point end out, I clutched scissors, a laughable little pair of pinking shears from Ma's sewing box.

I turned down Walker Street and found the vacant lot where Moishe's Pawnshop used to be. Across the street was the old Jewish Repertory Theater. The marquee listed dangerously over the entrance. In its glory days, it had been a Yiddish repertory theater that played such classics as *The Rabbi's Family* and *The Dybbuk*. Now the building was rented out to any group that could scrape together five bucks for the night, including fanatical Russians bent on freeing Mother Russia from the iron grip of the Bolsheviks.

I took a deep breath and braved the lion's den. The place was packed, the air so hazy with smoke from cigarettes and cheap cigars, I could hardly see the stage. It was worse than Sid's Paradise. As I made my way through the crowd, I scanned the faces around me. To my surprise, I wasn't the only female present. A couple of middle-aged women sat with their husbands, and I spotted a young girl holding her father's hand. The doggy smell of damp wool and body odor permeated everything, and the meeting hadn't even begun.

Once again, I had dressed inconspicuously. I wore a muskrat fur coat borrowed from a neighbor, Mrs. Stein in 2C, with the collar turned up; a gray scarf knotted high around my neck; and a beige cloche pulled so low it covered my eyebrows. From Ma, I borrowed reading glasses with heavy black Groucho Marx frames, which kept sliding down my nose. Since it was so cold, I figured no one would look twice at a girl all bundled up, but out of precaution, I gave myself a limp by inserting a pebble in my shoe. It was too hard to remember to actually limp, so the pebble was my very own stroke of genius.

I found a seat up in nosebleed heaven—in other words, the balcony—where I could see everything despite the smoke, without drawing attention to myself, and peered down at the crowd. There were two kinds of people who left Russia: The better-off types who had escaped the Bolsheviks and communism and arrived with diamonds stuffed up their noses or their asses and had the capital to start businesses were known as émigrés. Then there were the great unwashed, the destitute, the fanatical, and the uneducated who were terrified of Stalin and his violence but held to the socialist ideals of equality and justice. They were called immigrants and they were the people hunched over in their chairs below. This group wanted the old Russia back, with them running the country.

One after another, Russian fellows got up to speak. They stuck out their chests and paraded back and forth on the stage, ranting as bad as or worse than Pa. Why did only men rant? We women screamed and yelled and whined, but rant? No. The gist of the speeches was that Russia was one big fat gulag and the Sovietization of the country had caused widespread famine. Unless something was done to stop Stalin—the Butcher of the Ukraine, as one man referred to him—there was no hope for the future. Kaganovich's visit was mentioned and there were references to ongoing plans to sabotage Stalin, like Manka had said, but no specific details. As far as Kaganovich was concerned, obviously the subject of assassination was not for general discussion.

I only half listened as I searched the audience for Ivanov. I worked systematically, row by row, starting with the front. So many shiny bald heads, so many big bellies resting on thighs heavy as bolsters. The typical Russian man is sorely lacking in the looks department and often resembles a russet potato with teeth. Ivanov should be easy to spot. Not much to go on from the nosebleeds. He wore that ridiculous hat and was missing a finger, though many working men had lost a finger in factories and slaughterhouses. I examined both faces and hands. I spotted the two schmucks from the club, Curly and the one who made the crack about my foam bubbies, Baldy.

By the fifth speaker, the odor of unwashed bodies floated up like an unwelcome cloud, and the balcony filled with the stink of men who all needed a good soak in the bathtub. I burrowed my nose into my scarf as the young man on the stage introduced himself as Oleg Krietetsy. From his accent I pegged him as coming from near Kiev. Not a Jew. Not a Cossack. Not a kulak. He wore an old-country suit that looked like it had been cut out of brown butcher paper and stitched together by orangutans. I shouldn't judge or leap to conclusions. For all I knew, he was a decent human being.

"When you chop wood, the chips fly," he began. "We face two enemies. Two men so bloated with their own power they will do and say anything to hang on to it. Hitler and Stalin are two sides of the same horse," he said, slipping into English. The expression didn't work but I knew what he was driving at. "But," Oleg went on, "we must confront the Bolshevik using peaceful means. If we exert violence as many of you here tonight wish, we will then become as evil as they are."

He was greeted by loud taunts. These Russians were not what I would call a reserved people. The crowd stomped their feet and hollered insults as Oleg raised his own voice to be heard above the din.

I wondered what Arnold would make of Oleg's speech. Stalin was vehemently anti-Nazi, but he had turned Russia into a country where millions of innocent people had suffered and starved. I couldn't blame Ivanov for wanting to kill Kaganovich, a monster by any standard. After all, I wanted to punish Ivanov for raping my ma. But Oleg was asking where all this violence would lead. I didn't want to hear this liberal claptrap. My moral judgments would come after I found Ivanov.

I continued my inspection of the audience. A Slavic-looking fellow in an embroidered vest was sitting on an aisle seat. He resembled Ivanov, but when I leaned over the railing to get a better look, I realized he was too skinny. Damn it. There was no sign of Ivanov's coarse face or his hat, assuming he was wearing it. Maybe he hadn't come to this meeting.

Oleg finished speaking, and instead of applause, there were catcalls and boos. People started to leave. Resolving to return to as many meetings as it took to locate Ivanov, I headed down to the main floor, my foot aching from the pebble in my shoe. The entrance was jammed with people, so I limped toward the rear exit that led to the alley.

That's when I saw him. Ivanov was sitting beside the door. The same brutish profile and the jutting chin I remembered from the tram.

Carter wanted me to shadow Ivanov, to find out where he lived, so I slunk back, my eyes trained on his face. People were trying to make their way to the washrooms, but Ivanov headed straight for the exit. Apparently assassins don't stand in line to take a piss. Neither do spies, not this one, anyway. I elbowed my way forward and followed him as he dipped out of the theater and into the cold night.

I had assumed trailing him would be easy. In fact, over the last weeks, I had practiced shadowing people—following housewives with their shopping, men coming home from work, kids going to school or to the candy store. But now I realized that had been in broad daylight on commercial streets where all I had to do was look in the plate-glass windows of stores instead of at the subject and keep a half-block distance. On side streets, there were doorways to duck into if my target got suspicious and was about to look behind them.

Tailing a subject on a dark, deserted street lined with vacant lots was a different bucket of fish. If he turned around, he would see me before I had a chance to duck behind a lamppost, not that there were many of those. I let him get a block ahead of me. He was an energetic walker, swinging his arms, taking long strides, glancing neither left nor right. His jaw was set. Anger radiated from him. Everything about him looked furious, from the tightness of his shoulders to his scissorlike strides, as he fumed about the last speaker's words of moderation.

The pebble in my shoe was slowing me down and giving me a painful blister, but I couldn't stop long enough to take it out for fear I would lose him. For three blocks, he headed south, then he made a left at the intersection. After several minutes, my foot was throbbing so bad I had to stop and shake out the pebble. When I straightened, Ivanov was nowhere in sight. I ran to the corner, looked both ways. Not a soul. I backtracked a half block.

There was only one explanation: he had ducked down the alley. I'm scared of alleys. Not so much because they're dark and smelly but because they are always filled with rats. I squeezed the little finger of my right hand in my left. Such a goose, I was. My gun was in my pocket, and I had my scissors. Why wasn't that reassuring?

I peeked down the alley. Sure enough, there was a figure stopped at the end lighting a cigarette. He was in shadow, but the flame of his match illuminated his face. It was Ivanov. I entered the alley and inched along, trying to stay as close as possible to the wall.

The alley was lined with cellar doors built into the sidewalk for dumping coal. Some of these hatchways were yawning open, waiting to break the leg of an unwary pedestrian. It was so dark. When a rat scurried over my foot, I jumped and nearly crashed into a garbage can. I clamped a hand to my mouth to stop from screaming. Ivanov looked back and I held my breath. Could he see me? Did he suspect someone was following him? He was taking such a meandering route it made me fear he was on to me. Apparently not, because after a moment, he continued on his way. I exhaled in relief, then followed at a pace, determined to find where he lived.

He exited the alley and turned onto Park Street, then left onto Mott. I ducked into a doorway of a tenement and watched as he walked ahead, one block, then two. He stopped at a ratty-looking building and entered. Bingo. Once he was inside, I moved toward the building to get the address. On the crumbling brick facade was a faint sign that read "65."

I had tracked the fox to his lair.

# Chapter 14

I possessed valuable information: Yuri Ivanov's current address. I should immediately inform Carter, but he would notify the Secret Service and they would swoop in and arrest Ivanov before I had a chance to confront him. Despite my loyalty to Carter, I couldn't let that happen. After all, hadn't I been the one to track Ivanov down, not the Secret Service? I would tell them soon enough, and they could pick up Ivanov, interrogate him, and find out if he was acting alone or if he had confederates. Due process is the American way. Ivanov would be judged by a jury of his peers, convicted, sentenced to life in prison. But not before he and I had a little chat.

On all my other visits to Five Points, I had felt scared and vulnerable. Maybe it was my new dress of printed rayon and silk stockings that gave me confidence. Maybe it was the familiar sight of Mr. Saltzman's rag-and-bone cart as it swung around the corner. But my breathing slowed to normal. I felt calm and determined. Finally, I was going to get answers.

In broad daylight, I had no difficulty finding Ivanov's building on Mott again. Number 65 was one of the older tenements. From a crow's point of view, it would resemble a dumbbell, wide at the street end and the rear, with a narrow section in the middle with an air shaft to admit some air and light. That was the theory, anyway.

Inside the vestibule, the stench from the overflowing garbage bins hit my nose. Christ, it was rancid. I didn't know Ivanov's apartment number, so I loitered in the entrance, waiting for a neighbor to appear. On the crumbling plaster wall, some luckless resident had written, "Abandon hope all ye who enter here." A tenant with a sense of humor.

Just when I thought I couldn't take the smell anymore, an old woman, stockings drooping around her swollen ankles, staggered down the stairs, already hammered at eleven in the morning. I asked her where Yuri Ivanov lived.

"Four C," she muttered.

I brushed past her before she could put the bite on me for spare change.

The stairwell was dark. The lone light, swaying on a frayed cord, had been used for batting practice, and the jagged remnants of the bulb hung at eye level. The banister wiggled like a loose tooth, so I stayed as close as I could to the inside wall without touching it because it was streaked with something brown. As I climbed, the smell of cabbage rolls, goulash, bacon grease, and old fish mingled with the stench of trash. Finally, I made it to the fourth floor, not quite managing to dodge a cockroach the size of a lobster scuttling along a stair. I felt a stab of pity for the residents. This dump made my building look like the Plaza Hotel. I had to pee, but I'd wet myself before I used any toilet in this building.

When I reached his floor, an unexpected wave of panic washed over me at the sight of the narrow corridor. The walls seemed to be closing in, threatening to crush me like a vise. Claustrophobia, my old friend. I grabbed the little finger of my right hand and squeezed to calm myself. It didn't help. I searched for a gulp of air, but it wasn't there. *Stop*, I told myself. *This will pass. You will be fine.* After a moment, my pulse slowed and I moved down the hall.

As I approached 4C, I noticed the doorjamb was so splintered it looked as though someone had once taken a crowbar to it to force their way in. I knocked, bracing myself for the sight of the Cossack. But no one came to the door. I could hear the static blare of the radio and was taken aback by the sound of *Our Gal Sunday* coming from the other side. I knocked again harder. No answer. As I lifted my hand for a third try, the door swung open.

To my surprise, a young woman stood in the doorway. She looked to be a few years older than me, and her plaid housedress and gray sweater were stretched so tightly across her pregnant belly that I could see the outline of her navel. Her face was pretty but pale. If she'd been a tray of rugelach, I would have put her back in a hot oven for another ten minutes. A little girl with blond hair peeked out from behind her legs.

Had the slattern on the stairs told me the wrong apartment? "Is this the residence of Yuri Ivanov?" I asked.

The woman stared at me. I repeated the question in Russian.

She gave me a big smile. "*Da, da.* My name is Anya Ivanov. I expect you. Please come." Her English was slow and careful, with a Russian accent thick as borscht. "Please excuse English. I learn at night school when Yuri here to watch . . ." She gestured to the girl. "Svetlana."

I was taken aback. She was expecting me? Was Yuri onto me? I'd been asking about him all over Five Points. Had I walked into a trap? Confusion and fear rose in me.

I took a step back, but Anya grabbed my elbow and ushered me into the apartment. I dodged a wet diaper hanging from the clothes-line strung across the room.

"Your English is good," I mumbled.

"Thanks you very much." She closed the door and turned down the Admiral radio. "I listen and practice from radio. Soap opera is educational." Then to my surprise, she quoted *Our Gal Sunday.*

"Can young orphan girl from small mining town in Colorado find happiness in arms of wealthy England lord?" She giggled. "But what means *orphan?*"

"A person with no father or mother," I said, glancing about the room for signs of Ivanov, but unless he was hiding behind the tattered curtains, he wasn't home. "That's my mother's favorite, too."

"Sit, please." Anya cleared a stack of newspaper clippings off a wooden chair with missing rungs. "I have paper here."

Warily, I took a seat, still unsure who she thought I was. I had been so determined to confront Yuri, but now I found myself relieved he wasn't here.

As Anya poked through a drawer set into the kitchen table, I looked around. I couldn't imagine how any family could live here. The apartment was neat and clean, but as dark and spare as a jail cell. The one room served as parlor, kitchen, and bedroom. The bathroom and toilet would be down the hall. Judging from the drip coming from the sink, they had running water, probably only cold. A hot plate with a frayed cord served as their stove. Unlike Manka's apartment, this one was like an oven and stuffy. The radiator hissed out steam. I unbuttoned my wool coat and draped it over the chair, the gun making it list to one side.

"Where is shit paper?" Anya muttered to herself.

The girl, about two years old, tottered over to me, wearing a gingham dress that was too short for her and revealed her pipe-cleaner legs and scabbed knees. I didn't need to wonder if Ivanov was her father—she had his blue eyes and square jaw.

Anya found the paper she was looking for. "I finish. Just look." She waved the sheet triumphantly, thrusting it at me as though presenting me with a slice of Sacher torte.

The heading read: "City of New York: Application for Public Housing." Neatly printed in ink was all the information the city required for admission to government housing: name, age, occupation of head of household, current address, number of members of the household, and so on. Should I play along with her misunderstanding, pretend to be an official from the city, or tell her why I was really here?

I looked at Anya, who was sitting, chewing on her bottom lip. "My neighbor help me with spelling," she said.

Svetlana seemed to sense her mother's anxiety and moved next to her. Anya pulled the girl up, balancing her on her knee despite her swollen belly.

"How far along are you?" I asked.

"Seven months," she replied. "You see we are herrings in barrel in this apartment. Also, not safe for Sveta or baby." She pointed to a long narrow window at the level of Svetlana's knees. Chicken wire was nailed across it. "Yuri fix. He scared Sveta fall." She gestured with her foot at the scraps of lumber nailed over holes in the baseboards. "To stop rats."

This was what Ivanov had done with the supplies from the hardware store, I realized. Never had it occurred to me that Ivanov might have a wife and family—a child he cared enough about to protect from deadly falls and hungry rats. In my mind's eye, he was as I had seen him in Russia, with a whip in his hand, leaving in his wake misery and confusion. Nothing—not this young woman, or her child, nor this room—made any sense. The Cossack who raped Ma and burned our cottage and the man who bought a dime's worth of chicken wire and nailed it over the window so his little girl would not topple out could not be the same man.

"So," Anya said. "Can you help us, Miss . . . ?"

"Chernovtsy," I said quickly, using my mother's maiden name. "Rivka Chernovtsy." I glanced at the application. Yuri Ivanov was a common name, as common as John Smith in America. Maybe I had the wrong man. "Where in Russia is your husband from?"

"We come from small village Slavostok. Arrive in America in 1936."

Those facts corresponded with Carter's information. "What was his occupation in the old country?"

"He was in the czar's army, an *ataman*, a chieftain." She smiled proudly.

So he was a Cossack. And I had seen and recognized him at a Free Russia meeting, and he had returned to this building. Anya's husband had to be the right man, so why was I second-guessing myself?

"You wish speak to him?" Anya asked, setting Svetlana down. "At work now." She was talking more hesitantly now. The effort of speaking English was wearing her out.

"Shall we switch to Russian?"

"Da," she said, gratefully.

"Where does Yuri work?" I asked. "Your application form only says the Lower East Side."

"He moves things from this place to that place. Hooch, furniture, furs, anything."

"A delivery company?"

"Yes, Fletcher's Moving and Transport."

"And the address?"

Showing no hesitation, she rattled off an address by the docks.

The poor are used to meekly answering buttinsky questions from strangers. She thought I was from the city, so she replied without hesitation, for which I felt a small stab of remorse. Other questions occurred to me, but suddenly I wanted to get away from this nice woman and her daughter who soon might be without a husband and father.

I returned the form. "You have been helpful, Mrs. Ivanov. One of my associates"—how official I sounded—"will be in touch with you shortly to finalize your application."

I stood to leave. As I reached for my coat, to my horror, Svetlana pulled the gun out of my pocket. She waved it around in her chubby hand, then dropped on the linoleum floor, where it fell with a thunk. I scooped it up and shoved it back in my pocket, but I wasn't quick enough. Anya's hand flew to her mouth. "Don't be frightened," I said. "It's just that in this neighborhood . . ."

"Yuri does not like this neighborhood either. Or this building."

But I could tell from her face she was troubled and, now, possibly suspicious of me. "I'll see what I can do about the housing," I lied. From the visit, the pretending, the fibs, I was bushed. I would throw a goldfish to the cat and treat myself to a cab ride home. "About the gun . . . I had an incident recently. A man mistook me for a rent collector and tried to rob me." It was a transparent lie. I had never seen a female rent collector and doubted they existed. Anya was new to the country and evidently didn't know this, because she regarded me with a warm smile.

"Now I understand." Anya held open the door for me. As I turned to leave, she touched my arm. Then, Russian-style, with her fist she made a thumping motion over her heart. "Thank you, Miss Chernovtsy. You are a good woman. God loves you."

And did God love her, too? If so, he had a funny way of showing it. Svetlana, a gooey rusk in one hand, waved goodbye.

I groped my way down the tenement stairs two at a time, oblivious now to the stains and the cockroaches. I needed to get out of Five Points as quickly as possible. What had I been thinking coming here? Approaching a wanted assassin in his home? I had convinced myself that finding Ivanov would bring me peace and give Ma back her sanity, but now I wasn't sure. What was worse, I'd put a target on my back. I imagined Ivanov coming home tonight and Anya telling him about my visit and the gun, how I didn't take the housing application with me. She had trusted me, but he wouldn't.

The fact that Ivanov had a family he loved made him even more dangerous. Once he heard of my visit, he would come after me. I needed protection.

I needed to speak to Carter.

I stumbled on the last of the stairs. Carter would be so disappointed. I had just bungled our case, giving Ivanov notice we were after him. If Ivanov disappeared, we'd be back to where we were six weeks ago, with no leads.

# Chapter 15

———— ❖ ————

*Midtown, New York*

"I must tell you something," I said to Carter.

It was 2:00 a.m. and we were sitting in a quiet corner at the Anchor Bar. Carter had given me a joyful thumbs-up when I had tipped my pillbox hat earlier that night. Now his face was intent with anticipation as he shelled peanuts from a bowl on the bar, his knee bobbing up and down in a jittery way that was unlike him.

"There is a part to the story, however, you're not going to like," I added.

Carter took a sip of his martini. My own gin rickey sat untouched. I couldn't bring myself to drink it. I was afraid my hands would shake too much.

"If it's that Hattie knows we're seeing each other, then I'm already aware." He smiled. "She mentioned something in our last session."

What a little buttinsky Hattie was. I could strangle her. "I had to tell her something," I explained. "She was asking questions about Ivanov. I'm sorry. I know it's supposed to be a secret that we meet."

"It's fine, Giddy. We can trust Hattie's discretion. You were quick to think of such a believable cover story. That's one of the many reasons you're a great spy. You can think on your feet. Now, what's the report?"

"I found Ivanov."

"Oh, Giddy, my girl, that's great news. Why didn't you start with that? Tell me, where does he live? I'll alert the Secret Service and they'll bring him in. Time is of the essence. Kaganovich's ship, the *Nordvik*, will set sail from Russia soon."

"He lives in an old tenement building on Mott Street, number 65. But, Carter, I don't know how long he'll remain there."

"What do you mean?"

"Well . . ." I didn't want to tell him what an idiot I'd been.

Carter set down his drink. "What's happened, Giddy?"

In a rush, I confessed it all. How I had followed Ivanov home from the Free Russia meeting, but instead of reporting his new address, I'd gone back the next morning to interrogate him myself. Carter's jaw clenched and he looked ready to explode until I said, "Ivanov wasn't home, but I had a long talk with Anya, his wife. Did you know he was married?"

"We don't know anything about his private life," he replied, his voice tight. There was a painful silence as Carter appeared to count to ten, then he said, "Well, thank God he wasn't home. Who knows what he could have done if he found out who you were. Now, tell me exactly what happened. I need to know every detail."

I managed a small smile. "I thought you liked the essentials."

But Carter was all business. "Not now, Giddy, this is serious. Tell me what you two said to each other."

I relayed our conversation. "They have a child and she's expecting another. She thinks I'm with public housing, that I work for the city. She told me how Yuri fixed up their apartment to keep their daughter safe. He sounds like a good father."

"Good fathers can be assassins, too. Is that everything? It doesn't sound like you raised any suspicions."

"There's one more thing." I looked down as I told him about the gun.

"For the love of Christ! What kind of city worker carries a gun?" he said. "You've put yourself in danger, not to mention jeopardized our mission. We're trying to stop an"—he glanced around—"assassination here. The moment his wife mentions your gun, he'll know you weren't there to commiserate about their wretched apartment. He will disappear and we'll be back where we started."

"I know. It was stupid of me. But I did find out where he works." I slid one of my business cards over to him with the address of Fletcher's Moving and Transport scribbled on the back, a small peace offering.

"But why? I'm trying to understand, I really am. Why would you even consider approaching him, and with a gun, no less? I won't even ask where you got it."

"Having a gun in that neighborhood made me feel safe." I hesitated, then said, "I told you my brother and sister died in Russia."

"And I'm very sorry about that, but how does that justify your negligence?"

"They were murdered during a pogrom."

Carter put his face in his hands and was silent a moment. Then he looked up. "Oh, Giddy, I didn't know." His voice was soft, all trace of anger gone.

"How would you? It's not something I like talking about," I admitted.

"I'm listening now." He placed his hand on mine.

I took a deep breath for courage. Ma wasn't the only one who didn't like to speak of the past. I told him everything, about being in the henhouse when the Cossacks rode in, seeing them set fire to our house, and watching as they chased my cousins with their bayonets.

"How did you escape?"

"I hid in a cow carcass. I pretended the cow's ribs were my ma's arms holding me tight." My eyes begin to fill. I swallowed a lump in my throat at the recollection of the cold, hard ground through my thin nightdress, the vibrations of the horse hooves, my terror of the horses trampling me to death. "My brother and sister weren't so lucky. Baby Yossel's head was smashed open against a rain barrel. Bekka's body has never been found."

"My God."

"You sure you want to hear all this?"

When he nodded, I went on. "The bones froze while I was inside. I called for help, and my mother was running to me with my baby brother in her arms when the Cossacks returned. They were coming for me, but she fended them off. I tried to escape. I tugged at the ribs, clawing, breaking off my nails and cutting my fingers. I sliced my arms trying to reach between the bones. That's how I got these scars." I pulled up the sleeves of my white organza blouse, exposing my arms. Carter, to his credit, didn't recoil.

"Oh, Giddy." I let him hold me.

"A Cossack spied my ma. He reached down from his horse, grabbed her, and swung her by her braid onto his saddle." I paused. Her braid had been thick as a man's wrist. "Ma screamed bloody murder, pounding her fists on his chest, struggling to jump to the ground, but she couldn't get free."

Carter listened, nodding, his eyes not leaving my face.

"The Cossack let go of Ma's braid. And . . ."

"What happened?"

"I believe he raped her. And it's my fault." I downed my drink in one big gulp and wiped my mouth with the back of my hand. "You asked why I went to Ivanov's. That's the reason. I needed to confront him about what he'd done to my family. Carter, you've lived in America your whole life. I came here fleeing death and destruction, but the man responsible for that is walking free." I smoothed the sleeves down over my arms. "I'm the only one left in my family who can ensure that justice is done. I keep thinking, if only . . ."

If only what? I didn't know how to finish that sentence. What can a little girl do against a burly Cossack? In my head I knew there was nothing, but in my gut, I felt if only I hadn't called out to Ma at just that moment. If I had waited, the Cossack wouldn't have seen her, wouldn't have done what he did to her. I was selfish. I couldn't keep my mouth shut. All I could think of was that I needed her, needed her arms around me, and needed her to tell me everything would be all right. It was a hard thing to live with, knowing I was the cause, however innocently, of my Ma's rape and Bekka's and Yossi's deaths.

"So now you know why I wanted to find that son of a bitch so bad. But I am sorry. I've ruined everything."

"My poor girl. My brave darling. I can't think of anyone braver. I am so sorry you had to go through that. You must realize, though, that you couldn't have saved your mother. You were a child." He stroked my hair and then kissed the top of my head. His scent was a comforting aroma of aftershave, gin, tobacco, and leather. "I'm glad you told me. It helps me to understand a lot of things about you. As for Ivanov, we found him once; we can find him again. Agent Miller won't be happy, but I'll try to appease him. We'll sort this out."

We sat for a long minute in companionable silence as I tried to stuff down my memories of the past.

"We're a team," he finally said, keeping his arm around me.

I was so relieved, I wanted to kiss him, and so I did, catching us both by surprise. He didn't move at first, then his lips yielded. I raised my hands to his shoulders as our mouths moved together, soft, then urgent. His breathing quickened and he pulled back, flushed.

"Sorry," he said. "It's been a long time since I've kissed someone."

"Don't be sorry," I replied. "I'm the one who kissed you. I've been thinking of doing that for a while."

"Have you?" he said, surprised. "What else have you thought of?"

I straightened, emboldened by the look in his eye. "I've thought of how lonely you must be. I am, too. Lonely. I look forward to our trysts."

"As do I," he said, tracing my cheek with his finger. A loaded pause stretched between us, with me waiting to hear what he would say. "Suppose we stroll across the street? I bet I can convince the Marquis Hotel to give us a room."

What I should have done—what Ma would have wanted me to do—was button my coat over my chest, tell him he had the wrong girl, and empty the bowl of peanut shells over his head. But I wanted to say yes. After all, who knew how long this would last? How long would it be before the appeal of being with a mouthy Jewish girl from the tenements wore off? Once he'd arrested Yuri Ivanov, would I ever see him again? Ma always said, "Love is an illness for which the only cure is time." I wanted to remain ill a little longer. I accepted Carter's offered arm and together we marched across the street.

# Chapter 16

*Midtown, New York*

The Marquis Hotel had a plain brick facade, so solid and prim looking that I doubted an unmarried couple without a suitcase or valise
would be permitted to check in. If only I had a cheap wedding ring
to slip on my left hand the way some girls did.

Carter slid a ten-dollar bill across the counter to the desk clerk
and, in exchange, received a room key. How simple life was when
you had money. Then, with his arm around me, he dropped the key
in my coat pocket and whispered, "You go up first. I will be up in a
minute. I just need to make a call."

I scuttled across the lobby to the elevator, unable to meet the desk
clerk's eye.

Room 282 was much swankier than I expected. As I took in the
marble fireplace with its fire crackling in the grate, the Turkish carpet, and the four-poster bed, I suddenly felt uncertain. I remembered
what Hattie had said. Was she right? Was I kidding myself? Did it
amuse Carter to be with a working-class girl? Did he have what the
French called *un goût pour l'égout*, a taste for the sewer? I had come
across the phrase in a cheap novel. It was not too late. I could dash
down the service stairs before Carter arrived.

But hadn't I wanted this since the moment I first saw him at Sid's?
And despite my poverty and lack of education, he desired me, too.
The notes of "I've Found a New Baby" drifted in from the bar, the

Kit Kat Club, next door, and I relaxed. I sat on the edge of the soft bed and slipped off my shoes, thinking how Carter's hands would undress me soon enough. Then I remembered that underneath my blouse and pleated skirt, I was wearing a tatty brassiere and underpants. I couldn't let Carter see those. As quickly as I could, I undressed and stuffed my gray underthings in a drawer, on top of a Gideon Bible. Naked, I crawled into bed, pulled the sheets up to my chin, and waited.

The song at the bar next door ended and a new one began. What was keeping Carter?

Just as I thought he had changed his mind and I should get dressed and slink home, there was a knock at the door. I glanced at the room key on the nightstand. I couldn't very well answer naked, so I pulled the sheet around me, hoping I looked alluring, and went to answer.

"Come in," I said as I unlocked the door.

Carter entered, his eyes moving over me. "You're already undressed." He touched my shoulders. "Giddy, you're shaking."

"I guess I'm a bit nervous," I confessed, a little surprised at myself. After all, I had seen this man's penis in the washroom of Sid's.

"Why? It's just me."

"But you have been married. You've done this before. I haven't." There it was. The stark truth.

"You don't fool me." He lifted my chin. "You are not so tough as you like to appear."

At that moment I felt about as tough as the wings of a butterfly.

"You have nothing to worry about. I'll treat you as if you were a fragile Ming vase. Come, sit." He brought me to the bed and I sat. "I know how to bring a smile to your face," he said, stepping away.

I raised an eyebrow as he pointed one leg in a ballet pose in front of me. "What are you doing?"

He didn't respond, just began waving his leg to and fro as he inched up his pant leg to reveal a muscular calf. I began to giggle at the sight of this straitlaced immigration officer dancing for me like a Rockette at Radio City Music Hall. He kept it up, then finished with a high kick as I exploded into peals of laughter. Any nerves I had were gone.

He gave a small bow. "See what foolish things you make me do? I want to make our first time together unforgettable," he said, walking over to the bed. His hand went behind my neck to keep me close, and I felt the bristles of his chin on my face as our lips touched. He was less hesitant now and he teased my mouth open with his tongue.

As we kissed, I pushed his jacket off his shoulders and began unbuttoning his shirt, enjoying the expensive texture of the fabric, then the smooth muscles of his chest. He stood and shimmied out of his pants and shorts.

"Now you've seen all of me. I want to see all of you," he said, tugging at the sheet wound around me.

I let it fall from my body and saw the effect my nakedness had on him. He joined me on the bed and I wrapped myself around him, embracing him, holding him, giving myself to him, all ambivalence gone. At first there was some pain, but it soon passed. I wasn't sure what I was supposed to feel, so I let my body take over. Soon, a tingling, then a liquid, rocking sensation, like being on a boat but better. This was an idiotic way to describe what I felt but it was the best I could do.

Carter gave a groan of pleasure, then collapsed, spent. When he rolled off, I leaned over and kissed him deeply. Then we lay together, me with my head on his chest, enjoying the feel of the fresh sheets and soft, feathery quilt.

Carter touched my forearm, gently tracing a scar. "You should never feel embarrassed about these scars. They symbolize how resourceful, how brave, you are. You should be proud of them."

"Thank you." I wiped my cheek.

After a pause, he spoke again. "I've been thinking about Ivanov."

"Oh?" I said, a little surprised. For once my worries had receded to the back of my mind. I propped myself up on my elbow.

"We've been hunting him, but he consistently slips through our fingers."

"No thanks to me," I said.

"But you may have given us another strategy."

I felt suddenly very alert. "What is it?"

"You said yourself that Ivanov will be looking for you. So it occurs to me that to catch him . . ." He trailed off.

"You let him find me." *But what then?* I wondered.

# Chapter 17

Ivanov would find me. It was just a matter of when. Carter assured me that Agent Miller had a Secret Service man posted outside both my apartment building and my storefront on Broome. I was often at the shop, smartening it up for opening day. When Ivanov appeared, the agent would arrest him. The plan sounded straightforward, but it could put me in a hell of a pickle. Off the top of my head I could think of ten things that could go wrong. Suppose the agent was off sick, or taking a coffee break, or simply took his sweet time getting to me? Stalin wasn't the only one who was paranoid.

Miller's agents were working undercover and often changed, so I was never sure whether there was someone looking out for me or not. The Lower East Side was crawling with bums and loiterers with nothing better to do than to insult and harass passing young women. For all I knew, the agent was pretending to be one of them.

But the weeks ticked by and Ivanov didn't appear, which left me in a state of anxiety. I vacillated between disappointment, gratitude, and terror at the thought of the Cossack walking through the door. The only time I felt truly safe was when I was with Carter in our room at the Marquis Hotel, where we met every Friday night in what I came to think of as "our room."

As soon as I saw him, the world dropped away. There was joy in the power of knowing Carter wanted me, that in spite of our differences, he desired me, and I wanted him as much as he wanted me.

This was what I'd dreamed of from the moment I first laid eyes on him. We would make love on the smooth satin sheets and, after, lie in each other's arms. I wanted to hear him whisper endearments to me, tell me how smart and pretty and sexy I was. I wanted him to linger in the room while I bathed and got dressed. I allowed myself to imagine that there was a future for us. Maybe not as husband and wife, that was too much to hope for, but as loving, lifelong companions. But when I hinted at such an arrangement, he changed the subject or made a joke of it. Instead Carter wanted to discuss the case. He always reassured me that we would find Ivanov, but as time went by, even he seemed to be discouraged.

"The *Nordvik* has set sail," he said one Friday night in our room at the Marquis.

"When will he arrive?"

"Within a month." He was softly caressing my arms, but I could hear the urgency in his voice. Time was running out. I couldn't wait for Ivanov to come to me. I had to provide the bait and reel him in.

Before she died, my old bubbe used to say, "He who doesn't have a dog hunts with a cat." It was one of her more obscure expressions. It means use what tools you have to get what you want, even though those tools might be inadequate.

And so the following day I returned to Mott Street and left a handbill advertising the opening of my store in Ivanov's reeking vestibule. I scribbled the words "Anya, please come" and signed the note Rivka since that was the name she knew me by. Anya would figure it out and tell Ivanov I was her mysterious visitor with the gun. It wasn't a subtle approach, but I expected to hook Ivanov like a fish.

I didn't. In fact, very few customers darkened the door of Giddy's

Creams and Lotions in my first week of business, let alone a would-be assassin. I polished the counter, a slab of marble left behind by the previous tenant. The store was deserted. Outside, a couple of sweatshop girls holding a copy of my handbill stood on the sidewalk admiring my fancy-schmancy sign in the window.

The sign looked like a million bucks. It was in French script with bold, upswept characters like I'd seen on an old bottle of Eau de Lavender. The sign painter had been worth every penny of the five dollars I'd forked over. My shop's location was perfection, just like I'd figured. Every woman on the Lower East Side sooner or later ambled past my place on the way to the market, the tram stop, or the sweatshops. There was one problem. I'd only made a handful of sales since opening, despite Arnold and me handing out over fifty handbills. No one was buying. A forest of tall green bottles stood on the shelf, staring at me, challenging me to sell them.

The bell over the door tinkled and some sweatshop girls marched in. They noticed the price of the jars, shook their heads in disbelief, then spotted the free samples. They each grabbed one and left.

This scene was already familiar. Everyone wanted something for nothing. No one was splurging on vanishing cream or skin food with pictures of the Eiffel Tower at a buck a jar. With Arnold's help with the math, I had my expenses and overhead all worked out. I considered slashing the price to seventy-five cents, but my production cost was fifty cents a unit because I used only the best oils and top-quality fragrance. That would give me too small a profit margin. Vey, retail. I wasn't sure my business was going to survive.

The bell over the door rang again, and Hattie entered wearing her pearls and a new fur jacket.

"How's by you, Giddy?"

"I'm doing good." Not the whole truth but close enough. Some of my life was going well. Carter and I were a team now, as well as lovers. I was growing more confident of his affection for me. It wasn't love yet, at least not on his part, but his warm feelings for me were something I could build on. And that would do for the moment.

I eyed Hattie's jacket dyed to look like mink. It was only muskrat, but still swell looking.

"Your ma works here?" She gestured to the back of the store, where Ma was bent over the hot plate stirring a container of coconut oil. "I thought she never left the apartment?"

I smiled. One bright spot was that Ma had become quite the chemist since she helped me perfect my formula for eyeliner. Now she insisted on coming into the store to experiment with my other concoctions. I had my tried-and-true combinations—lanolin, rose water, and coconut oil—but Ma thought she could improve on them. She'd even cut back on her drinking. "Ma has crowned herself 'chief of research and formulation.' She has a talent for knowing just how much stearic acid and beeswax to add to the oils to make a stable emulsion."

I motioned to the jars bearing my labels of the Eiffel Tower. "Ma formulated a night cream that leaves a lovely sheen on the skin. Crushed pearls, she adds, if you can believe." I was pleased she'd taken over the formulating and mixing. The smell of the coconut oil was making me sick. I could swear it had gone rancid, but Ma insisted it was fine.

"Your customers must love your creams."

Hattie was being so kind, it cracked the optimistic facade I was trying to maintain. "Look around. Do you see any customers?"

"Rome wasn't burned in a day."

"Built in a day."

"Sure, but—"

Hattie sat down as Ma bustled in from the back, her eyes clear and bright, a spatula in one hand. "Hattie, you're talking and you haven't said hello to me? What am I? A chair? A dish of coldslaw? One of your spirits from the Other Side?" She gave Hattie a hug and then, sidestepping her crutch, which poked out from under her chair, turned to me. "Have you bought that scale for me yet?"

"It's on order," I said, then explained to Hattie, "Ma demanded I get her one of those professional scales like the pharmacists use to compound their medicines. Who has the persistence to win an argument with Ma?"

"So all you lack is customers for these outstanding products?" Hattie asked. "Anyone explain to you we're in the middle of the Great Depression?"

"Anyone explain to you I need some emotional support?"

I gestured at two ladies who paused briefly by the store, then hurried on. "It's been like this all week. I feel like flinging myself in the East River and getting it over with."

Ma threw me a hurt look, and I remembered her attempt with the gas oven and felt lower than a hoop snake.

"Always the melodrama," said Hattie.

"You'd feel that way, too, if you had the rent to pay on this store," I said, my eyes on the empty sidewalk out front.

Ma wound a strand of hair behind my ear. "But look at the place, so pretty, and my Giddy? No other girl in the world could have done what she did, and on a shoestring yet."

"Thanks, Ma," I said. She didn't know where I got the money for the six months' rent and knew enough not to ask.

Ma waved her spatula. "*Nu*, I just wanted to say hello to Hattie. I got a glass vessel on the hot plate. I got to check it, make sure it doesn't overheat." And off she went.

"Vessel?" Hattie raised an eyebrow in need of plucking.

"Vessel," I repeated. "She's gotten very hoity-toity since becoming a chemist."

Hattie laughed, then grew serious. "Is it only customers you're looking for out the window?"

Hattie always saw right through me. I couldn't mention Ivanov, but she already knew about Carter and me, so I said, "I had hoped Carter would breeze in with his dazzling smile. Say hello, meet Ma, buy a jar or two for a sister or his mother." I tried to conceal how disappointed I was.

"I've told you what I think of Mr. V."

Her superior tone of voice irritated me. "I feel the presence of a green-eyed monster." The moment the words were out of my mouth, I could have kicked myself. It was a nasty thing to say. Thank God I didn't add, *You'll never find anyone to marry you because you're mean as a skunk*. I stopped myself in time.

"That's not fair, Giddy, and you know it. Love has blinded you. You have no perspective."

"Let's not fight."

"I know you're under a lot of pressure." But Hattie looked about to cry. "I never see you after the show at Sid's anymore. Between this shop and all your so-called 'meetings' with Mr. V., you're never around."

I put an arm around Hattie. "I miss you, too."

Hattie just harrumphed and reached for her crutch.

At the door, she paused. "If anyone can make a success of this store, you can, Giddy."

I held the door for her and watched as she made her way slowly up the street. My thoughts returned to Ivanov. Wherever he was, I knew he hadn't forgotten about me.

# Chapter 18

—◇—

*Lower East Side, New York*

I woke to a rusty squeak outside my window. I glanced over at Ma's bed and saw the outline of her chest rise and fall under the covers as moonlight streamed through the crack in the window shade. The sound came again—something was on the fire escape, too heavy to be a stray cat. I slipped out from between the sheets and tiptoed to the window. There was the clump of feet, then the shriek of the metal step. I sprang back, heart pounding.

When I yanked the cord of the roller blind, it flew up with a loud snap.

Cupping my hands to better see, I peered out. A face, a few inches from mine, stared back, nose pressed against the soot and coal dust coating the pane. In the light of the moon, I made out his bulky form and strange hat. Ivanov. He had come for me, and in his hand, he was holding a gun. Stifling a scream, I let go of the cord and retreated into the room.

He tapped the glass once, then twice. Behind me, Ma stirred. I went back to the window, my mind racing. He must have crawled up the fire escape on his hands and knees, crouching low so he couldn't be seen from the street, and peered in every apartment window until he reached ours. He motioned me to open the window, but my hands were shaking so bad that I couldn't have released the latch even if I had wanted to.

"Meet me on the roof," he mouthed in Russian, pointing upward. Did he take me for a fool? I shook my head.

"Hurry, or I shoot her." He gestured to Ma.

How had Ivanov found me? I hadn't given my address to Anya. I looked past Ivanov's shoulder to the sidewalk. Cherry Street was deserted except for an old man huddled for warmth under a pile of newspapers. The Secret Service agent assigned to protect me was nowhere to be found, not that I would recognize him if I saw him. I looked back at Ma. I had no choice.

"I'm coming," I mouthed.

Heart pounding, I wrapped my chenille bathrobe around me, and from under my mattress, I withdrew my gun. I'd never fired it, but tonight I just might have to. I slipped it into my pocket, then tiptoed into the parlor, careful not to wake Arnold. I grabbed my galoshes, only stuffing my bare feet in them once I was out in the hallway.

As I raced up the stairs to the roof, all I could think was if Ivanov killed me, who would fix Arnold's breakfast and make sure he got through his final exams? I'd bought him a graduation suit on the layaway plan at Poppenberg's. What would become of it? And who would thread Ma's needles and tell her that she needn't drink so much and that I loved her? Even Pa came to my mind. He'd been without work for a year. How was he surviving? Hattie and Sid at the club. My fledging store just opened. And Carter. My love grew with every tryst at the Marquis Hotel.

Revolver in hand, I stepped out onto the roof, which was wet from a recent rainstorm and deserted except for the lone figure of Ivanov waiting by the chimney. I couldn't see his gun, but I knew he would have it within reach. Beads of sweat formed on my forehead despite the cool night. As he strode toward me, I raised my weapon. "Don't come any closer."

But he kept coming. I called out for him to stop. "I'll shoot," I shouted. I had imagined this moment so often. After all these years, face-to-face with the man who had caused my family so much heartbreak. I fumbled with the gun, aiming it at his chest. No one around to hear a shot. He would fall to the ground like the bodies of my cousins in the Russian snow so many years ago. It made me want to kill him even more, and yet I had promised Carter I wouldn't.

And that was my mistake—hesitating. Ivanov closed the distance between us, yanked the gun out of my hands, and tossed it over the side of the roof, where it fell with a thud onto the street below.

Shit.

Ivanov towered above me, so close I smelled the garlic sausage on his breath and the stink of his cheap cigarettes. In Russian he said, "We both know you're not a killer . . . Giddy, is it?"

"How do you know my name and where I live?"

"I found you with my mouth."

"Whatever that means."

I flinched as he reached into his pocket, thinking he was going for his gun, but he pulled out the handbill I had left in the vestibule for Anya to find.

"I asked around. You have a business on Broome Street, just opened. Congratulations, or should I say mazel tov?"

"So you followed me home from my store?"

He ignored my question. "You come to my house. You question Anya. You lie to her, saying you were from city hall. You've been looking for me. Why? What you want?"

Was this man the golem of my nightmares? I couldn't be sure. Then I noticed the leather pouch around his neck. It was the one I remembered, swinging back and forth on his chest as he galloped toward me. This was the Cossack.

"You don't remember me, do you?" I said. "I'm Gitel Brodsky from Stulchyn. In 1920, you and your Cossack thugs burned our homes, our barns, and our shul. You stole our livestock. You killed our neighbors. You killed my baby brother and my beautiful sister. And you raped my mother. I saw you. She was trying to save me. Many times, I dreamed of meeting you, rehearsed what I would say to you, what I would do to you." On and on I spewed my hatred. It was like lancing a boil, the relief was so great. And for his part, Ivanov stood there and listened. "Do you ever think of what you did—all the people you killed and tortured?" I stopped for air.

"You have the wrong man." The green light from Siegel's Pharmacy across the street made his face look all bones and hollows, an unreadable mask.

"You're lying. I remember you. I remember your face. Your stupid hat and your drawstring bag of children's bones."

"This?" He held up the pouch. He loosened the rawhide string and shook out the contents, then held it out to me. It was a tattered black-and-white photo of a young woman holding a child of about three or four on her hip. "My first wife, Saskia, and our son, Mischa." There was a long pause. "Stulchyn, you said? Yes, I was in your village, but my job was to confiscate food and livestock and deliver it back to the barracks. I was forager, a procurer. I didn't hurt anyone."

"You set my house on fire. The only reason I survived was because I hid inside my grandmother's dead cow."

Ivanov's face changed then. "A dead cow? A pile of bones?" He studied me for a moment. "Now I remember you, those brown eyes of yours, the serious eyebrows. You wore a red wool cap and a thin nightdress printed with flowers. Tell me, do you remember how you got out?"

"I clawed my way out," I said. "I have the scars to prove it."

"Nyet. I pulled you out."

"No, that's not what happened. You were going to kill me. I bit off your finger."

He shook his head. "You couldn't get free. The carcass was frozen solid and you were mewling like a kitten. I broke the bones. And, as thanks, yes, you bit my finger." He held up his right hand, missing the tip of the little finger. "You had no warmth in your mouth. It was like getting my hand caught in a wolf trap. You were freezing to death but you fought like a demon. I wrestled you onto my mare, then wrapped you in a horse blanket to give you to your mother."

Was Ivanov telling the truth? Had he saved me from freezing to death? My memory was a jigsaw puzzle with missing pieces. I remembered biting his finger. I remembered being in Ma's arms, but nothing in between.

"I didn't rape your mother," he said.

"Then who did?"

"My comrade. While I was pulling you out of the cow bones, he attacked her."

I remembered the older Cossack with rings of fat around his neck. My mother had hit him with a piece of burning timber. He had swung her up by her braid onto his saddle.

"Why should I believe you?"

"Ask your mother."

"She can't talk about it," I said.

"Then I don't know what to say. Believe what you want to believe."

I scrutinized Ivanov's face, looking for traces of Arnold. There was that Slavic nose that Arnold had and the sharp cheekbones, but that was all. Different shape of face, different eye color, different hair. Ivanov was telling the truth—about the rape anyway. But none of this absolved him of guilt. He was there. He was complicit.

"What I believe is what I saw," I said. "You destroyed my home. Why? What did we ever do to you?"

Ivanov stepped back, reached in his pocket. He pulled out a cigarette and lit it. "I was a boy of eighteen. I did not know any better. I thought only of my fellow soldiers, my horse. Cossacks are warriors. Our life was hard but we were like a family. We ate and drank together." A note of longing crept into his voice.

"And killed and pillaged and raped together," I said.

"I did not rape anyone. Killed, yes, but only men fighting me. Never children. Never women."

"Why us Jews?" I pressed.

"I was taught that you were parasites, sucking the life's blood out of honest Christians. When I was a young recruit, our ataman used to say, 'If God didn't want us to kill these people, he wouldn't have made them Jews.' He said you Jews had gold in your cellars, that we had only to help ourselves."

His words made me nauseated. "Gold? You must have seen how humble our village was. Hunger, disease, and poverty were the only things we had in abundance. Few families owned even a cow or a horse. You attacked us for sport. We couldn't fight back—we had no guns, no bayonets, only pitchforks and shovels."

"It is not an excuse," he said, flicking the ash from his cigarette. "Just an explanation. I was following orders. Understand that hatred was injected into my veins like morphine. We were told Jews were not human."

"And you believed that?"

"From the beginning of time, all soldiers are taught this. It is the only way they are able to kill." Ivanov's hand was steady as he brought the cigarette to his lips.

"I can't imagine thinking that." But despite myself, I understood. Until I met Anya, I hadn't thought of Ivanov as human, just a rabid dog that must be put down.

"That is because living in America has made you soft. In Russia, where there is always violence, killing is as normal as taking a shit.

But what we did was wrong. Now I am ashamed that I was such a coward, that I attacked your people, who had never harmed me. Over the years, life has taught me remorse and compassion."

Compassion. I had seen that in how he cared for his daughter. "What made you change?"

"For fourteen years, the Bolsheviks had a campaign to kill thousands of Cossacks. We were considered 'counterrevolutionary.' A few years after the attack on your village, Red Army soldiers entered our barracks in the middle of the night and began shooting. The only reason I escaped was because I was in the latrine. When I heard the screams of my companions, I dove into that pit of piss and shit so they wouldn't see me. I crouched there in the stink for hours, listening to my fellow Cossacks being slaughtered. As they left, the Bolsheviks toppled the outhouse, and I was buried alive in human filth. That is how I learned what it's like to be hunted down for who you are, not what you have done."

As he spoke, I remembered Hattie's reading of him, the terrible smells. How uncannily accurate her vision had been. "Where did you go?"

Ivanov lit another cigarette using the tip of the first one. "I escaped to the town of Veshenskaiia Stanitsa, where I lived within a community of Cossacks. I married Saskia, and our son, Mischa, was born. It was not an easy life but we survived. Then, in the winter of 1932, the Red Army—under the orders of Kaganovich—locked all the Cossacks out of their houses. Seeing them ride in on their glossy, well-fed horses, I remembered what we had done to so many Jewish settlements. Except this time, it was my family who was losing their home. Saskia and our son were out in the cold. They said a train was coming to take us to a new town, but there were no trains for weeks. If our neighbors helped us, they suffered the same fate. Saskia and I lived in parks, on the roadside, in pig sheds and cellars, in the streets, and in gardens. We ate dogs, rats, diseased animals. Saskia died first—froze to death—then Mischa died from starvation. Neighbors ate their bodies before I could bury them. Somehow, I survived. But I wished I hadn't. I tried to hang myself, but God was not ready to put an end to my suffering. The rope froze and the knot refused to tighten. I longed for death, but to spite me, my heart kept beating."

I wanted to rejoice in his torment, but all I felt was sorrow. I knew what it was like to lose people I loved. "What did you do then?"

"I took this as a sign that God wanted me to leave Russia. I managed to get my hands on a dead neighbor's internal passport and residency permit, documents that did not identify me as a Cossack. But still I had to be careful. The government controlled where everyone had to live. If I got caught, I would be sent to prison. I traveled from Russia to Holland, begging rides from farmers on hay carts on their way to markets, sometimes sneaking into train boxcars. I walked hundreds of kilometers in the shiny Cossack riding boots I'd once been so proud of. By the time I reached Holland, they were strips of stiff leather, lashed to my feet with scraps of cord. My feet were so calloused I could walk without pain over broken glass. In Rotterdam, I found a freighter bound for New York. I had no money, but I was still strong despite everything, so I got a job as a stoker in the boiler room of the ship. Three weeks later, we landed at Ellis Island." He shook his head at the memory. "Three years it took me, from the time I left my village, to arrive in New York, where I met Anya."

We stood there in silence as he smoked, the weight of his story hanging in the humid air between us. After a moment, I spoke. "How you must hate Kaganovich."

"He is the only man in this world I cannot forgive. Kaganovich—Stalin's lackey. The Butcher's butcher. But he will pay. I will ensure that when he comes to New York."

"And how will you avenge yourself on him?"

"Opportunity will present itself."

I understood his need for revenge. Until five minutes ago, I had wanted to kill Ivanov, but Oleg Krietetsy's speech from the Free Russia meeting rang in my ears: Ivanov's plan would only lead to more lives lost. "Kaganovich is a powerful man," I said, choosing my words carefully. "Even if you do kill him, you won't get away with it. And then what? You've already lost one wife and child. What will happen to Anya and Svetlana and the baby without you?"

"Do not worry about them. They will be taken care of." Ivanov looked as if he was about to say something more but thought better of it.

"By who? Your Free Russia friends?"

"You know nothing."

"Ivanov, you speak of compassion and yet you have not renounced your anger. Violence only begets violence. This is America. The land of new beginnings. Leave the ancient hatreds behind."

"You are such a hypocrite," he said. "If I was the man who raped your mother, you would have killed me when you had the chance. Or maybe not. Maybe you are still the frightened little girl pissing herself inside a dead cow."

He was right. I was frightened, but the only way my fear would leave was if I got answers. "Your comrade. Where is he now?" I asked.

"He's dead. After I rescued you, a crazed man came at us with a pitchfork. I galloped away, but my comrade wasn't so lucky. The man chased him down and killed him."

There was no reason for Ivanov to lie and so I believed him. I felt a tremendous sense of relief. Ma's rapist was dead. Good. I could not have killed him. I knew that now. Someone else had done the job for me. To that unknown person I sent a prayer of thanks.

"You didn't try and save your friend?"

Ivanov shrugged. "Sure, but he deserved his fate." He took a last drag of his cigarette, then snuffed it out with his boot. "I've told you what I know about the pogrom. We have no more business, you and I. You must stop following me. Next time, I will use my gun."

"One more question. My sister, Bekka—tall, beautiful, about sixteen? Do you know what happened to her?"

"The village was chaos, people running back and forth, screaming. I have no recollection of your sister."

With that, he lifted a hand in a mock salute, turned, and clambered down the fire escape.

I waited several minutes, taking in great gulps of air, and then went to search for my gun, but it was nowhere to be found, and the street was empty of people. The bum from earlier had gone. I could only hope he was indeed an undercover agent and had left to follow Ivanov.

Carter was right. Ivanov would not give up until Kaganovich was dead.

# Chapter 19

---◆---

*Midtown, New York*

I replayed Ivanov's story over and over in my mind, trying to make it square with my own memories of that day. Some pieces fit, but others were still missing. Was the Cossack who attacked my mother truly dead? I wanted to believe Ivanov so I could finally let go of the hatred inside me. While I sympathized with Ivanov's losses, his experiences had made him ruthless and vengeful. He would say anything to get me to leave him alone. There was only one person, other than Ma, who could tell me the truth, and I had a pretty good idea where to find him.

I closed my store early. There were no customers anyway, although I was hopeful trade would pick up when the weather thawed, if I could last that long. I headed for Fifth Avenue and 42nd Street. Pa was a creature of habit, certain to have a conniption fit if Ma served him coffee in a cup other than the chipped white one he'd stolen from the Aristocrat Diner on Hester Street, always folding his newspaper exactly in half, always dressed in the same drab gabardine, so I headed to the New York Public Library, where I had run into him last winter.

I climbed the library stairs and scratched each paw of the stone lions, Fortitude and Patience, who guarded the entrance, and made a wish that Pa would be exactly where I'd spotted him the last time. Fingers crossed, I entered the main reading room on the third floor, only to be assaulted by the smell of dirty, wet socks. Slumped in chairs, scattered throughout the room, skinny men with stubble-covered chins and unwashed clothes dozed. The library had long been a refuge for those living on the streets. The librarians didn't have the heart to boot them out—they'd be sleeping over the subway vents when the library closed for the night—so they let them stay, only shaking them awake when they snored too loudly. President Roosevelt was trying his best with the New Deal, but a lot of men were unemployed. Still, I didn't remember the room stinking this bad last year. The smell made me queasy.

I surveyed the room, checking each long table, looking down aisles, stacked with books on either side. Sure enough, there he was, same chair, same posture, same green scarf I'd knit him in third grade, dozing beside a bunch of other men living on the bum. His chin rested on his chest, and a Zionist newspaper was spread-eagled on the table in front of him beside a balled-up brown bag that showed the grease stains from his pastrami sandwich. He'd aged since I last saw him. Once he'd had the bushy-haired, wild-eyed look of a young Trotsky. Now his dark eyes were sunken and his cheeks, once round and full, were hollow. He looked ready for a taxidermist.

I touched his shoulder. He startled. It took him a second to recognize me. "Gitel?"

"I need to talk to you, Pa."

A worried look came over his face. "Nu, is it about your Ma?"

He spoke in Yiddish, like always. He had no use for the English language, and the English language had no use for him. His few attempts to learn English by night school had ended with him screaming "Capitalist lackey" at the teacher and stomping out of the classroom.

"Something else." I rustled a brown paper bag in front of his nose. "Do you still like hamantaschen?"

"Is the chief rabbi of New York Jewish?" He pulled out a chair for me, but the air in the reading room was making me nauseated.

"Why don't we go downstairs?" I suggested.

He followed me down to the main entrance, the flapping soles of his shoes making a hollow sound on the stairs. We found a wooden bench in a corner near a steam radiator and I handed him the cookies, then pulled off my scarf. The air was better here. Nearby, a window was open a crack, and there were fewer people milling about.

As he chewed, crumbs fell into his beard, which was whiter and shaggier than I remembered but still featured a patchy spot under his jaw from his fiddle. It reminded me of happier times before the pogrom, when our house was filled with his music and Bekka, Ma, and I would twirl each other around our cottage in time to a mazurka.

An image floated back to me—Ma strumming her mandolin, cradling it like an infant, a curtain of golden hair falling on either side of her face as Yossel slept in a laundry basket at her feet, me and Bekka dancing and whirling around the kitchen, knocking over pots and pans and wooden candlesticks, and laughing like lunatics. Before the Cossacks. Before Bekka disappeared. Before America. Before Ma shrunk into a pale imitation of the woman she once had been. The memory broke my heart.

"I see you're still playing your violin," I said.

"I busk at the Bleecker subway station. Most days I make enough for food."

It pained me to think of my pa, along with the ragtag Gypsies and the hurdy-gurdy man and his monkey, trying to coax a few cents out of unemployed men and women. "And where are you living now?"

"A boardinghouse in the Bowery run by a Mrs. Fogarty. Not too bad. Running water. Clean sheets."

"I figured maybe you'd sailed to Palestine, like you always wanted." Zionism was one of the many things he and Ma fought over. He wanted to settle there while the British were still running the show and be a pioneer in the new Jewish state. Ma said she was too old to be a pioneer. Peace was all she wanted, and there was no peace in Palestine and never would be.

"You know me, Gitel. Zionist head, Jewish heart, American passport. Besides, where would I get the money for passage?" In his voice was the defeat of a dream abandoned, but he was still an observant Jew, judging by the kippah perched high on his shiny bald head and his tzitzit dangling from under his jacket. "But I can't complain. How's by you?" He pinched my cheek. "You've always been so pretty."

I was amazed. Pa usually threw compliments around like they were manhole covers.

"I'm fine, Pa."

"Your ma?"

"You would know if you came home." I needed him home as much as I needed a third armpit. I don't know why I said that. To show I loved him despite everything? Or to make him feel guilty?

"Just because I left doesn't mean I don't still have feelings for her."

"You got a funny way of showing it."

"Did you come here to lecture me?" he asked, rooting in the bag for another cookie. He didn't ask about Arnold. It seemed like the only one in the family who gave a damn about my baby brother was me.

"No." I shifted, uncomfortable on the hard bench. "I've been thinking about our life in Stulchyn, about the pogrom."

His hand stilled in the bag, then he set it down. "Look to the future, Giddy. Don't dwell in the past. You can't remake the past any more than you can unbake a cake."

"The past is here," I said. "I saw one of the Cossacks on the streetcar."

"*Schmegegge.*"

"It's not baloney." I dug in my pocketbook for my sketch and set it between us.

To his credit, he fished his wire-rimmed spectacles out of his pocket, wound the curved stems around his ears, and studied my drawing.

"Do you remember him? He was with another Cossack, an older man with a thick neck."

He tossed the sketch in my lap. "Some things are best left alone."

"And some things fester." I pressed on. "Did you see him pry me out of Laska's carcass? Did you see Ma get—" I couldn't finish.

Pa looked at me with tired, bloodshot eyes. "I brought us to America to escape the past and here you are bringing it up again. Why? Why must I relive this?"

"Because I need to know the truth."

"You want to know the truth? The truth is that I wasn't there when the Cossacks rode into our village. I was off in the countryside . . ." He trailed off.

I blinked, my memory foggy. I remembered searching for Pa outside the shul and not seeing him, but he was there when I woke up in Ma's arms. "I need you should tell me what happened."

"I was away on an errand. When I returned to our village and saw what was going on, I was horrified. One of the young men wanted us to stand and fight. We all gathered in a group, but when they came for us, I froze. I could not fight. The Cossacks beat me, then cast me to the side, and I stayed down, but I was not dead, not even close. But doing nothing was the only way I knew to survive. I'm not proud of that. I laid there and watched as the soldiers murdered my friends and their children, and I did nothing, not even when you cried for help, not even when our Yossi was thrown through the air."

A tear slid down his cheek. I looked out the window, embarrassed. Silence stretched between us.

"Pa," I said. "Who freed me from Laska?"

He pointed at the sketch in my lap. So it *was* Ivanov.

"Did he rape Ma, too?"

Anger stained his face red. "No, that was his friend."

Ivanov had been telling the truth, which meant . . . I looked at Pa, now white-haired and frail. But years ago, he was well-built and still strong. "What did you do?"

"It was the sight of your brave ma, who had never so much as raised her voice at me or anyone else, spitting in that brute's face that jolted me into action. If she was still fighting, then I had no excuse. There was a pitchfork on the ground. I picked it up and ran, screaming, toward them. He gave chase but I was faster. I caught up to him and drove the pitchfork through his chest, pinned him to the ground. I'll never forget him lying there, hands wrapped around the handle, blood seeping through his gray overcoat."

It echoed what Ivanov had told me. The "crazed man" who killed his friend.

"I've been trying to find the man responsible so I could get justice for Ma, maybe bring her some peace, but he's been dead this whole time. And she's known that," I said slowly, the realization sinking in. "I don't know what else I can do to make her better . . . other than persuade you to come home."

He fidgeted with his beard. "I can't. I told you last time we talked."

"Why not? You two still love each other. She needs you."

"She's the one who asked me to leave."

I leaned back, shocked. "What? Why?"

"That's something you must ask her. I gave her my word I wouldn't tell you—that's the least I owe her." He was on his feet, agitated now.

"Pa, you're not making any sense."

"Just know that everything I did was for my family. I wanted you to have a better life in America. You're young, Giddy. You should get married, have babies, make a life for yourself. Instead you're spending your time dwelling on the past. The past will devour you, then shit you out. Trust me." It was almost word for word what Ivanov had said to me on the rooftop. Their words rang true. Every time I touched my scars, I relived the pain. Now that I knew what had really happened, I could go forward with my life. Make a new beginning. I looked down at the sketch of Ivanov in my lap. I could tear it up if I wanted, but I still had to find him—for Carter. I might need the drawing. I folded it up.

Pa began walking away.

"Wait, Pa." I fumbled with my pocketbook, withdrew a few bills, and stuffed them in the bag with the remaining hamantaschen. I caught up to him, grabbed his elbow. "At least take the last pastries." I pressed the bag into his hand. "I'm sorry, Pa. Sorry to bring this all back to you." I repeated something Carter had said to me. "Sometimes it helps to talk about ugly memories."

"And sometimes it makes it worse."

He looked so old, so defenseless, so much the aging lion grown toothless. "You did your best, Pa. You killed him. Be kinder to yourself. Give yourself a break."

"I didn't protect you. I didn't protect your ma or—" He broke off and I knew he was thinking of Yossel and Bekka.

"But, Pa, you gave me the best gift in the world."

"And what was that?"

"You brought me to America."

At last he smiled. "You know, Giddy, from the day you were born you were always the troublesome one, the rebel, the *pisher* with the big mouth. Never obedient, never the rule follower. I shouldn't say this, but always you were my favorite."

"I love you, too, Pa." I leaned down—he was half a head shorter than me—put my arms around him, and gave him a hug. "Take care of yourself, Pa. Your luck will change. This depression can't last forever. Soon every woman in Manhattan will want a Persian lamb jacket made by you."

"From your lips to God's ear." He headed for the stairs leading to the reading room.

I trudged home, stopping at the newsstand to read the headline in the *Post*: "Kaganovich to Meet with Secretary of State Next Week."

At the curb was a dead rat, flattened by a passing car, guts pink and glistening. I walked on a few paces, then vomited into the street. I wiped my mouth, still feeling nauseated. This was not like me. I'd grown up on the street, seen plenty of disgusting things. Even as a kid I rarely threw up. Was the stress of the past months getting to me? But no, I'd gone through worse. Then the realization hit me. Hands shaking, I counted the days on my fingers. I had something else to worry about besides Kaganovich.

# Chapter 20

———— ◈ ————

*Marquis Hotel, Manhattan*

I paced room 282 of the Marquis Hotel, waiting for Carter to arrive. How quickly things had changed. A month ago, I had been aglow with anticipation at the thought of seeing him, knowing how he would touch me and kiss me. Now I was filled with dread because tonight I had to tell him something that would either unite us forever or break us apart. My stomach was roiling and I felt muddleheaded. I made it to the bathroom just in time. When I came out, wiping my mouth on a tissue, Carter was in the room.

"You're pale. What's wrong?" Carter reached for me, but I wrapped my arms around myself and walked away. "Is this about Ivanov?"

Always the talk of the Cossack. The first question out of his mouth every time we met. But I shouldn't be resentful; after all, it was Ivanov who brought us together.

"Giddy, please, talk to me. What's happened?"

First business, then the personal. I swallowed my feelings and tried to compose myself, remembering the speech I had rehearsed. "Ivanov came to me, just like you said he would." I watched for his reaction. "It was the middle of the night. He appeared outside my bedroom window with a gun."

He rushed to me. "Oh, my darling, no wonder you're upset. Did he hurt you? Did you hurt him?"

He had never called me darling before. "No, he didn't hurt me.

He thinks I'm a girl from Russia with a grudge, not a spy for the US government." I eyed him. "But you said Secret Service was shadowing me. I assumed the agent saw him at my building and followed him when he left."

"That's what Agent Miller promised." Carter retreated a few steps. I could almost see the wheels spinning in his head as he tried to work out what had gone so terribly wrong. "He knows how important this mission is. He would have ordered protection. Unless . . ."

"Unless what?"

"Unless Miller was negligent and ordered his agent to guard you at your store on Broome Street but not your apartment, or maybe he didn't have the manpower for guards at both places . . . Miller has slipped up before. That's the only explanation I can think of for why he wouldn't have alerted me immediately." Carter returned to me, guided me to sit on the bed, and knelt at my feet. "Giddy, I am so sorry. I will have a few choice words for Miller when I meet with him next. My God, what a fright you must have had." He touched my cheek. "I knew you were brave, but now I'm convinced you have more—how do you say—*hutzpah*, than all of the Secret Service."

My shoulders came down from around my ears and I managed a faint smile. "The word is *chutzpah*. The *ch* sound is like you're clearing your throat."

"You must tell me everything," Carter said, taking a seat next to me. "What happened?"

I told him about Ivanov yanking the gun from me, but I glossed over our discussion of the pogrom and Ivanov's suffering at the hands of Kaganovich. "You were right about him. He's dead set on killing Kaganovich. He as much as told me so. I tried to dissuade him, but it was useless."

"Did he disclose details of his plan?"

"No, all he said was that 'opportunity would present itself.' And that he was doing this for Anya and Svetlana, though I can't imagine how this benefits them. If anything, they'll be left destitute."

"Svetlana?"

"His daughter. Anya has another baby on the way, too."

"Yes, well, we can't understand the mind of a man like Ivanov," Carter mused.

I thought of Anya struggling to make ends meet without Ivanov in that lousy apartment. I put a hand on Carter's knee. "You said you knew some city officials who were aiming to build low-cost housing. Can you put in a good word for Anya, once you arrest Ivanov? She'll need the help."

"Yes, of course."

"Good." I was eager for this to be finished. It was time for the Secret Service and Carter to take over. "When do you think you'll do it?"

"Do what?"

"Arrest Ivanov. He doesn't know why I was really following him. He thinks he's safe. But you have his address at 65 Mott Street and also his work address with the moving company."

Carter said, "We're not quite ready to act."

"What do you mean? Kaganovich is going to be here next week."

"But here's the problem. If we arrest Ivanov prior to that, what proof do we have of criminal intent? The only so-called proof I have is hearsay from informants. Agent Miller insists that to get a conviction for conspiracy to murder, we need more substantial evidence."

After all the risks I'd taken, it still wasn't enough. I stood, hands on hips. "If you're asking me to find him or act as bait again, I refuse. Ivanov told me he would kill me if I followed him. I believe him."

"I will speak to Miller about providing more security. We are so close, Giddy. We can't give up now. Come now, sit," Carter said in a tone meant to be soothing.

"No," I said, my voice rising in anger. "I won't be a part of this anymore."

"What about what Ivanov did to your family?"

"I have made peace with the past. Nothing will bring my brother and sister back."

"What can I do to persuade you?" He got out his billfold.

I felt sick. I had taken his money willingly because I was devoting so much time to chasing down Ivanov, but now? We were friends, lovers, partners, or so I thought. Our relationship had deepened since he hired me that day at Cholly's over lunch, hadn't it? "I don't want your money."

"Don't you need it for your shop?"

I hated that he was right. I'd placed an ad in the *Forward* and Arnold passed out more handbills to the sweatshop girls as they came and went to work, but still the store stood empty, the neat rows of creams and lotions undisturbed. What did I expect? We were in the middle of the Great Depression. Everyone was broke. Without Carter's stipend, I would have been in the ketchup.

"Why are you getting so upset?"

I sat down, biting off a piece of cuticle. "Because I'm pregnant."

It wasn't how I planned on telling him, but there it was. My words hung in the air between us.

Carter was silent, his face as pale as mine probably was. "Are you sure?"

"I haven't been to a doctor, but I'm certain. I'm late, and I'm never late. I've been throwing up. I can't keep anything down except seltzer and saltine crackers."

"Maybe you're just tired, overworked from juggling Sid's, your store, and me."

"Look, this comes as a shock to me, too." I hadn't planned on having a baby for a long time. I wanted to be a career gal, and then after I'd made a success of my career, I would find a husband, and not one that Ma or the shadkin found for me. But what's the expression, "Man make plans and God laughs"? In happier moments I speculated that a baby would be the very thing to complete our relationship. I'd held out hope that Carter might feel the same, with time, but now I sensed how naive I was. He was pulling away, emotionally and physically, now on his feet, pacing.

"How is this possible?" he was saying. "I have been so careful. I always withdrew before climaxing. I never came inside you. How could this have happened?" He lit a cigarette and inhaled deeply. "You should have used a diaphragm, or Dutch cap, or whatever you call those devices."

"Don't put the blame on me. It took two to make this baby. You should have used French letters." I almost hoped he would say more stupid things so I would have an excuse to hurl something at his smug, disapproving face.

"Well, you cannot continue with your pregnancy," he said, exhaling a lungful of smoke.

The room grew still. I waited for him to go on, but he didn't. Was that it? Just that bald statement? Nothing to cushion the blow, like "I love you and nothing would please me more than to get married, but it wouldn't work"? Did what we have together mean so little to him?

A lump formed in my throat. "I thought we loved each other," I said quietly.

Carter seemed to soften then. "Giddy, I do care about you. I do. But—"

I held up my hand. I didn't need Carter to spell it out. "I'm a poor immigrant girl without any education or class and therefore not marriageable," I said, tears coming to my eyes. "Other couples marry and overcome bigger obstacles than we face." There was resentment and self-pity in my voice. I was glad Ma wasn't here to hear me.

"Marry?" Carter said, incredulous.

Of course he didn't want me. I thought bitterly of the opening lines of *Our Gal Sunday,* "Can a poor girl from a mining town in Colorado find happiness in the arms of a wealthy English lord?" I had my answer. But it's one thing to know a truth in your head and another to know it in your heart. I wiped at my face, feeling the smeared mascara sticky on my cheeks.

Carter took my chin in his hand. "Giddy, you and I have something more precious than the threadbare convention of marriage. I cherish you, my darling. Your lovely body, your smile, our times together in this room, your wit, your humor, your brilliance. You located Ivanov, something even the best-trained detectives failed to do. We are working together on such a vital project, and the timing of our investigation is crucial. Nothing must interfere with our duty to America. Not even this . . . turn of events. Don't you understand? To accomplish what we are both committed to, something must be done about the pregnancy. I can't have you chasing after a murderer if you're expecting. You must have a . . . procedure."

"An abortion?" I drew my face out of his grip, feeling faint. We had conceived a child together, but he treated my pregnancy like an annoying inconvenience—a stumble on a stair. The thought of an operation, maybe bleeding to death, terrified me. I recalled poor dead Ruth Pokorny in apartment 3D—her uterus perforated, the blood, her moans and cries of pain; Ma, me, and Arnold dragging her blood-soaked mattress to the curb.

"I do not know anything about these things, but I have heard it is not risky if done sooner rather than later. I will cover the cost, of course." Carter took a final draft on his cigarette, then snuffed it out. "You must get the best. Money is of no consequence."

"You make it sound so simple."

"I think it is. A simple, safe procedure. Commonly performed. Over in no time."

It is difficult to think when your heart is breaking. Hard to do anything but sit and weep, but I tried to pull myself together.

Carter rubbed my knee. "I'll bring you here when it's over so you can recover in comfort. It'll be fine. You'll see, honey."

He had never called me honey before. It was a homey word, the kind of endearment a husband calls a much-loved wife. But Carter said it in a cajoling, half-desperate tone. I looked up into his eyes. They were filled with concern, but not for me—for himself. And suddenly I had a sinking feeling.

"You're married, aren't you?"

It was a guess, but there it was. When he dropped his gaze, I knew it was true.

I'd been such a chump. In the beginning, I'd wondered if Carter had a wife, but when he told me she'd died, I was filled with compassion, knowing what it meant to lose a loved one. I was so blinded by his interest in me, I believed every word he told me.

In espionage stories, that's a classic blunder all spies make. They think the person who recruits them cares deeply for them, wants to protect them like family, that they are part of a circle of love. I had made that elementary mistake. Confused love with manipulation. To Carter I was just a convenient means to an end.

Carter still hadn't spoken. What a craven son of a bitch he was. I shoved his hand off my knee and crossed my legs. "What do you have to say for yourself?"

"I'm sorry."

"Sorry you lied? Or sorry you got caught?"

"Sorry I have hurt you."

"Why did you tell me your wife was dead?"

"She might as well be. Our marriage is a charade. She's one of those society ladies like Madame X in the painting at the Met who would rather be attending tea dances at the University Club than be a companion to me. It is a lonely thing to live with a woman you have nothing in common with. When I met you, I felt excited in a way I hadn't in a long time. You had passion. You were willing to hunt down assassins, tell jokes, tease me, introduce me to a world I knew nothing of. My wife would rather play roulette and baccarat in the casinos in Biarritz."

"Hattie was right. You kept me hidden for a reason."

"That was to preserve the secrecy of our mission," he said. "Giddy, I do care for you. With my wife, it's obligation, but to be with you is a joy. I'm in a loveless marriage."

"A loveless marriage." I laughed. "Do you have enough clichés to last through the rest of this discussion?" And yet, a part of me believed him, believed that the connection we had was real. "Are you ever going to leave her?"

"No, I soldier on for the sake of the children. And then there is my reputation and my position at Ellis Island."

Children. He had children, too. I had heard enough. I knew what I had felt for him was love, but it didn't matter. He wasn't mine and never would be. I had been a fool. And now I was pregnant. How right my bubbe was when she said, "When you eat with the rich, you end up paying the bill."

Carter was pontificating about duty and the fate of America. "We must put our personal problems behind us and concentrate on thwarting Ivanov. Please, Giddy. Do not let me down when we are so close to capturing him." He pushed up my sleeve, exposing my scars. "Have you forgotten what he did to you? To your mother? No child should have been subjected to such atrocities."

I rose. How dare he use my trauma against me. He was a master manipulator. "Enough. I want nothing more to do with you."

"I have betrayed you, but think of what we've accomplished together. We are working for a better future for America. That has not changed. I know you're furious with me. Use that anger but direct it at Ivanov."

I shook my head. "You said Miller needs evidence, but Ivanov will not disclose his plan—I've tried. There's nothing more I can do."

Carter looked grim. "Miller won't arrest him now. He is intent on building a solid case that will stand up before a judge and jury. Miller needs to catch Ivanov in the act. The problem is we don't know when or where he plans to strike. You're the only person who knows Ivanov. The agent I mentioned who disappeared—I've learned that he was killed. I need you, Giddy. America needs you."

"I'll help. On one condition."

"Name it."

"I want to meet Agent Miller. I don't trust you. All these months, you've kept me in the dark and fed me horseshit. I want to know what's really going on and what you stand to gain out of it."

"And the termination?"

"I'll take care of it." Which meant confiding in the one person in the world I didn't want to know.

# Chapter 21

❖

*Lower East Side, New York*

When I woke up the next morning, there were a few blissful seconds when I forgot my conversation with Carter, forgot I was pregnant, forgot my life was a mess. Then morning sickness hit me. I threw back my covers and rushed to the bathroom down the hall, hoping no one would hear my retching. Yesterday, I'd felt scared but hopeful about Carter's reaction to the baby. Now, knowing the truth about him being married, I just felt plain scared. Undergoing an abortion terrified me; even if I did survive, it was illegal, and if I was found out, I could go to prison. But I couldn't dwell on that. It was nine o'clock. I had to open my store in an hour.

I left the washroom and stumbled into the kitchen, where Ma sat sewing. Arnold's cot was put away, his blankets neatly folded. He must have already left for school.

For a change Ma seemed calm, stitching together a pair of police trousers for Mr. Portnoy. She had set out a glass of tea for me and a bagel with farmer cheese. It seemed as good a time as any to drop the bomb.

"Ma, I have a problem."

"Mm-hmm?" She continued basting the pants.

When she was lost for words, my bubbe used to say, "I feel I have swallowed grass snakes." That's how I felt now and I said as much to Ma.

"Well, is it a big problem or a small problem?" she asked.

"Right now, it's a small problem, about the size of the head of that needle in your hand." It was silly to be so indirect, but I didn't know how else to start. I picked at my bagel, trying not to feel sick. "But it's getting bigger every day."

"Talk sense."

"Ma, I'm pregnant."

She looked up quick, pricking herself with the needle. "Gitel, you're kidding. It's April Fools' Day or some American holiday I don't know where the trick is to give your ma a heart attack."

I tried to smile. "If only it was a joke."

She set down her sewing. "You sure?"

I nodded, "I'm sure."

"So that was you I heard just a minute ago vomiting in the toilet down the hall? Here I thought it was Mrs. O'Riley again." She bit off a piece of blue thread and put her thimble down. "How did it happen?"

"In the usual way."

"I don't believe you. You don't have a fella. Were you . . . interfered with maybe late one night on your way home from Sid's?" She reached over, stroked my cheek. "You can tell your ma. I would understand."

Her eyes got a distant look, and I knew she was remembering what the Cossack had done to her. Is there a musty warehouse in the mind where bad memories are stored, memories that come in flashes out of nowhere, when we least expect them? Can this warehouse be walled off with a sign nailed across the front, like building inspectors do with condemned buildings—"Do not enter. Not fit for human habitation"? If so, this recollection of Ma's rape would be the first I would put in such a warehouse.

Tears threatened, but I blinked them back. I wasn't going to cry.

I'd done enough of that yesterday with Carter to float the *Titanic.* "Nothing like that, Ma."

"I don't understand. Who's the father?"

"It doesn't matter who the father is."

"Of course it does. Do you love him?"

"I thought I did." And now? I didn't know what I felt for him. Love, infatuation, or just a crush? Whatever you call it, it can't be turned off like the flame under a pot, but I was furious at his deceit. And as everyone knows, anger drives out love. "It's not going to work out between us."

She started to pace and wring her hands. "Give me a moment to take this in. I can't believe what I'm hearing. Of all my children, I had the most hope for you, Giddy. You were the ambitious one, the smart one, the one who was going to make something of herself, to make this whole struggle in America worth it."

I dropped my head so she couldn't see my eyes fill.

"You were my shining star, the last one I thought would make a mess of her life. A credit to the family, you were going to be. Now you have done what even the most stupid, shiftless girls in the neighborhood have managed to avoid—get pregnant."

I felt sick, not the morning sickness I was now so familiar with ever since this tiny human had set up camp in my body, but sick at heart. "Stop, Ma. I feel bad enough already."

But she wasn't through with me.

She threw her glass of tea against the wall and it shattered. "Do you hear that noise? That was not a glass. That was my heart breaking."

I would have given anything to be somewhere else right then, even back sewing buttons in Grossinger's sweatshop.

"Why isn't it going to work out?" she asked. "Who is the father? Tell me."

"His name is Carter."

"What kind of name is that?"

"A goyish name. He's a Gentile." Then to twist the knife, to pay her back for that crack about me being her shining star, I added, "Blond, fair complexion, blue eyes."

"A mixed marriage is not the end of the world," she said, steadying herself on the edge of the table, trying to picture such an improbability. "You wouldn't be the first bride to give birth to an eight-pound baby six months after the wedding."

Even though it was still morning, I got the bottle of schnapps from under the sink and poured a splash into two shot glasses and put one in front of her. "He doesn't want to marry me." It wasn't quite the whole truth, but close enough. I had wanted to marry him, just as I wanted him to want the baby. But only on the soap opera *Our Gal Sunday* did those dreams come true.

"Then he is a fool and should burn in hell. No, burning in hell is too good for this playboy." Her shoulders slumped. She looked gray and worn, every minute of her fifty-five years. "You gotta get married, Giddy. You can't end up like that Irish girl in 4A, the talk of every yenta in the neighborhood. No decent man will have her now."

"I don't need you to remind me."

"And, just so you know, I can't wash diapers and tend to a baby during the day while you work at the store. I'm too old." She heaved a great sigh. "I'll call Mrs. Lowenstein, the matchmaker. Maybe she can find—"

"That's some demotion. All of a sudden I go from being your shining star to secondhand goods to be pawned off on the first schmendrick who'll take me?"

"All right already, no Mrs. Lowenstein. What are you going to do?"

"God forgive me, Ma, I hate to say this, but I can't keep it." Carter had made that very clear.

"I'm supposed to pass your baby off as my own? No one would believe it," Ma said, misunderstanding me. "I don't know who else could take it—we have no relatives here, and you can't give your own flesh and blood to some stranger."

I shook my head. "I'm not going to give it up for adoption. I think you know someone who could . . . get rid of it for me."

I had expected some protest, some words of outrage, but Ma was silent, considering.

"Someone who is safe and discreet?"

After a moment, she said, "Mrs. Stein's daughter found herself in trouble last year. She went to a man. I don't know if he was a doctor or an intern—maybe he just went to medical school for a year, or maybe he read how to do it in some book, but she didn't have any problems afterward. Not like poor Ruth." She paused. "If you're sure this is what you want, I'll get his name."

"I don't know if this is what I want. It doesn't matter what I want. I can't afford to have a baby on my own. I need to concentrate on my business and supporting Arnold through college." If things had been different with Carter . . . But no. "How do I know I'm making the right decision?"

"You don't," she said.

"Maybe if I have an abortion, I'll regret it my whole life."

Ma opened her mouth, then clamped it shut.

"What?" I asked.

"You want to know about regret? For years I regretted *not* having an abortion."

"What are you talking about?"

Ma made a face like she was sorry she had spoken.

I wiped at my eyes. "You didn't want me?"

"Talking about you, I'm not."

And then the obvious hit me between the eyes like a dead mackerel. "Arnold?"

Her face crumpled. When Ma cried, I wanted to open a window and jump out. Instead, I put my arms around her as she sobbed.

Then for the first time, she spoke about what had happened to her during the pogrom. I had long known the truth, but I had never heard her describe her experience, and so I listened, letting her tell it in her own way. Haltingly, she recounted the rape and how Pa had found her afterward. "There were days when I wished he hadn't. Other women in the village who had been violated felt the same way. After the pogrom, we women who'd lost everything wandered aimlessly, not eating, not sleeping, not bathing, not caring if we lived or died. When I realized I was pregnant, I was frantic. I didn't want to carry a rapist's baby. I wanted my Yossel back." She looked at my face. "You're not surprised. Have you always known?"

"No. It was only later when I was old enough to understand the timing of it all . . . and to see how you were with Arnold," I explained. "No one could help you end the pregnancy?"

"My sister gave me a tincture of slippery elm, but all it did was make me vomit. Soon it was too late. Everyone in Stulchyn guessed the truth. We had to emigrate to avoid the shame. When Arnold was born, the midwife—she lived by Delancey Street—was known in the neighborhood as the Black Stork. She asked me if she should cut the cord. That's what they did in those days. If the birth cord isn't cut, the baby bleeds to death."

I added another splash to her schnapps glass.

"But I couldn't. Arnold was a beautiful baby. He reminded me of Yossel when he was born. I told myself I would learn to love this infant."

My poor brother, so eager to please, so in need of love and approval. How hard he studied to make Ma proud of him. Somehow he had sensed the truth and tried to show that he was worthy of Ma's love.

"And do you love him?"

"Vey, what choice did I have?" She put her hand on my knee. "For many years, every time I looked at Arnold's face, I saw the Cossack, but the memory of what happened faded after a while. I had no choice but to go on. Life got better. I could see the admiration from other women when I pushed him down the street in his buggy. Always the compliments about how sweet he was, how smart, how adorable. I knew it was true, but in my heart I could never feel that. I tried."

"So you resigned yourself to the situation?"

"I did what I had to do. I was an adequate mother to him. He deserved better. I know in my head that Arnold is a blessing. Never has he caused me a minute of worry. I am lucky to have such a boy, so healthy, so fine looking."

"I believe you, Ma. You did your best." For a moment, I wondered if Arnold was the reason Ma had asked Pa to leave two years ago, but the timing didn't make sense. They had made a life together for years. What had happened two years ago?

"I tell you about Arnold not to unburden myself," she was saying. "I tell you because I didn't have options, but you do. This is America. Here you have choices. But even so, you never know if you're making the right decision. You do your best. You hope for the best. If you have decided wrong, you accept your fate." She wiped her eyes, then mine. We were both crying like idiots. "You are my heartbeat, Giddy. My gift from God. With Arnold, I did the best I could." She downed her schnapps. "I apologize. Mrs. Lowenstein I should not have mentioned."

"I'm so sorry I failed you, Ma."

"We'll get through this," she said. She held her hanky to my nose like I was five years old. "Now blow."

Just then, Arnold came out of the front parlor, a pencil stuck behind his ear, a chemistry book under his arm. "Any more tea, or shall I make some more?"

I glanced at Ma. We were both thinking the same thing. "I thought you had left for school," I said.

"I was studying. I have an exam tomorrow."

"How much did—"

"Everything."

Ma reached for him. "Arnold, I'm sorry. This isn't the way I wanted you to find out."

He let her hold his hand for a second, then pulled away. "I figured it out a long time ago. I'm a genius. Remember?" He gave a short, hard laugh. "I just didn't know my real father was a Cossack. That's great. Now I have two fathers I don't like very much." There was such bitterness in his voice. Before he turned back to the parlor, I saw the tears in his eyes.

# Chapter 22

*Manhattan, New York*

The worst part was the anticipation. I was afraid as I had never been afraid before. I envisioned a grimy basement, dirty instruments, and an ignorant old woman poking at me with a dirty knitting needle. But Ma assured me that this doctor, if that's what he was, knew his business. And so I was going ahead. What hope was there for a bastard child, half Gentile, half Jewish, raised in poverty? Only a Hollywood screenwriter could graft a happy ending on to that miserable set of facts.

I told Ma that Carter insisted on driving me to the doctor and was then taking me to a hotel to recuperate after. She wasn't enthusiastic. She wanted to take care of me herself, but she helped me pack an overnight bag and, to my surprise, promised to mind the store.

Carter picked me up in his Packard in front of the entrance to Seward Park—I didn't want him to see my tenement building—and right away, I could tell something was wrong.

Carter wasn't acting like himself. He was tense, edgy, his fingers too tight on the steering wheel. I would have liked to think he was worried about me, but something else was eating him. Before, I would have reached for his hand, regaled him with stories, but now I was silent as we drove to the Wooster Street address Ma had written on the back of a bakery receipt in her shaky scrawl.

It was a narrow three-story brick building, neat enough, the sidewalk swept, the door painted blue. I expected Carter would accompany me, but he just reached into his coat for an envelope and passed it to me. Inside were several bills.

"I'll wait in the car for you," he said.

Once, I had looked at him uncritically. Now when he turned to pass me the money, I noticed his face, usually so clear and pink, had an angry red boil on the cheek, topped with a crater of pus. I wished I had one of Ma's basting needles so I could lance it.

I slammed the car door behind me and entered the building. On the second floor, I found office number 205. An opaque glass window in the door bore the hand-lettered sign KNOX'S IMPORTS. I knocked and a male voice called from the interior, "Come in."

I squared my shoulders and pushed the door open. Standing in the reception area was a tall man wearing a white lab coat and a head strap with a light affixed to it. A surgical mask hung down around his neck.

"I'm Morty," he said, not offering his last name.

Ma used a false name when she made my appointment, but I couldn't remember what it was. "I'm Giddy," I finally said.

"Pleased to meet you." He smiled in a professional manner and shook my hand. His brown eyes, behind black-framed glasses, seemed sympathetic and free of judgment. Though his eyes were creased with lines, there was a boyish look about his face. I guessed he wasn't much older than me. He reminded me of a classmate I'd had a crush on in fourth grade. I could tell he was Jewish from the accent, the dark eyes, and the schnozzola. This should have been a comforting thought but it wasn't. NYU medical school had a strict quota on admitting Jews, which made me wonder if Morty was a full-fledged doctor.

I handed him the envelope from Carter.

I could quiz him about his qualifications, ask how many of these operations he had performed successfully, but what good would that do? You bought your ticket, you jumped on the tram. You didn't ask the conductor to show you his driver's license. I wasn't about to return to the car, where Carter waited. I had no option but to stay and hope for the best.

He gestured for me to follow him.

"Mrs. Stein gave my ma your name," I said as we walked down the short corridor. "You helped her daughter."

He nodded noncommittally. "So you live on the Lower East Side?"

"Cherry Street."

He led me into an examination room with a table in the middle, a sink in one corner, and a bare light bulb hanging from the ceiling. The table had once been a dining room table. Old burn marks bore evidence of scorched pans and long-forgotten family dinners. Morty went to the sink and scrubbed his hands with green soap. Over his shoulder, he said, "We have a lot in common. I grew up on Hester next door to my uncle and cousins' appetizing store, Fraiberg & Sons—lox, herring, some chopped liver, even caviar." He was chit-chatting to relax me. "What kind of work do you do?" he asked.

"I used to work by Grossinger's loft in the needle trade as a button sewer." About Sid's Paradise, I said nothing.

"Hard work, long hours," he said, placing a duck-billed instrument in a machine that looked like a steamer for keeping food hot. "My mother sews leather purses and handbags at Pomerantz's, on the next block."

"Now I have my own business. Giddy's Creams and Lotions on Broome." I thought of my new store, freshly painted and fully stocked with products. Pride crept into my voice. I wished I could tell him the store was flourishing, but he seemed a nice fellow and I didn't want to lie to him. Under different circumstances, I would have fibbed and told him how swell my store was doing.

"That's wonderful. I wish you every success. You're an entrepreneur."

I assumed that word was a compliment and tried to smile. It didn't work out. My face was too stiff from apprehension. I didn't want to talk anymore. I just wanted to get this over with as fast as possible and get the hell out.

"Before we get started, Giddy, I must ask if you are sure you want to go ahead with this termination."

*No,* I wanted to scream, *I do not want to go ahead with it.* I was terrified. The cemeteries were filled with girls who'd had abortions and died slowly and painfully from fever and blood loss. If I did survive, I might face criminal charges and a prison sentence. But now that I knew the truth about Carter, I didn't want to be carrying his child. Of that I was certain. In a voice that bore no resemblance to my own, I said, "Yes."

"You're sure?"

I nodded.

Morty snapped on rubber gloves, then after removing the lid reached into the steamer contraption behind him, removed the lid, and held out a thin rubber tube with a tiny hole at either end. The speculum was in the autoclave but she didn't notice it. "Let me explain my technique. I'll insert this catheter through your cervix, the mouth of the uterus. The catheter will cause your womb to contract, cramp, and then expel the fetus. How far along are you?"

"Only a few weeks."

"Good, you didn't wait too long. The catheter should remain in place for about twenty-four hours. Tomorrow night if it has not dropped out of its own accord, I want you to return and I will remove it. In a week or so, you'll be fully recovered. Do you have any questions?"

"Will it hurt?"

"Yes. I wish I could give you a whiff of ether for the pain, but in some patients, it causes the heart to stop. We can't take that risk." His eyes were dark with long lashes, which made him look less nebbishy. A handsome man he was not, but he was calm, and I had the feeling he wouldn't get rattled if I screamed or yelled from the pain.

"I'll be as gentle as possible."

I nodded again, not wanting to prolong the conversation. *Just get on with it.*

"This is hard for you, I know, but I've done this operation a dozen times. I'll take care of you."

*Don't be so nice to me,* I wanted to say. *You'll just make me cry.*

He handed me a clean bedsheet, then pointed me to the bathroom where I could undress. The bathroom was tiny but clean. With shaking hands, I took off my dress and stockings and hung them on the back of the door, then wrapped the sheet around me. I peered at my reflection in the mirror above the sink. I cupped my hand under the water faucet, took a gulp, and then splashed some on my face. Many Jews believe a child becomes human at the sixth month of pregnancy. In my heart I felt different. I was doing wrong, a neces-sary wrong but a wrong all the same. Would I ever forgive myself? I had to try, but I knew from experience that forgiving yourself is harder than forgiving someone else.

When I came out, Morty had covered the table with a white sheet. A shroud already in place. If I died, he could wrap me up like a loaf of challah, first folding the corners of the sheet over my head and feet, then rolling me from side to side to tuck the points of the sheet under me. I climbed up and lay down.

Morty adjusted my knees, then draped another sheet around me. "Ready?"

"The faster this is over, the happier I'll be."

"I'll do my best," he said.

*Stop with the morbid thoughts,* I told myself. *This will be over soon. I'll be fine. Ten years from now I'll hardly remember this night. Besides, I can't die even if I want to. If I do, my death will get this nice man, who might even be a real doctor, charged with manslaughter.*

By turning my head to one side, I could watch Morty—he now wore the white mask over his nose and mouth—as he took the duck-billed instrument from the steamer. I looked away. I stared at a crack in the ceiling as he elbowed my knees apart and inserted the instrument into my vagina. It didn't feel uncomfortable until, with a rattle and the turning of a screw, he opened it, stretching me in two. I squeezed my eyes shut.

"I'm going to insert the catheter now. Try to relax."

I tried to do as he said, but a sudden stab of pain took my breath away, and I gasped. I knew it would hurt, but this was excruciating. I thought I would faint. I wished I would faint, anything to make the torment stop. I bit down on my fist. Screaming would only distract him.

"Sorry," Morty said from behind his mask. "You have a tight cervix. If you need to yell, you can. There is no one to hear you. But better you should breathe deeply in and out."

But breathing would do nothing to stop the sharp waves of pain that ran through me like an electrical current. My vision blurred. My ears rang. I felt hot, then cold.

Just when I could no longer bear it, when I would have to shout at him to stop, that I would bear this infant and damn the consequences, Morty said, "There we go. It's in." He pulled the sheet down to my feet and peeled off his rubber gloves. "It's all over."

Sweet relief. The pain stopped. Three beautiful words. Possibly the most beautiful in the English language. Right up there with *I love you* and *Let's get married.* I wanted to sob. Instead, I just lay there, panting. I let my legs collapse onto the table.

Morty mopped his forehead with a white cloth. "Sometimes it

takes a while to insert the catheter. Sorry about that. You were very brave."

"I don't feel brave." I remained on the table, waiting for the ringing in my ears to stop.

"You will bleed for several days. It will feel like a heavy menstrual period. Don't do anything strenuous. Can you take some time off work?"

"A few days." I tried to sit up. The room spun.

"Easy there," Morty said, coming to my side. "Take your time. You've been through an ordeal."

I leaned back, letting him hold me steady. His arm was solid and firm. I wanted to stay that way, feeling his arm around me, but Carter would be waiting for me downstairs. It was several minutes before the table, the chair, and the overhead light stopped whirling. I swung my feet over the side of the table.

Morty brought me a glass of water and a pill. "For the pain," he said.

I swallowed it down, then gulped the rest of the water thirstily as he filled a small envelope with more pills. "I'm giving you four more. Take them four hours apart." He scribbled something on the back of it. "This is my phone number. If the catheter doesn't fall out by tomorrow, then call me for an appointment. It must be removed, otherwise you run the risk of infection."

"Thank you." I took the envelope. "Garfield 4109," a Brooklyn exchange, was scrawled in pencil.

"If, after that, you develop a fever, or if the bleeding is excessive or you have yellowish discharge, go immediately to the nearest hospital and tell the doctor you have had a miscarriage. Once the catheter is gone, there will be no evidence of a surgical intervention. The difference between a spontaneous miscarriage and an abortion is clinically indistinguishable."

"I understand." His penalty for performing an abortion was many years in prison and, of course, the death knell to whatever career he might have as a doctor, if that's what he was. Morty had taken a tremendous risk for me, a woman he didn't know from a bar of soap. It made me wonder why, so I asked him.

"My sister nearly hemorrhaged to death from a back-alley abortion. I was a third-year med student at the time. I managed to staunch the bleeding and get her to the hospital, but it was touch and go for weeks. I don't want other girls to go through what she did."

He spoke in such a compassionate and sincere way, as if it was only right and decent to help girls who got into trouble. I warmed to him. "Morty, can I ask you something else?"

"Shoot."

"Will I be able to have children in the future? When I'm ready?" Meaning when I had a man who would want to marry me and raise a family. It was a question that had been troubling me.

"Yes, if you take care of yourself. This means making sure the catheter is removed. An infection could make you sterile."

"Thank you," I said. "I'm feeling better now. I should go."

I tried to stand, but I was still a little woozy and had to brace myself against the table.

"Stay where you are." Morty fetched my clothing from the bathroom. On top of my underpants was a Modess pad and a belt to secure it between my legs. Even though he had performed a most intimate operation, he tactfully turned his back as I pulled on the pad and belt and then hooked it between my legs. It felt bulky but secure. I struggled into my garter belt, panties, brassiere, and then my dress.

Exhausted from the effort, I sat back on the table. "I could use some help with my stockings," I said.

"Of course."

Morty bent down and slid my stockings on. I clipped the tops on to my garters. He held out one shoe, then the other for me to ease my feet into. I should have been mortified by how shabby and scuffed my shoes were, the black leather so worn and patchy it no longer held a shine, but I wasn't. Morty hadn't grown up with a silver spoon in his mouth. He'd probably worn shoes just as shabby as mine. He held my ankle in his hand as he fastened the straps and the buckle. His touch was so gentle, I felt like I was five years old. A tear slid down my face. It splashed my shoe, and Morty wiped it away with his thumb without looking up. He was diplomatic, a *Reader's Digest* word for "kind."

He helped me to my feet. "Do you have a ride home?"

"Yes, my—" I was going to say *husband*, but I stopped myself. "Someone is waiting for me outside in his car."

"You're still shaky." He looped his arm around me. "I'll see you out."

We inched our way downstairs, me holding his arm with one hand and the banister with the other. Outside, the wind had picked up and the smell of rain was in the air. I pointed to Carter's Packard, where he sat waiting, a fedora pulled low over his face, a gloved hand on the steering wheel. The car motor was running. When he saw us, he sprang out and held open the passenger door. If Morty was surprised I was with such a high-class, well-dressed man, he gave no sign of it.

"Don't worry. Tomorrow won't be as bad as tonight," he said in a low voice as he helped me into the front seat. "Don't forget, if you have any trouble, call me."

Morty straightened and Carter shut the door, neither of them making eye contact.

When he got back in the car, Carter put his hand on my knee, but I moved away. I was glass. The slightest touch would cause me to shatter into a million pieces.

"It wasn't so awful, was it?" he asked, studying my face. "You look fine—pale, yes, a little unsteady, but not too bad."

I said nothing, just collapsed against the cold, slippery leather upholstery. I felt so hollowed out that every action, from putting my purse on the floor, to combing my fingers through my hair, to pulling my coat over my chest, was an effort. I considered telling Carter about the procedure, explaining how painful it had been, how humiliating to be naked and to open my legs to a strange man, but I was too exhausted to bother.

"Let's just get out of here," I said.

"Of course. We can talk later."

He shifted into first gear and drove down the street. Through the haze of the pain pill Morty had given me, I heard Carter say, "Have a good snooze. We have a long drive ahead."

Before I could ask where we were going, before we'd even turned the corner, I dozed off.

# Chapter 23

— ❖ —

*Long Island, New York*

I don't know how long I slept, but when I awoke, a trickle of drool wetted my chin. I sat up, wiping my face with the sleeve of my coat. My mind felt foggy from the pill Morty had given me, but behind us, I recognized the Manhattan Bridge.

"Where are we going?" I looked at Carter. "I thought we were going to the hotel."

He kept his eyes on the road. "There's been a change of plans, Giddy. We are going out of town."

"What? No, I can't." What if I needed to call Morty? What if I developed an infection? I couldn't be out of town. "Carter, it's vital that I return to the city tomorrow night."

He glanced over at me. "Agent Miller says he has new information about Ivanov's plan. I've arranged for him to come to my family summer home on Long Island tomorrow, but it's best if we drive up tonight. Don't worry. I'll have you back home after our meeting."

"Why couldn't we have met in the city?"

"We need a secluded place where we can talk with absolute privacy. Lobster Bay is a small town, and this time of year, it will be deserted, with only a few local people—fishermen, shopkeepers, and so on." He shifted into third gear. "There is no time to lose. Kaganovich's ship, the *Nordvik*, arrives in two days."

I wanted to protest, but a dull ache seized my lower belly as if I was beginning my monthly. I didn't have the energy to refuse.

He went on. "Agent Miller will give you instructions on your next move."

I had insisted on meeting Miller, and Carter had complied. I wanted to ask what part I would play in Miller's plan but I couldn't form the words. I was muddled by the heat inside the car. My eyelids drifted shut, but I couldn't get comfortable enough to go back to sleep.

The Packard, gleaming with a new coat of Simoniz, purred along the streets. Through the window, which was steamy with condensation, I watched as the wind blew lids from trash cans, tumbling them down the sidewalks as though they were tiddlywinks from a children's game. Dirty newspapers and garbage lay scattered everywhere. Leafless elm trees whipped back and forth. The ground was brown and blanketed with sodden leaves and horse manure from the delivery wagons. In the air was the scent of rain.

Morty had mentioned as I was leaving his office that the cramping would start within a few hours. He was wrong. I could already feel the wetness on the Modess between my legs. There was nothing I could do about it at the moment. I would have to wait for a chance to change the pad. Ma had filled my overnight bag with white sanitary pads.

"How far is Lobster Bay?" I asked.

"A couple hours."

I clutched my stomach as a new cramp rippled through me. Carter was oblivious, focused on the road as we left the city behind.

Breathing through the pain, I tried to focus on the changing scenery outside my window. I'd never been farther from the Lower East Side than the Metropolitan Museum, where I had met Carter. That was only a few months ago, but it felt like a lifetime. Now we were driving through tiny villages, some with nothing more than a gas station, a post office, and a general store. There were a few farmhouses with kerosene lamps burning in the front window; others looked abandoned. Barns and tall silos were silhouetted against the evening sky.

The tires of the Packard crunched along a gravel road that seemed to have no beginning and no end, only steep ditches on either side. There were few other vehicles. In short, we were in Hotseplotz—the middle of nowhere—and my belly was on fire. Should things go wrong, and there were many ways in which they could, there was no one to turn to for help. I was far from everything familiar to me, completely alone and dependent on Carter. This isolation felt more dangerous than my visits to the slums of Five Points. I needed to look after myself, to remain alert, to be cautious. The trouble was, all I wanted to do was sleep.

Night fell and it began to rain. Carter turned on the wipers, but even so the downfall was so heavy, it was impossible to see more than a few feet ahead of the car. The headlights picked up the deep potholes in the middle of the road. Abruptly, Carter swerved to avoid them.

"This might not be the most opportune time to discuss this," he said, "but there are some things you need to know about Agent Miller."

I tried to focus. "Yes?"

"I have been having doubts about his bona fides for some time. This is why I was reluctant for you two to meet, but you demanded it, and, well, he's requested you be there, too."

Between the haze of the pill and the pain in my stomach, I tried to understand what Carter was driving at. "Because he dropped the ball on providing adequate security for me?"

"Miller may be disloyal, or he may simply be incompetent."

Did Carter mean that Miller wanted the assassination to go through? None of this made sense. "Carter, go back to the beginning—how did you become involved in this, this manhunt?"

"Miller came to me months ago and said one of his agents, a man named Harris, had infiltrated the Free Russia group and suspected an assassination conspiracy was afoot. I was then tasked with looking through our records to find recent Russian immigrants who might conform to a certain profile. I hired extra men to examine every entry involving Russians for the past year. But we had nothing to go on. I have mentioned to you how many thousands of Russians wash up on our shores each year. I had just about given up hope when you came to my office—the answer to my prayers."

The story as I had understood it was that first I confirmed Ivanov's identity, *then* Carter learned from the Secret Service that Ivanov was a wanted man. Carter hadn't mentioned anything about extra help to vet files. It wasn't exactly a lie, but rather a lie of omission, like neglecting to tell me he was married.

I looked out the window. The wipers couldn't keep up with the deluge of rain and they were slapping as fast as they could. They seemed to be saying "What to believe, what to believe?" over and over.

"Why didn't you tell me your suspicions about Miller sooner?"

"I would have, but I didn't put two and two together until now. It was when I learned Miller hadn't provided you with protection that I began to doubt him. I suspect that when he came to me, he was actually looking for an undesirable immigrant from Russia who he could use for his own ends. I showed him your sketch. I think he's been in touch with Ivanov and encouraged him to go through with this plot."

Was Carter saying Miller was a fascist sympathizer? In taking my sketch to Carter, had I directly incited Ivanov to murder Kaganovich?

No, Ivanov didn't need me or anyone else to fire him up, I thought, recalling my rooftop conversation with him. Or was that precisely what Miller was exploiting? Ivanov had said he had protection for Anya and Svetlana if anything happened to him. Was it Miller's protection he was talking about?

"But why involve you and me?"

"We are Miller's cover. And when things go awry, as he plans, we will take the blame. But we can't let that happen." He paused. "Giddy, there's a small pistol in the glove compartment. Take it."

I opened the glove box and fumbled through old receipts for gas, empty matchbooks, and crumpled Pall Mall packages until my hand touched cold metal. "Why are you giving me a gun?"

Carter downshifted as we rounded a curve and didn't answer until we were on the straightaway. "It's for your safety. Yes, I was upset with you having one before, but I see now that you need it. Ivanov is unpredictable, and so is Miller . . ."

"I thought you needed Ivanov alive."

"I do, but that was before I realized the truth about Miller. Ivanov is his puppet. He will let him go free. It might be up to you to stop Ivanov. For that, you'll need a gun."

Carter's words shook me. I held the pistol, which felt oddly comfortable in my hand, as though it had been custom made for me. "Is it loaded?"

"Yes."

It was just the right size to tuck into my pocketbook, unlike the pistol I had stolen from the customer at the Paradise.

The car slowed. "Here we are," he said.

# Chapter 24

*Lobster Bay, New York*

I took in the heavy wrought-iron gates, which were fastened with a padlock and chain. Beyond was a long driveway flanked with poplars. I could just see a rambling white house with green shutters. What Carter called a summer home was to me a mansion, one that could shelter ten families on the Lower East Side. "This all belongs to you?"

"My family, yes. The house was one of the original farmhouses in the area, built in 1866, just after the Civil War. We have enlarged it, of course. It has been in my family for a couple of generations." Carter pulled out a ring full of keys. "I hope everything is shipshape. In the winter, after the summer people leave for the city, nature reclaims its own. The wolves howl and grow bold, foxes rush into the henhouses." He removed the key he was after. "Local people grow bolder, too. One man in particular has broken into our house so many times we have nicknamed him the Woodsman. Mother put a note on the door: 'Dear Sir, please have the kindness to tell me what it is you desire. I shall arrange to have it left out for you on the veranda.' Even though she used her best Crane writing paper, she never received a reply." He laughed. Despite the dire circumstances we were in, he was clearly delighted to be here. I caught a glimpse of the old happy-go-lucky Carter.

He hopped out of the car, unlocked the padlock, then drove

through. Once we were on the other side, he stopped again and closed the gates. I watched from the side-view mirror as he twisted the chain through the bars and snapped on the lock, then tucked the key in the mailbox fastened to one of the gateposts, no doubt for Miller. I felt like telling him that box would be the first place the Woodsman would look, but decided against it. I needed to get into the house and take another pain pill.

We proceeded down the driveway until we reached a white-shingled garage, big enough to park five cars, a smaller replica of the house. Carter parked inside. Even in the dim light, I could make out canoes suspended from the rafters, paddles, bicycles, an old croquet set with rusty wickets, an iron-railed baby's crib, and a Ping-Pong table.

I reached around to the back seat and retrieved my suitcase and shoulder bag. Carter opened the car door for me, and when I stood, a drop of blood trickled down one leg. I needed a bathroom, but Carter had moved to the trunk and was now rummaging around. *Hurry up, for the love of God, before I embarrass myself.* He picked up a calfskin briefcase and tucked it under his arm, and then picked up in both hands a wooden crate that looked to be filled with groceries. He led me up the flagstone path to the house, which I could now see was three stories and featured a complicated roof covered with cedar shakes and bare vines clinging to clapboard siding.

As if by magic, the rain had stopped, and the air was fresh and cold and salty. The Lower East Side stank of tanneries, coal furnaces, and livery stables, but Lobster Bay had the crisp, clean smell of money.

We mounted the front steps. Carter set down the crate and fished yet another key from the multitude on his key ring. "Welcome," he said, holding open the door with a smile.

For a moment I felt wistful, remembering a movie I'd recently seen where the leading man carried his bride over the threshold of their new house on their wedding night.

It felt colder in the foyer than it had been outside on the veranda, colder than the atmosphere between us. "Isn't it a lovely house?" he said. "I have so many wonderful memories of this place."

I was in pain, but all Carter seemed to want to do was show the place off. I shuffled behind him through the foyer, past a huge staircase, and into the living room, which was papered in blue-and-white toile—scenes of shepherds playing lutes and girls dancing in peasant costumes. I had once seen such wallpaper in the window of B. Altman's department store. Chintz drapes hung from the bay window facing the ocean, but the furniture was draped in bedsheets, looking like the lumpy bodies of sleeping giants. From the ceiling, two enormous paddle fans hovered, still and silent as birds of prey.

"These floors are chestnut. Made from trees grown on the property and milled a few miles away. The mills are long gone now." On and on he chattered.

He wanted me to marvel over the dusty wonders of the place, but the whole house made me feel like such an innocent. Even if Carter wasn't married and wanted to marry me, I could never have fit into this elegant place. The house confirmed what I already knew: Carter and I were as different as pickles and caviar. I was glad he was married, hopefully to some anemic former debutante who presided over ladies' teas, dull dinner parties, and—this last detail hurt—small children blue with cold in wet bathing suits.

Now all I wanted was a bathroom, another pill, and a warm bed to curl up in. A little sympathy would be welcome, too. But I made a slight effort at civility. "It's swell."

Just then, a cramp seized me, and I steadied myself on a high-backed wooden chair, a wave of dizziness washing over me. Carter seemed to remember himself then, or maybe he was just afraid I would throw up on the Persian carpet covering the parquet floor. "Where are my manners? You must be exhausted. You've been through a lot. We both have."

Both? I tried not to find his words galling. All he'd had to do was open his wallet. I'd had to risk bleeding to death. Carter was indifferent to what I'd been through and was relieved I hadn't inconvenienced him by dying. Maybe that was too harsh, but that's the impression I was getting from him.

"I just need a bathroom," I said.

"Right through the library." He pointed to a doorway.

"Thank you."

"I'll get the furnace going. We keep electric space heaters on in the winter to prevent the pipes from freezing, but the coal furnace is more efficient. We have a caretaker who fires it up a day in advance so the house is toasty by the time we arrive, but I did not have time to write him and he doesn't have a telephone." Over his shoulder he called, "Make yourself at home. I'll be back in a jiffy." He clattered down the stairs. "Soon we'll be snug as two bugs in a rug."

As soon as he was gone, I crossed the living room and entered the library. Bookcases reached from floor to ceiling. There seemed to be as many volumes as in the New York Public Library. Despite my pain, I could appreciate the sheer luxury of such a collection in a summer house. I didn't covet rich people's sailboats, fancy cars, or gloomy paintings, but this—dozens and dozens of books, slim, fat, and in between—this I did covet, not for myself, but for Arnold. He would go nuts over this collection of leather-bound tomes.

Along the far wall of the library, behind a small door in the wainscoting, I found the bathroom—a tiny sloped-ceiling room with a toilet and a small triangular sink fitted into the corner. I sat on the toilet and unhooked the sanitary pad. It was sodden with clotted blood. My ears rang. Carter's gun peeked out of my purse on the mosaic-tiled floor. What had I gotten myself into? I had thought myself so strong, so steely, and where had it led me? Into the middle of a dangerous plot with a determined assassin and a compromised Secret Service agent. I wished I had never laid eyes on Ivanov, I wished I had never met Carter, I wished none of this had happened. I would give anything to be back at home with Ma right now, having a shot of schnapps.

I had survived the worst pain in my life. I would survive whatever lay ahead of me. I could meet with Agent Miller, figure out if I could trust him, figure out the truth of what was going on. I had no choice. I had no way of getting back home.

I placed the bloody pad on the basin between an elegant flacon of Arpège perfume and an Elizabeth Arden powder compact. I fixed on a new pad. I started to wrap the used pad in toilet paper and tuck it in my purse but, on second thought, decided instead to leave it on the sink for Mrs. Van der Zalm to find in the summer, when she came in to powder her nose. Let Carter talk his way out of that.

Then I flushed. There was a chugging, balky noise, then the bloody water swirled and disappeared without a trace. *Plumbing— another problem that money can solve.* There is no accounting for the thoughts that enter your head when your heart is breaking. At the sink, I washed my hands and downed another pain pill.

Then I went to find Carter.

# Chapter 25

*Lobster Bay, New York*

I made my way up the staircase, clenching the banister. I wanted to move faster but I didn't have the strength. I pressed my legs together, conscious of my leaky, unreliable body.

"Carter?" I called.

"In here," he replied.

I followed the sound of his voice down the hall. The walls were hung with photos, scenes of happy family occasions—weddings, birthdays, christenings. I averted my eyes. I couldn't bear to look at them. Some pictures must have included his wife.

I found Carter in the master bedroom, holding out a flannel nightie patterned with sprigs of flowers. "Here, put this on. It's one of Mother's."

"Give me some privacy, please." I didn't want him to see the pad between my legs.

"Don't be silly. You are so wan, I am afraid you will faint. Let me help you undress. Lift your arms."

I was so weak from loss of blood that I didn't argue. I raised my arms, palms turned so he wouldn't see the scars.

"Attagirl."

It seemed a million years ago that Morty had helped me put this dress on. Now Carter hung the garment with more care than it deserved on a wooden hanger, adjusting it this way and that, before placing it in the closet. Grasping the hem of my slip, he tugged that off as well. I unhooked my bra and slipped the nightie over my head. He walked to the closet, retrieved the dress, and hooked the straps of the thin slip and bra over the hanger.

"We need to talk, Giddy. I wanted to during the drive, but when you dozed off, I didn't have the heart to wake you."

I brushed past him. "I'm going to bed. I'm freezing."

"I'll tuck you in before you catch a chill."

He took my arm to assist me into bed, but I shook off his hand. I wasn't that helpless, even if the four-poster was so high I had to hop to get in. The horsehair mattress squeaked and gave way beneath me. He plumped up two eiderdown pillows, then arranged them under my head. He straightened the quilt, pulled it up to my chin, and tucked it tightly under the heavy mattress. The sheets clung damply around my legs, pinning together my thighs and ankles. I was swaddled as tightly as a baby.

"Please, tell me what's wrong," he said. So he had noticed the tension, my lack of eye contact.

"I'm exhausted and in pain."

"Of course, my darling, I understand."

First *honey*, now *darling*. Such schmegegge. Such malarkey. He'd lost the right to call me anything but Giddy.

He went into the bathroom, and to my fury, when he returned, he slid in next to me. Being in bed with a man I was so angry with was absurd. My teeth were chattering despite the heavy quilt. Carter didn't seem to feel the cold. He was not shaking; his lips were not blue. Under the covers, he crossed his legs at the ankle, perfectly at ease, and he turned his head on his pillow to gaze at me with an unblinking stare, resembling something reptilian, a creature that felt neither heat nor cold. Before I could move away, he stroked my forehead, then my cheek with the back of his hand. His touch repelled me, making me shiver even harder.

"Please, Carter. There must be somewhere else you can sleep in this vast house of yours. I can't fall asleep with you here. Whatever you have to say can wait until the morning."

He had the nerve to look hurt, but he threw back the covers and stalked off. From down the hall came the sound of a door slamming.

Mercifully, the pain pill began to take effect. My eyelids drooped and I fell into a doze. I dreamed I was in a field of tulips like the ones I had seen once in Seward Park. When I bent down to pick one and shove it in an empty milk bottle to take to Ma, the tulip turned into a baby and started to wail. I started and sat up, pain seizing my belly, but it was milder than before, and I felt hungry, always a good sign. I stumbled into the washroom to change my pad. I gulped down another pill—I only had two left now—and stumbled back to bed and fell asleep.

*  *  *

The next morning, I awoke to sunlight crisscrossing the coverlet. I yawned and stretched, and felt pretty tip-top, all things considered. I went to the window and got my first good look at Lobster Bay. The sun reflected off the fresh green of the new spring leaves, washing the world in a dazzling light. The ocean resembled a tarnished silver tray covered with white froth. Huge breakers crashed and clawed up on the shore, greedy for anything to sweep into the sea. There was the cry of a gull, and the growl of a motor vehicle far away. There was no sign of another house in either direction. Lobster Bay was a place where rich people came to swim and sail and play volleyball on sandy beaches in the summertime. It was not a watering hole for spies.

I bathed, brushed my teeth, tidied my hair, and started to feel like a human again and not like something the cats had been at. I left the nightie on a hook behind the bathroom door. On the back of the nightie was a blotch of blood I noted with malicious delight. When the smell of bacon wafted up the stairs, I realized how starving I was. I couldn't remember the last time I had eaten. As I descended the stairs, I heard Carter call, "I am just rustling up some eggs and beef sausage for breakfast. It will be a few minutes. Make yourself at home."

I wandered into the library, taking the opportunity to do what I do best—snoop. I tilted my head to read the titles. Some looked familiar. I spotted the bestseller *Gone with the Wind,* which I had read with pleasure. Feisty Scarlett O'Hara was my kind of gal. I pulled out *The Great Gatsby* and leafed through it. Hattie had said it was a perfect description of how badly rich people behave. I shoved it back onto the shelf. I didn't need Mr. F. Scott Fitzgerald to tell me what was as plain as the nose on my face.

As I returned the novel to its spot, I saw another book had been jammed in horizontally. I pulled it out and ran my hand over the gray cover: *Protocols of the Elders of Zion.* On the front was a caricature of a Jew—hook nose, fringed prayer shawl, and fleshy lips. Arnold had wised me up to this book—a fabricated account of the so-called Jewish conspiracy to dominate the world by seizing control of the press and financial institutions. Henry Ford had promoted this and quoted it in his publication *The International Jew.* As I flipped through the pages of the *Protocols,* I experienced a different kind of sickness in my belly, a pain that had nothing to do with what I had undergone in Morty's office. It was a new copy, but a thoroughly read one, judging by the underlined passages and notes penciled in the margins. Was Carter reading this, or may God be listening, did it belong to someone else in his family? I checked the flyleaf and my heart sank.

There, on the bookplate under the words *ex libris*, was Carter's name scrawled in his loopy cursive with the year 1936. This was his.

I stepped back, scanning the shelves. In the next bookcase was *The Conquest of the World by the Jews*. Next to that was an ancient pamphlet bound in heavy leather entitled *On the Jews and Their Lies* by Martin Luther. I found more titles, including *The Layman's Guide to the Practice of Eugenics*. All bore Carter's name. I wanted to scream and hurl them all into the fireplace, but I resisted the urge.

My hand stopped over *The Collected Speeches of Oswald Mosley*. I knew who the Fascist Mosley was, thanks to British Pathé newsreels and Arnold. We had watched Mosley, the founder of the British Union of Fascists, and his Blackshirts goose-stepping through the streets of East London giving the stiff-armed Nazi salute and yelling "Heil Hitler." With a sense of foreboding, I opened the book and read the inscription: "To Carter Van der Zalm, our stalwart American friend. Regards, Oswald."

Carter knew Oswald. They were friends. Carter was a fascist. I felt like an ice truck had come out of nowhere and flattened me.

I closed my eyes and tried to breathe. How could I have been so mistaken about Carter? What was it Hattie used to say? "The signs are always there. It's just a matter of whether we choose to read them." I thought back to my meeting with Carter at Ellis Island when he talked about "undesirables" entering the country, his description of the Madame X painting at the Met as "degenerate." Is that how he saw me? Perhaps quoting Roosevelt at Cholly's was a lot of bunkum to win my approval. Whatever his true feelings toward me, he wasn't above sleeping with me. As Hattie had pointed out, I was just another working-class girl to be used for his own pleasure. I felt sullied now and foolish for allowing myself to be played so easily. I had succumbed to his charms, fallen into his arms. Once again, I was thankful I had gone through with the abortion.

I went to the tiny bathroom and threw cold water on my face. The walls seemed to sway around me, closing me in, suffocating me, making me dizzy and claustrophobic. My heart beat fast as a wave of panic took hold of me. I felt like something had its hands around my throat. I thought I would choke. My forehead pricked with sweat and I was trembling. But it wasn't the physical symptoms that were so bad. I was detached from myself. I felt that all of this was happening to someone else and there was nothing I could do about it. I looked down at my body, but it seemed to belong to someone else. I grabbed my little finger and squeezed it, but this did not calm me. I looked in the small gold-framed mirror over the sink and wondered who the girl was with mascara running down her cheeks, and why she was staring at me.

I fumbled for the window, unlocked it, and pushed it open. There was a blast of salty air and the sound of the ocean. I could breathe now. "It will be over soon." Those were Ma's words when something bad happened. My brave ma, who had not given up, who hadn't surrendered, who had not allowed herself to be broken. Nor would I. I had Ma's example and the examples of all the women in our village in Russia who had carried on, no matter what. In spite of rape and bloodshed, loss of their children, loss of husbands and loved ones. I would somehow survive, too. I fixed my face and returned to the library.

I bent to retrieve Mosley's book from where I'd dropped it on the floor. That's when I spotted Carter's calfskin briefcase tucked under a wing chair. Why had he taken such care to conceal it? I listened for Carter—he was still futzing around in the kitchen, whistling a cheery tune—then I slid out the case. It was locked, but that was no challenge for me. Working as Hattie's snoop had given me a host of useful skills, including picking a lock. I pulled a bobby pin from my hair, straightened it, then wiggled it back and forth. I heard a click. When I opened the briefcase, I found a letter on top of a stack of manila files, in an envelope marked "Top Secret." I unfolded the letter. It was written in the Palmer method of penmanship, perfectly symmetrical, as easy to read as the headlines of the *New York Post*.

Dear Mr. Van der Zalm,

Thank you for your timely decision to join us. I need not tell you that if all goes well with this chap you have hired, Yuri Ivanov, you will have earned the undying admiration of Sir Oswald.

Our friends in Germany inform us that their foreign minister Ribbentrop and the Soviet foreign minister Molotov are discussing the terms of a nonaggression pact between their two countries. The essential term of the agreement is that neither would invade the other country nor align itself with the other's enemies. The Soviets have shown willingness to sign, probably because they anticipate the successful purchase of arms from the US. Just to be clear, it is vital that this pact not go ahead. Stalin will use it to buy himself more time to accelerate production of tanks, planes, and artillery. He must be stopped. The threat of communism is a threat to Nazism and America. Hitler is the only one with the courage and capability to face down Stalin.

So, old man, ensure Ivanov does what is required. As you point out, he is an "unpredictable zealot," but he is *our* unpredictable zealot.

I agree the girl could be useful. Although, for safety reasons, I am usually opposed to recruiting civilians, the fact that she is Jewish makes her expendable. It also gives a nice ironic touch to our operation. Say and do whatever is necessary to ensure her loyalty and cooperation.

As you know, all this is hush-hush.


Wilfred Risdon,
Director of Propaganda, the British Union of Fascists
London, SW 1


I steadied myself on a nearby table. So Carter had hired Ivanov. Everything he told me yesterday about Miller being a double agent was really about himself. Unless they were in cahoots. If that was the case, I was about to be trapped in this house with two fascists. My heart began to race again. What was I going to do? What was their plan for me?

I glanced down at the letter. It was dated three weeks from the day I went to Carter's office at Ellis Island, and that was the day I'd walked right into the lion's den.

Carter had manipulated me from the get-go, and I, who prided myself on my street smarts, had been blinded by my need for revenge. Carter had played the part of the patriot, the hero, the rescuer. Because he was handsome, well-dressed, and well-spoken, I'd assumed he possessed all manner of sterling qualities—honesty, patience, and chivalry. I'd forgotten that virtue knows neither class nor gender.

They say it's always better to know the truth no matter how painful, but it didn't feel that way. *Expendable*—of little significance, use once, then discard. I was a single-use spy. They had me running all over New York chasing a dangerous assassin. Had there ever been a Secret Service agent keeping an eye on me? I doubted it. I rubbed my arms, feeling the ropey scars. Carter was playing the white knight and, at the same time, playing me for a sucker.

Ivanov could have killed me that night on the rooftop. I thought through what else I knew: Carter wanted Ivanov to kill Kaganovich. That's why I was not to harm him. If Kaganovich was dead, an international incident that not even FDR could contain would blow up.

And Free Russia? Their fantasy was to drive out Stalin and take back their country from the Bolsheviks. This was Ivanov's demented logic.

Ivanov might be willing to die for his beliefs, but Carter thought only about his own hide. I was sure now that he had made false promises to Ivanov about taking care of Anya and Svetlana. He wouldn't risk a connection between himself and Ivanov's widow. And where did I come in? Carter couldn't take the gamble of Ivanov being arrested, interrogated, and implicating him. Carter needed Ivanov dead.

That's when it hit me. Carter was grooming me to kill Ivanov. He'd given me a gun, stoked my past hatred of Ivanov, my duty to my country. What I didn't know was how Miller fit into these plans. Was he a friend or a foe?

The whistling grew louder. Carter was approaching the library.

"Giddy," he called from the hallway. "Where are you? Breakfast is ready."

Quickly, I refolded the letter and returned it to the case.

"Giddy?" he repeated, a note of impatience in his voice.

"Coming." I snapped the hasps closed and shoved the case back under the wing chair. There was no time to relock it with my hairpin. I looked quickly around at the floor and bookcases, making sure everything was back in its place, then I said in a breezy tone, "In the library."

I pulled *Gone with the Wind* from the shelf and pretended to be reading when Carter walked in.

"Ah, there you are," he said. "You looked flushed. Are you all right?" He held me by the shoulders and looked into my eyes.

I reminded myself that his concern was bogus. Once I would have welcomed his thoughtfulness. Now his gestures had the tenderness a lion shows a gazelle he has just captured and has pinned between his paws. I was a means to an end—expendable—nothing more. "I'm fine," I replied, then managed a smile. I couldn't let him suspect that I knew the truth. "Must be the sea air."

"Yes, it does wonders, doesn't it?" he said. "Well, I've made coffee. Shall we eat? Miller will be here soon."

Everything in me wanted to run out the door and back to New York, but I couldn't do that. I had to stop Ivanov—and Carter. So with all the resolve I had in me, I nodded. I replaced the novel on the shelf, then followed Carter out of the room.

# Chapter 26

Had the Academy Award for Best Actress been given out this year? This breakfast would require all my acting skills, I thought as I sat down at the table to a plate of toast, eggs, and beef sausage accompanied by a steaming cup of coffee. Should I have stolen the letter? No, Carter would have discovered it was missing. And who would I show it to? Agent Miller? Carter said Miller was a fascist sympathizer, but was that true? There was no mention of him in the letter. Was Carter just trying to throw suspicion off himself and create distrust between Miller and me? Was that why he told me two different stories about finding Ivanov in the immigration records? If I could get Carter talking, maybe I could catch him in a lie.

"So how are we going to stop Miller?" I asked, curious to hear what horseshit would drop out of that beautiful mouth of his. "Should we notify his superior?"

"I had thought of that, yes, but we run the risk of him finding out. If his back is up against the wall, he might do something drastic. And Ivanov is unpredictable. When Miller arrives, say nothing that might make him suspect we are onto him. Come to think of it, it's probably best you don't say anything. Let me do the talking."

I sipped my coffee. The beans were freshly ground, and I had poured in plenty of cream. "But we can't just do nothing."

"No, of course not. Today, we'll hear Miller out. You'll find him a bit of a diamond in the rough. We need to discover what he knows of Ivanov's plan—then we'll figure out how we can trip him up."

"Fine, but we're playing a dangerous game."

"I have a feeling Miller will do something to give himself away," Carter said.

*Do something like what?* I wanted to ask. Goose-step up the drive-way with a copy of *Mein Kampf* tucked under his arm? Wear socks patterned with swastikas in the red, black, and white colors of the Third Reich?

Carter may have used me shamefully, but I couldn't let that cloud my judgment. Miller might very well be a Nazi as Carter said. I needed to be objective and put aside my feelings of resentment and humiliation.

I heard the motor of an approaching car.

"That'll be him. Remember, mum's the word."

"Sure." I rose from the table, my legs no longer wobbly. Breakfast had done me a world of good. Even the cramping was more bearable. I was tempted to take another pain pill, but I knew it would make me drowsy and I had to be alert.

The bell rang loud and clear, echoing throughout the house. Carter went to the door and I heard a murmur of male voices. I moved into the foyer and, to my surprise, saw two visitors. One man was stout and dressed in a heavy overcoat, an astrakhan hat, and clumsy-looking boots. He sported a soup-strainer mustache and close-set, wary eyes. He was clearly Russian. Only a Russian would wear such ill-fitting, cheap clothes. I was certain I had seen that chubby face before, but where? It was hard to say. I confess that stout middle-aged Russian men look pretty much the same to me.

Next to him was a tall, skinny man with a cardboard tube under his arm whom I took to be Secret Service Agent Miller. He was clean-cut and professional looking, and appeared to be the real McCoy, but I knew better than most that looks could be deceiving.

"Sorry we're late," he said. "Our car crapped out on us outside of Coeursville. Fan belt. Not a soul in sight. Had to improvise with the wife's stocking I found under the back seat." He shivered and rubbed his hands together. "What a desolate place! I'll be glad to get back to the city." Miller unwound a scarf from around his neck. "You must be Miss Brodsky, the girl who drew the sketch. Mr. Van der Zalm has told me a lot about you. I heard what Ivanov did to your family. A damn shame. The Service is grateful for your help in catching him." His voice was pure Brooklyn. I had to suppress a smile when he referred to me as a "goil." He'd been raised on the streets just like me. Carter was going to need me to translate but not for the Russian. "I'm Agent A. J. Miller, by the way." He shook my hand in one firm, no-nonsense motion.

"Pleased to meet you," I said. "Please call me Giddy."

The Russian stood stiffly by Miller's side, waiting to be introduced.

"Oh, jeesh, where's my manners? This," said Miller, "is Igor Oblomov."

"How do you do?" said Carter. A flicker of surprise passed over his face—he evidently wasn't aware of Oblomov's existence, never mind his attendance this morning.

"Oblomov works at the Russian embassy as a cleaner," Miller explained, "in addition to moonlighting as a spy for the Secret Service. In the course of emptying the wastebaskets, he learns many interesting things, don't you, Igor?" Miller gave Oblomov a friendly elbow in the ribs.

Evidently in the Secret Service, even the snoops had snoops, or maybe *informant* was the expression. Oblomov said nothing, just looked watchful and slightly puzzled, his wary eyes flitting from one face to the other.

"It's a long, boring drive with a fella who speaks not a word of English," Miller went on. "I might as well have been traveling alone."

I glanced at Oblomov to gauge his reaction to this comment. An irritated look passed over his face and then quickly disappeared. Perhaps he didn't speak English, but I bet he understood plenty. Interesting turn of events. With neither Miller nor Carter speaking Russian, I was the one-eyed man in the country of the blind. I could turn this to my advantage.

In Russian, I said to Oblomov, "How do you do?"

"Hello, I am honored to meet you," Oblomov replied. He didn't offer to shake hands, which was fine by me.

Carter cleared his throat. "Gentlemen, let me take your coats and show you into the living room."

Oblomov kept his scarf on but handed me his hat. Miller shrugged off his raincoat, revealing shoulders so angular it was as though he'd forgotten to remove the hanger before putting on his shirt.

As we walked to the living room, I asked Oblomov in Russian, "You speak English?"

"*Da*, but not much."

"But you understand it?"

His intelligent eyes fastened on mine and a small smile played on his lips. I suspected in Russia he'd been something more than a cleaner. "I keep my eyes open and my mouth shut."

In the old country they say, "In a quiet lagoon, devils dwell." Did that describe Oblomov? Was he a devil? I would reserve my verdict until I chatted with him a little.

Carter had uncovered the living room furniture, which last night had been draped in bedsheets. He'd even set out a plate of Danishes on the round table. The perfect host. We all stood around the coffee table. Oblomov drummed his fingers on his thigh, looking like he wanted to smoke one of those Russian cigarettes that smell like burning tires.

"Where are you from?" I asked. "I'm from Stulchyn." What I really wanted to know was why Miller had brought him to the meeting.

"Kelcmea," he replied.

I wasn't familiar with that village. "Is that in Poland or Russia?"

To my surprise, his face creased into a smile, all but making his eyes disappear into the folds of his cheeks. "I am glad you asked," he said. "After the Great War, borders shifted back and forth so fast that it seemed that some years our town was in Poland, sometimes in Russia. One day I asked an official from the capital if we were in Poland or Russia. He stared at me like I was a dunce and said, 'In Poland.' 'Thank God,' I replied. 'I couldn't stand another Russian winter.'"

Oblomov began to laugh and I joined in, even though I'd heard this joke a million times from Pa. Humor builds trust. And trust, not love, not money, not hope, makes the world go round. So, God help me, on the basis of his tired old joke and his harsh peasant accent that was so like my bubbe's, I decided to trust Oblomov.

I was just about to ask about his job at the embassy and whether Miller was the straight goods, but Carter, obviously feeling excluded and annoyed I hadn't kept silent as instructed, demanded to know what was so funny.

"Just a Russian joke," I said.

"Giddy, we have important matters to discuss." He gestured for everyone to take a seat.

Once we were settled, Agent Miller said, "Miss Brodsky— Giddy—I won't beat around the bush since we are running out of time. Kaganovich's ship docks tomorrow. We need to arrest Ivanov before he assassinates Kaganovich. An international incident would have catastrophic consequences, as I'm sure Mr. Van der Zalm has explained."

"Giddy is aware of the stakes and she's willing to help however she can," Carter answered for me.

"Do you know what Ivanov is planning?" I asked, annoyed at Carter's presumption.

"I'm happy to say I do, thanks to our friend Mr. Oblomov here." He gave a fist-pumping gesture in Oblomov's direction. "Kaganovich is the guest of honor at a welcome reception with the secretary of state, Cordell Hull, at the Russian embassy in two days. Ivanov will strike then."

Carter raised his eyebrows. "You seem very sure."

"It makes sense. Hundreds of people. A quick shot at close range. Ivanov tosses his gun into the lily pond in the back of the property. When we question him, he plays the innocent guest."

"Can you trust . . . ?" Carter gave a nod at Oblomov.

"Oblomov infiltrated the Free Russia group and befriended Ivanov, who asked him a bunch of shitty—sorry, Giddy, pardon my French—a whole lot of questions about the layout of the embassy."

The penny dropped. Of course. That's where I had seen Oblomov. The Free Russia meeting. Carter had mentioned an agent who was tracking Ivanov but who had been killed—another lie to make me think I was his only hope at stopping Ivanov. But here was Oblomov, not only a reliable informant but a man who knew the embassy inside and out. What the hell did they need me for?

"Go on," Carter said.

"The embassy reception is a perfect opportunity. Ivanov can slip in, kill Kaganovich, and then slip out. The trick will be to nab him before he makes his move. Here are the blueprints of the embassy. We'll have two men stationed at the entrance to check guests. No one enters or leaves the building without being frisked, from the ladies to the secretary of state, Mr. Hull."

"So you'll arrest Ivanov when he shows up?"

"We need proof of his intention to kill Kaganovich for charges to stick. Only if Ivanov is packing a gun can we arrest him."

"Agent Miller, what do you need me for?" I asked. Carter threw me a dirty look.

"Glad you asked. At the Secret Service, we always have a backup plan. That's where you come in. If Ivanov does, by some miracle, manage to slip in unnoticed past security, we'll need you to trail and separate him from the guests so we can arrest him without fanfare." Miller opened the long tube he'd brought and pulled out a scroll of parchment paper. "Here are the blueprints of the Soviet embassy." He unrolled the paper on the table, using the plate of Danishes and an ashtray to hold down the sides. He pointed out the entrances, the reception room, and the garden. "We'll have agents at all these locations. Each of them will have a cigarette tucked behind his right ear. That's how you'll recognize them, Giddy. We want you to pose as one of the serving staff and circulate among the guests with trays of hors d'oeuvres and canapés. When you spot Ivanov, give the high sign to one of our boys by scratching your nose. Then—and for a bombshell like you, it should be a breeze—lure Ivanov into the garden. We'll have more men waiting there. They'll handcuff Ivanov and whisk him out through the garden door to a car waiting in the alley behind the embassy grounds. Think you can handle that?"

I was puzzled for a second until I realized Miller didn't know that Ivanov already knew me, and that my presence would alert him to the fact that I was onto him. Carter must not have mentioned Ivanov's rooftop visit to Miller. The Secret Service had no need of me, not with Oblomov working for them. If anything, I was a liability.

I looked at Carter, who had gone pale. The embassy must have been Carter's master plan. With his iron-tight security and the help of Oblomov, Miller had unwittingly thwarted it. Carter and Miller weren't working together. Miller was on the level. When he arrested Ivanov, all Miller would have to do to get Ivanov to spill the beans would be threaten to deport Anya and Svetlana, then Carter would be exposed. His leg was jiggling up and down like a piston as he tried to think of a way to salvage the situation. Carter hadn't counted on Oblomov; he hadn't counted on Miller being so well briefed. Did Miller suspect Carter was not what he seemed? Hard to tell.

Miller took my silence as apprehension. "We hope it doesn't come to this. Our goal is to coldcock Ivanov at the entrance, but if that fails, we'll need your help. But don't worry. Secret Service agents will be all over the embassy like flies on sh— like ants on an anthill. Just whistle, I mean scratch your nose, and one of my boys will come running, I promise. We'll take care of the rest."

If I had any hope of stopping this assassination, I had to trust Miller. And, I realized, Miller needed me to run interference with Carter because he had just inadvertently revealed his entire strategy to the enemy.

"Fine, I'll do it," I said. An idea had been niggling at me ever since Miller mentioned frisking the guests for weapons. I recalled the odd assortment of things Ivanov had purchased at the hardware store in Five Points: chicken wire, wood boards, nails, plaster of paris, and cheesecloth. The first three items made sense—boarding up the window so Svetlana wouldn't tumble out. But the plaster of paris and cheesecloth had puzzled me. Now I understood. I knew how Ivanov was going to smuggle his gun into the embassy. To warn Miller, I had to get him alone.

Miller smiled. "You're one tough broad. I was hoping you would say that. Here's your disguise."

He retrieved a package from his briefcase and handed it to me. Inside was a uniform the color of wilted celery, with a yellow apron stenciled with the hammer and sickle, the insignia of the Soviet Union. Modest. No short, sassy skirt, no low-cut bodice with plenty of room for tips, no red open-toed pumps. It confirmed what I already knew: Communists are a puritanical bunch of poker-up-the-ass goody-goodies.

The business concluded, Miller proceeded to eat a Danish, oblivious that his plan had a fatal flaw. I needed to tell him about Carter's letter. I needed to tell him how Ivanov intended to conceal his gun. But how to get him alone? Miller munched on a second Danish.

"No breakfast," he mouthed apologetically, brushing crumbs off his chest.

I turned to Carter. "Perhaps Agent Miller would like some coffee to go with those pastries. How about making some? And I could drink another cup, too."

Miller perked up at the mention of coffee. "Coffee, great," he said, pronouncing it *caw-fee*.

Carter winced, not for the first time, at Miller's accent. What a snob. "Sorry," he said, "but it's time Giddy and I head back to the city. We have lots to do before the embassy reception."

"Yes, you're right," Miller said, not sounding too happy but helping himself to one more Danish before rolling up the blueprints.

"Giddy, can you get their things?" Carter asked.

"Sure," I said. My moment alone with Miller wasn't going to happen. My mind raced through other options as I retrieved Miller's coat and Oblomov's hat. Then I landed on an idea.

Back in the living room, I held out Oblomov's hat and spoke to him in Russian. "Your agent pal thinks you don't speak English, but I bet it's better than you let on. I suspect you understand plenty. I need you to give him a message from me. Tell him that my handsome friend here is working for the British Union of Fascists in

London and is determined to see the assassination go ahead. He's the one who hired the assassin. I have seen a letter that proves this. And now that my friend knows how you plan to stop the assassin, my friend will change his strategy. Your agent must be on alert." As I spoke, Oblomov's face remained as impassive as a plate of blini, but his eyes were drilling into mine. "Also I have an idea how the assassin will smuggle his gun into the embassy. Can you tell all this to your agent?"

It was a cumbersome, maybe confusing, message, but if I used proper names, Carter would figure out what I was saying even if he didn't speak a word of Russian.

"*Da,* I will try."

Miller and Carter looked at me expectantly. "I was just explaining to Mr. Oblomov where my store, Giddy's Creams and Lotions, is located so he can bring his wife and daughter by. I'm developing many fine products in addition to face creams. My latest formulation is a collection of eyeliners that will be very popular. Available in brown, sable, and midnight black. Perhaps Mrs. Miller would also be interested?" I handed him my new business cards, listing my products, "La Tour Eiffel"—with two *f*'s this time.

"Thanks," he said, dropping it into the cardboard tube.

"We are open from—"

"That's enough, Giddy," Carter said.

"Yeah, we gotta get the show on the road," said Miller.

"And may I have your card?" If Oblomov bungled the message or Carter's plans changed, I had to know how to get in touch with him.

Miller fished out a business card from the inside of his jacket pocket and handed it to me. It read "Agent Miller, Secret Service," with an address on West 45th and a phone number.

I tucked it in my brassiere.

I should have felt a sense of triumph that I was one step closer to exposing Carter, but I felt like crap. I was responsible for saving the lives of two men who didn't deserve to be saved: Ivanov, who had brutalized my village, and Kaganovich, who had overseen the massacre of thousands of men and their families as part of Stalin's program of "de-Cossackization." But now, I had an ally.

At least I hoped so. I hadn't been doing too swell lately in the judging-of-character department.

# Chapter 27

⸺◈⸺

*Lobster Bay, New York*

"We must get back to Manhattan as soon as possible," Carter said in a rushed, distracted manner, tossing the sheets over the living room furniture and packing the leftover beef sausage and bread into a grocery bag.

Fine with me. I needed to see Morty. The catheter hadn't dropped out and I didn't want to get an infection. I took pleasure in arranging the appointment using the fancy telephone in Carter's vast living room. It made a nice change from the urine-recking phone box at the end of my street that I usually used.

Our ride back was quiet. Carter was thinking, or more likely panicking, now that Miller had anticipated the details of his assassination plot. No doubt Carter was trying to figure out a way to dodge security.

I couldn't resist needling him. "So how are we going to trip Miller up?" I asked.

"What's that?" he asked. It was the first time I had seen him look flustered.

"His plan for the embassy reception? It's obvious he's going to find a way to sneak Ivanov in past the security with a weapon, then blame me for not identifying him in time."

"Yes, right. That's likely what he's thinking."

"So how will we stop him?" Should I explain how Ivanov was going to bring in his gun in plain sight, right under the noses of Miller's men?

"I'll think of something."

"He's got us in a pretty pickle, hasn't he? I won't even be able to smuggle in the gun you gave me with this level of scrutiny."

Carter's face looked as if he hadn't considered that. When he didn't say anything, I jostled him. "Carter, come on. What are we going to do? We can't just do nothing."

"I don't know!" he said. "Let me think, for Christ's sake. Just shut up for once in your life."

He was doing his best to hold himself together, but the cracks were showing.

After a long pause, he spoke. "For now, we continue on as planned. We can't let Miller suspect we're onto him. We'll find a way to hide the gun on you. He said guests would be frisked, not staff . . . And, by the way, at the embassy reception, you report to me directly when you spot Ivanov, not Miller. Promise me. I won't have anything happening to you."

Once, I would have been flattered by his concern, but now his words sounded so phony-baloney, the cheap sentiments of a master manipulator. But he was also desperate. I could use that to my advantage. After all, hadn't I learned from the best?

"Carter, I don't know if I should do this. I agreed to help Miller but I'm having second thoughts. It's so risky—"

"How much?" he asked.

"How much what?" I asked, hanging on to the handle of the door as he swerved around a corner too fast.

He looked at me. "How much money do you want?"

"For blowing Ivanov's brains out because you're too chickenshit to pull the trigger yourself?"

He nodded, all pretense of being a decent human being gone.

"A hundred and fifty. Up front." It was enough to stock Giddy's Creams and Lotions for months to come with glass jars, shea butter, lavender water, and almond oil. My little shop would no longer be undercapitalized—that is, if I survived this whole ordeal. And if I didn't survive, and I had to consider this possibility, then Ma could take over the store.

Carter agreed without even haggling. So this was what our supposed love affair had been reduced to—a business transaction.

I doubted Carter could salvage his plan, but I had no intention of killing Ivanov or letting Ivanov assassinate Kaganovich. However, I had to play along so I could keep Miller abreast of what was going on. If I didn't hear from the agent, I would attend the embassy reception, but I would not waste time sweet-talking Ivanov out into the garden for Miller's men to arrest. No, I would be at the entranceway waiting for him. They would arrest Ivanov, and under threat of deportation, he would sing like a canary about Carter's involvement. It sounded easy but there was a lot that could go wrong. For one, I was banking on Miller believing me. If he didn't, I had a juicy morsel of information that would persuade him I was on the up-and up.

It's funny the way I can sometimes figure things out by putting together miscellaneous facts that seem to have nothing in common. Years ago, I helped Pa study for his American citizenship test. One of the questions was: Who was the American president who was assassinated in Buffalo in 1901 by an anarchist with a hankerchief draped over his hand, which concealed a handgun? Answer: Mr. William McKinley.

I bet Ivanov had taken the same test as my pa. Except Ivanov was smart. Instead of merely a hankerchief, he would fashion himself a plaster cast.

When Carter started to pass the turn for Wooster, I said, "No, you have to drop me off at the doctor's."

A muscle in his jaw twitched. "Fine, but I can't wait for you. Make your own way home. I have business to attend to on Ellis Island."

That was just fine by me. We rode the rest of the way without speaking, Carter in sullen silence, me secretly elated. Money has that effect on me.

Carter pulled over in front of Morty's building and took out a wad of bills. I was astonished. He was going to develop sciatica carrying a roll that big in his hip pocket. Not even Sid went around with that much. "Lucky for you a long shot came in for me at the racetrack this week—Amos the Famous, paying fifty to one."

I hadn't known him to be a gambler, but nothing really surprised me at this point. After forking over my money, he sped away.

I climbed the stairs to Morty's office. He greeted me at the door and ushered me in. I took off my skirt and stockings and climbed up on the table. He went to the sink in the corner and washed his hands. As he scrubbed away, using a nail brush, he absently hummed "Night and Day."

"I love Cole Porter," I said.

"Me too," he replied, putting on his gloves. "Lie back now and try to relax." He gently parted my knees. "This won't take long. Breathe. Better still, hum along with me."

And so I did, gazing once more at the ceiling. And he was right, humming did relax me, and before I knew it, he was saying, "There you go. The catheter's out. Everything looks fine, Giddy. No sign of infection. Did you have a rough time?"

*You don't know the half of it,* I thought. "A lot of pain, but the pills helped," I said.

I sat up, and Morty held out his hand to steady me, but there was no dizziness this time. I got dressed as Morty cleaned up, humming once more. I felt a flood of gratitude toward this man, this stranger who had changed the course of my life. Because of Morty's skill and kindness I could go on with my life and pursue my dreams. I thought of his sister, who had nearly bled to death from an illegal abortion. I wondered what her life was like now, whether she was happy, if she had found someone to love and have children with.

"Morty, I didn't have a chance to thank you before. You've performed a mitzvah. You should know I appreciate the risk you've taken for me."

He seemed embarrassed by my comment and looked at the floor. "I'm glad I could help. Take care of yourself. If you need contraceptive advice, there's a clinic in Brooklyn I can refer—"

I didn't let him finish his sentence. "I won't be needing that, thanks anyway." I sounded very prim. Sex had turned me into a knucklehead; it wouldn't happen again. But Morty meant well, so I didn't mention any of this.

I didn't linger. Just said goodbye and hopped on the streetcar, my other Cole Porter favorite, "You Do Something to Me," playing in my head.

I reached my block. Like usual, Cherry Street was strewn with garbage, the fire escapes draped with dirty pillows and blankets, and stray dogs nosing at a bone. But it looked a beautiful sight to me. I was so glad to be home I could have kissed one of the bums snoring in the entranceway.

It was late afternoon. The apartment was dark when I let myself in. Ma was lying on the sofa with a damp cloth over her eyes, which meant she had one of her headaches, but she sat up when I came in.

"Giddy, is that you?"

"Yes, it's me, Ma," I said, pulling up a chair next to her. "I had the operation. It went fine."

She took my face in her hands and kissed me. "I've been worried sick."

"I'm all right."

"And your goyish boyfriend?"

"Gone and forgotten." I spanked my hands together, like I was brushing off stale cake crumbs.

"Good, about him we shall speak no more."

Arnold came over to Ma. "A headache?"

She nodded.

"And you, Giddy? You could probably use a nice glass of tea?" He paused a moment. "I'm sorry you had to go through that."

From the look of sympathy on his face, I could tell he knew everything. Before I could respond, he said, "I'll make you some tea." He went into the kitchen and soon I heard the kettle boiling.

"Such a thoughtful boy," I said.

Ma gave me a little smile. In a low voice, so Arnold wouldn't hear, she said, "Arnold and I had a chance to talk while you were away. I told him the truth about my feelings for him, that I had tried hard to be a good mother but I was sorry I had failed him. He said I hadn't failed him, that I had always been present for him. He said he loved me and that both of us should let the past go and forgive each other. He said, making a joke of it, 'If you can forgive me for looking like a Cossack, I can forgive you for not being a milk-and-cookies kind of ma.' It was funny the way he said it."

"I'm very happy to hear that, Ma." At last, here were the two of them talking frankly and putting to rest the pain and resentment between them.

"Ma, there's something I need you should tell me." There was no gentle way to ask this. Soon I would be confronting Ivanov. There were questions that had been gnawing at me, things I needed to know. "I saw Pa at the library."

She looked at me like I'd stabbed her. The damp cloth fell from her forehead into her lap. "You're kidding."

"About such things, I don't kid." I described how we had visited over the hamantaschen.

"And? Has he found another woman yet? Some nice shiksa with varicose veins?" she said, attempting a joke, but I could see she was hungry for details.

"He's busking with his fiddle and living in a boardinghouse on the Bowery. He looks like the wrath of God, if you want to know the truth. And judging by the rips in his filthy jacket and trousers, there's no woman, shiksa or otherwise."

"Poor man."

I rubbed my thumb across her swollen knuckles. "I asked him about returning home, Ma. He told me you kicked him out, that you'd never allow him back. Now, tell me why you asked him to leave." If I didn't make it back from the embassy reception, Ma needed someone to take care of her, make sure she took her medicine, got enough rest, ate, and didn't drink too much. Arnold would make a life for himself—finish school, get a job, and marry. Ma couldn't function on her own. She needed Pa.

"You and me have talked about the pogrom." Ma paused. "I had almost succeeded in closing that chapter of my life. The nightmares had stopped. I could sleep without waking up screaming. Then I found out what your pa did and I asked him to leave."

Arnold came out with glasses of tea for me and Ma, then he went off to the bedroom to study.

I took a sip of tea. Arnold had added just the right amount of sugar. "What did Pa do?" I prompted. "I need the truth."

She took a breath, then said, "It's about Bekka."

I sat back. My mother never spoke of my sister. "Bekka?"

Ma had a wistful look in her eye. "Do you remember how lovely she was? That thick hair and those eyes?"

"Yes, I remember," I said softly, then waited for her to go on.

"Your pa did it for the money, Giddy." Ma looked so exhausted, so tense, so tight around the mouth and eyes. "I hated him for it, for letting me believe all those years that she died in the pogrom, letting me think she had died a brutal death at the hands of those savages."

I shook my head. "Please, Ma, talk sense. Bekka's not dead?"

She wiped her nose on the sleeve of her cardigan. "Count Oshefsky—who, you remember, owned our village—had a son, Stefan. He was in love with Bekka, had been for years. I would never have consented to the match, nor under normal circumstances would your pa, but he wanted us to immigrate to Palestine. That's what the money was for. You know what a fervent Zionist he's always been. He was desperate. The day the Cossacks attacked, Pa was delivering Bekka to Stefan like a side of beef. That's why your father wasn't in our village when the Cossacks came. He was too ashamed to tell me where he was."

I swallowed down the lump in my throat. "He sold her," I said, my voice hoarse.

"In Russia it was called *vykup nevesty*, bride price."

"Call it anything you want—he sold her." I felt ill. I remembered Bekka speaking fondly of a boy named Samuel who lived in a nearby village. She would have refused to go to Stefan. She would have kicked and screamed.

"I knew nothing. I thought she had died at the hand of some Cossack. It tormented me that we never found her body, never gave her a burial, never sat shiva for her." She sighed. "A couple of months later, I realized I was expecting. Everyone in Stulchyn who could count to nine figured out the father must have been a Cossack. We had to leave. Then your pa told me about his money for passage to Palestine. But he said his brothers gave it to him."

"So that was a lie? Pa's brothers giving him the money?"

She nodded. "But that's what he told me. He already had the money and this was his explanation. I agreed to immigrate but not to Palestine. Our life would have been twice as hard there as it was in Russia. I insisted on sailing for America."

"Thank God you did." I sat in stunned silence as the weight of Ma's words sank in. "Wait, this means Bekka is . . . alive?"

She managed the smallest of smiles. "Yes, I believe so."

Bekka was alive. It felt too good to be true. "So for years you thought Bekka was—"

"Put it this way. For years I was dancing with a corpse."

"How did you find out the truth?"

"By a dumb accident. Two years ago, I got a letter from an old neighbor in our village, the midwife who'd delivered Bekka. She wrote to ask how I was adjusting to life in America and asked if the streets were really paved with gold." Ma laughed ruefully. "At the end of her letter, she mentioned that she had seen Bekka at the Oshefsky estate outside of town and congratulated me on my fine-looking grandson, Mikhail, who was now helping his father manage the estate."

"But all those years . . . I don't understand. Couldn't Bekka have run away? Come home to us?"

"The count had a priest come and perform a marriage ceremony."

"But . . ."

"Giddy, I have spent a lot of sleepless nights thinking about this. I think they must have kept Bekka confined until we left for America. After that she had no one to help her. You wouldn't remember, but the Oshefsky estate was miles out of town along a bad road. My poor Bekka has led a very isolated life."

"Oh my God. What did you say to Pa?"

"I showed him the letter. Eventually, I forced him to tell me the whole story. I was so angry that he had let me suffer all these years, thinking my oldest girl was dead, that I packed up all his clothes into a grocery bag and threw it into the air shaft. I should have thrown him in, too. I know what you're thinking. You think I should take him back, but you see how impossible it would be?"

I knew Pa was difficult. What man isn't? But I'd never thought of him as cruel. There are things in this world you don't come back from, tragedies you can't get over, people you can't forgive. Lying about the death of your firstborn child is one of them. Pa said at the library that everything he did, he did for us. What a hateful lie. He was the one who wanted to go to Palestine, not Ma. And yet, I had also benefited from Bekka's bride price. I felt sick at the thought. Without Pa's deceit, we would never have made it to America. I owed him nothing, not my love, not my loyalty. He was dead to me. In my heart, I sat shiva for him. And yet, overriding my anger at Pa's treachery was the joy of knowing Bekka might still be alive.

"Better for me to know the truth than hope any minute he's gonna walk through the door with a half pound of pastrami under his arm," I said, trying to make a joke of it. But she was right; reconciliation was out of the question. "Have you written to Bekka?"

She took a sip of tea. "Of course, but she is so furious with Pa she won't have anything to do with either of us, not even to write a postcard to say if she's alive. This is what my neighbor reported in her second letter."

"I can't say I blame her. But, without Pa, aren't you lonely?" What I really meant was *Who will look after you if I am killed by Ivanov at the reception?* "I love you, Ma. You haven't had an easy life. But you've been brave and you've never given up. And that's the important thing." I took a deep breath. "You need someone to take care of you."

"Well, it sure won't be your pa." She gave my hand a squeeze. "Tsikele, I will be fine. You worry too much about me."

"Bubbe use to say, 'The same heat that hardens steel melts butter.' In our individual ways, Ma, you and me are both steel."

"Me, steel? I'm more like leftover gefilte fish."

"There's no such thing."

# Chapter 28

*Lower East Side, New York*

I was troubled with the truth about Pa and questions about Bekka when I woke the next day. But I couldn't sit and stew. I had a business to run. I got washed and dressed and went to my store. Promptly at 10:00 a.m., I rolled up the shutters, unlocked the door, and hoped that Agent Miller would drop by.

Around noon, a giggly sweatshop dolly strolled in. She was interested in the new eyeliner in midnight black, so I plunked her on a stool in the front window and showed her how to apply it. My demonstration attracted attention from passersby who gathered at the window outside to watch. A couple of them came in. They turned out to be paying customers, not just lookie-loos. By late afternoon, it began to rain, which drove more people inside, and I made a few more sales. Maybe my business had a fighting chance.

But on the issue of Agent Miller I struck out. The whole day my eyes were glued on the street, willing him to show up. Had Oblomov bungled my message? I had to talk to Miller, explain I was in over my head. Carter was no dope. Sure, he was panicky now, but he would come up with an alternate strategy—he had to.

It was still pouring when I locked the front door for the night. Out of nowhere, I felt a tap on my shoulder. I whirled around, certain it was Miller. But Anya Ivanov stood on the sidewalk, her hair hanging in wet snakes around her face. Sticking out of the pocket of her coat was the handbill I had left in the vestibule of her building. Svetlana slept in her arms, clasped diagonally across Anya's pregnant belly. Thick blond hair, huge blue eyes, and flawless skin. Even in this disheveled state Anya was beautiful, despite the tense, worried look on her face.

"I must talk," she said in English. "Please."

"What is it?" I asked.

She hesitated, the rain dripping down the collar of her coat. I was getting drenched myself. Might she know of Carter and Ivanov's plan? I had to find out.

"Let's walk back to my apartment and have a tea," I suggested. "It's only a few blocks away. Can you manage Svetlana?"

Heads bent against the rain, we hurried down the street toward my building. Once inside, I drew her into the kitchen and pulled out a chair for her.

"Ma, this is Anya." I didn't explain who this young woman was who wore a coat far too thin for the weather. Ma would figure it out. I had reluctantly told her about Ivanov, feeling she should know in case anything happened to me. "Anya, this is my ma."

Anya was out of breath from climbing the three flights to our apartment and the weight of an eight-month belly. I hung her wet coat on a peg behind the door, then I took Svetlana from Anya's arms and carried her into the bedroom Ma and I shared. I passed by the parlor, where Arnold was sitting with a chemistry textbook propped open on his bent knees, listening to the radio. WNYC played a fox-trot, but the news would be broadcast in ten minutes. He nodded at Svetlana. "Who is she?" he mouthed.

"I'll explain later," I said.

In my room, I peeled off Svetlana's damp clothes. She didn't protest as I wrapped her in my bathrobe and tucked her into my bed, covering her with a quilt. She just stared at me with round eyes, clutching her moth-eaten stuffed rabbit. "You'll be all right, little one," I whispered.

Returning to the kitchen, I saw Ma had poured Anya a glass of tea and was buttering a slice of rye for her. From the way Anya gobbled it down, I wondered when she had last eaten. Was she here to scold me for lying to her? No doubt Ivanov had broken the news that I wasn't from the city housing department of New York, about to install her in a spanking-new apartment on a tree-lined street where her children would attend a wonderful public school and learn to become real Americans.

I poured myself a tea and sat down, letting the warmth of the cup seep through my cold hands as I waited for Anya to explain why she was here. Ma threw me a look that told me although she realized this was Ivanov's wife, she pitied her, shivering and pregnant as she was.

Anya brushed the crumbs from the bread off her lap. "Yuri says to me you do not work for New York City," she said, speaking with greater fluency than the last time we met.

"I let you believe that. I'm sorry I deceived you, Anya. My real name is Giddy Brodsky. I—"

"Not important. I come for different purpose. Not about that." Anya spoke without shyness. When I went to her apartment, she had seemed so young and uncertain of herself, eager to make a good impression. Tonight, she was blazing with a kind of urgent confidence. "I need help. Miss Giddy, a man came to my home today. A nice, well-dressed man, tall and handsome, a gentleman. I hear him talk to Yuri. After the man left, Yuri said to me, 'I don't give up. The Kaganovich ship is in harbor. Maybe better this way.'"

I could venture a pretty good guess who that man was.

Anya went on. "Yuri would be angry if he knew I was here. But you are a woman with a good heart." She made the familiar fist-to-heart motion I remembered from my visit to her apartment. "Yuri is good husband but he is difficult."

"Why have you come to me, Anya?"

"Where I live, no one speaks Russian, only Polish and German. I have no friends. I know no neighbors. My English not so good, but . . ." She faltered.

In other words, I was not just her last resort, but her only resort.

Arnold came out of the parlor, his chemistry book in his hand, finger holding his place. "I couldn't help but hear you mention Kaganovich. They just said on the radio that his ship's being detained until the doctors can test the passengers for typhus. It's in quarantine, docked at the Chelsea Pier. I think that's at the foot of West 21st. No one except Immigration personnel are allowed on or off."

"Who is this Kaganovich?" Ma asked.

As Arnold explained, my mind raced ahead. There would be no reception at the Russian embassy tomorrow night. The waitress uniform Agent Miller had given me would continue to hang in my closet, along with the blueprints of the Russian embassy, the names of agents who would be there, and $150 in crisp five-dollar bills. I was off the hook. For a moment, I felt relieved, yet oddly deflated. Some part of me had been looking forward to locking horns once again with Ivanov.

And then I realized what Carter was up to. He had issued the detention order. He had Kaganovich in lockdown until Ivanov could get to him. Ivanov could execute the whole scheme himself. All Carter had to do was stand by and watch. This was his squeaky brand-new plan, which he didn't need me to take the fall for. Did Miller have any inkling of the magnitude of what Carter was planning?

"Anya, I need you to think hard. What did you hear Yuri and the other man say about Kaganovich and the *Nordvik*? Think, this is important."

"They talked fast in English so I do not understand much, but I know Yuri plans trouble. He left house tonight with a large suitcase. I fear he will do something."

"But what? What is he up to?" Ma said, leaning forward.

Anya shrugged. "I do not know. Dynamite? Bomb?"

"Did you heard him use that word, *dynamite*?" I asked.

Anya shook her head. "I am not sure."

"Giddy, what's going on?" asked Arnold.

"Anya's husband is a former Cossack with Free Russia, and he's part of a plot to assassinate Kaganovich," I said.

"How do you know this?" said Arnold.

"It's a long story. The important thing is stopping him."

Arnold spoke again. "About twenty sticks of dry dynamite would be enough to blow the Chrysler Building to kingdom come—that amount would fit just fine into a suitcase. All he'd need is a kitchen match; the gunpowder would do the rest."

It all sounded so far-fetched. Where on earth would Yuri Ivanov get sticks of dynamite? I paced, trying to reason this out. Then I realized any contractor who built highways or bridges and needed to blast through heavy terrain would have a ready supply. Road builders used it instead of hiring expensive earth-moving equipment. It might well be that Ivanov's transport company delivered dynamite from the manufacturers to building sites.

"Anya, does Yuri have access to dynamite?"

"I do not know." Anya hugged her belly and began to cry. "Maybe there are guards on the docks. Maybe Yuri's plan is not possible. I cannot lose Yuri. He is all I have. I cannot live alone in America. I do not know how things work here."

I put my hand on her shoulder. Let her think what she wanted. I knew how determined Carter was and how determined Yuri was. Yuri would succeed unless someone stopped him.

Ma looked at me. "Giddy, do not let him kill all those people."

Arnold was nodding. He understood the political repercussions. "You gotta help her. Go to the police. Translate for her. Make them believe her."

"Please." Anya gripped my arm, her lovely face pale and resolute. "Please, if you don't go, then I go alone. Without him, I have no money, no food, no life."

I'd underestimated Carter. Yes, he and his fascist pals wanted Kaganovich dead, but the entire shipload of passengers? Would he condone, even instigate, a massacre? Was his loyalty to the Bund stronger than his loyalty to America and to the free world? The answer looked like yes. I had to warn Agent Miller.

"I will do my best to help." I said to Anya, "You stay here with my mother. I'll phone a man I know. He'll know what to do."

Arnold started to say he would come with me, but I just threw on my coat and dashed out the door. There was no time to waste. Yuri would already be on his way to the docks by now.

Outside the rain came down in sheets, turning the sidewalk black and slick. I dodged the puddles as best I could as I ran to the pay phone at the corner. I flung open the door, and once in the shelter of the booth, I slapped my pockets, found a nickel, and dropped it in.

The Bell Telephone operator answered, "Number, please?"

I rummaged for the card Agent Miller had given me in Lobster Bay and read off the phone number, wondering what the chances were that he would be in his office at this hour.

"One moment please." She spoke in a bored nasal voice.

The phone rang and rang. I imagined it echoing throughout empty corridors of a huge office building. After several more rings, just as I was about to hang up, a female voice said, "Good evening."

"Hello, I must speak to Agent Miller."

"I'm sorry but who is calling, please?" I imagined a middle-aged dame, badly permed red hair, lips pursed in a "just sucked a lemon" expression. "Agent Miller left the office hours ago."

"This is an emergency," I said in my most businesslike tone. "My name is Giddy Brodsky." I spoke like my name should mean something to her. "If Agent Miller is not there, may I have his home number?"

"I have no authority to disclose that information." The receptionist spoke with the indifference of a woman with more important things on her mind, like getting home to a warm bed and a brandy.

"Listen, I have reason to believe a serious crime is about to be committed in New York Harbor involving a Russian ship, the *Nordvik*."

There was a long pause as she mulled this over. I wanted to scream with impatience.

The line cracked and hissed, maybe due to the pouring rain.

"He's . . ." I fought the temptation to blurt out that he was my last chance, that I hoped to hell he was on the level because if not, I was in double Dutch trouble. Instead, I said, "We work together on an immigration case. An informant contacted me tonight to warn me of an attack on the ship, the *Nordvik*." I spelled out the name, waited while she wrote it down. "May I have his home number?" I asked again.

"I'm sorry, but no."

I wanted to scream expletives, starting with *bitch*, into the phone but made do with "Please, I wouldn't ask if this wasn't urgent. Could you at least pass along my message?"

She cleared her throat. "I will try. But there is no guarantee I can reach him."

I was stymied. What should I do? The ride to the dock would be more than an hour, assuming I could persuade a cabbie to take me. But I had no choice. I had to stop Ivanov.

"Thank you. Please do your best. The lives of dozens of people are at stake."

I replaced the receiver and raced back upstairs to my apartment, where Ma and Anya were eating soup at the kitchen table. They glanced up as I came in, but I motioned I didn't have time to talk.

I entered my bedroom. Arnold followed me in.

"Where are you going?"

"To the docks."

"Let me come with you. It's too dangerous for a woman alone down there."

"I can't risk your life as well. I got myself into this, I'll figure a way to get myself out. If anything happens to me, you must be here to look after Ma." He opened his mouth to argue but I interrupted. "If you want to help, then lend me some clothes, a pair of pants and a work shirt."

Arnold rummaged through his drawers, handed me his clothes, and then went back to the parlor.

I tore off my dress and tugged on Arnold's corduroy pants and belt, along with his jacket and a cap. Carter's gun was at the bottom of my bureau drawer, under a pile of underwear and my best slip. The gun glinted dully in the dim light coming from the kitchen through the open doorway. It fit into my hand like it was custom made for me. I jammed it under my belt, then I took a bunch of dollar bills and stuffed them in my pocket.

As I was leaving the bedroom, Svetlana rolled over onto her back, murmuring in a sleepy voice, "Where are you going?"

"To find your father."

She held out her moth-eaten rabbit to me, her blond curls falling over her face. "Give this to my da when you find him," she said in Russian.

"I will," I promised and crammed it into the pocket of Arnold's pants.

When I walked quickly through the apartment to the door, everyone looked up. Arnold had given up the pretense of reading and looked at me with a worried expression. Anya's face was blank; she seemed too tired to feel anything. Ma got up and hugged me tightly. "You are my shining star, Giddy. The bravest of the brave." Then I left, taking the stairs two at a time until I was back in the street. I ran west down Cherry toward the Hudson River to flag down a taxi.

I had never been to the docks, never had any interest in going, knew nothing about ships, knew nothing about explosives, guns, or anything that would be useful to know at a time like this. I longed for an ally. Someone to tell me what to do, explain to me how you blow up a huge ship, explain to me how men can be so evil, and then tell me how I could prevent the worst from happening.

I had been wrong about Carter. If I was wrong about Agent Miller, I was walking straight into an ambush, an ambush from which there would be no escape.

There wasn't a vehicle in sight. Two bums loitering on the corner eyed me in a way that gave me the jimjams. I was very much alone.

# Chapter 29

*New York Harbor, New York*

Ivanov was nowhere in sight when I arrived at New York Harbor on the mouth of the Hudson River. In fact, if it hadn't been for two hookers teetering on dangerously high heels along the wharf, it would have been just me and a few screaming seagulls circling the garbage floating in the water. The place was as empty as my wallet after paying the taxi to get here. Even the customs brokers' office was closed. Their sign advertised "fast, quick service." I bet the hookers did, too.

It was a cloudy night but the rain had finally stopped. I tried to pinpoint the *Nordvik* among the dozens of ships scattered willy-nilly in the harbor, but the moon wasn't cooperating. The air was heavy with salt, tar, rotting fish, and filled with the sounds of bilge pumps, crashing waves, diesel motors, and the slapping of rubber fenders. Beyond the ships, I could just barely make out lower Manhattan, with its skyscrapers stenciled against the sky, the Jersey City waterfront, Governor's Island, and faintly in the distance, the lights of Brooklyn.

The working girls advanced on me. Both were about Ma's age but with meaty legs and huge bosoms with cleavage deep enough to park a bicycle in.

"Don't worry, ladies," I said. "I'm not muscling in on your territory."

They gave me the once-over, taking in Arnold's old trousers and work shirt, and giggled.

"You're not much competition," the one wearing a too-tight red taffeta dress said. "What are you doing out here?"

"Looking for someone," I said. "There should be no one around."

The stouter of the two flipped her cigarette butt into the water, where it landed with a hiss. "Yeah, there's usually at least guards."

"Must be the ball game that's on tonight," the first one said. "It's the opening game of the season, between the Red Sox and the Yankees. Give a fellow the choice between a Buffalo handshake and watching Spud Chandler pitch? We don't stand a chance. Time to call it a night, toots," she said to her friend. She turned to me. "You be careful out here."

I nodded.

She fumbled in the pocket of her rabbit jacket, which had once been white but now, even in the dim light, looked gray and pawed over. She held out a flask, giving it a jiggle. "Here, hon, something to warm you up." I didn't want to seem standoffish, so I took a sip, then wished I hadn't. I handed the flask back, and with a cheerful wave, they clattered off into the night.

After the hookers disappeared, I turned back to the harbor, squinting at the names of the ships. Just then, the moon peeked out from behind a cloud, casting a silvery glow over the water, and I made out the white letters of the *Nordvik* on its huge, black hull. It was moored several hundred yards from the wharf. Even in the lousy light, I could tell it was a bit neglected. The paint was peeling and the iron sheeting that covered the sides was rusted.

Now to find Ivanov. I crept closer. The pilings holding up the dock reeked with the piney stink of creosote. I moved along the pier, wishing I had a flashlight as I stumbled over the ropes, which lay tangled, hanging half in, half out of the water, thick as snakes. The moon disappeared again. I narrowed my eyes, straining to see anyone on the horizon.

A few feet away, packing crates were stacked one on top of the other. I climbed up, peering in all directions. I was wrong about the wharf being deserted. Dozens of big and fearless water rats, the size of cats, scampered up the anchor chains from the water to cargo holds in search of grain. What I thought was a heap of discarded rags was two hoboes curled up under a filthy blanket.

I was losing hope when I spotted a figure at the end of the wharf. From his erect posture and the shape of his hat, I knew it was Ivanov. He was headed toward a freighter sitting low in the water, probably waiting to be unloaded. Tethered to this ship was a small rowboat, its oars resting invitingly on the gunwales. In both hands, Ivanov carried a black suitcase, which he carefully placed in the rowboat's stern. Whatever was in the suitcase was heavy judging by the way he was struggling. Then the unmistakable smell of kerosene hit my nose. So that was his plan. Set fire to the ship with kerosene. Not so dramatic as a dozen sticks of dynamite in the boiler room, but it would do the job.

Ivanov glanced up once or twice, but he was so intent on his task, he didn't notice me squatting among the packing crates. I groped for my gun. I didn't want to kill Ivanov, just slow him down with a shot to the leg or shoulder, but my inexperience in using a gun made me hesitate. What if I hit the suitcase by accident? It might combust and set ablaze nearby ships. I knew from Pa, who always kept a kerosene lantern in the house to use during power failures, that kerosene has a higher flash point than gasoline. The flames could set Ivanov's rowboat on fire and then, in turn, ignite the ship it was tied to, causing a chain reaction. The explosion would turn the ship into a bomb of such magnitude the entire dock would catch fire. I couldn't take the chance. I had to get closer. But Ivanov was already taking up the oars.

A terrible thought occurred to me. Was Ivanov on a suicide mission? The newspapers were filled with stories and lurid photos of ships burning to the waterline when their fuel tanks exploded. This is exactly what would happen when the *Nordvik* caught fire. The tank would blow up, and the ship would sink. The downward suction would create a whirlpool that would pull the ship to the bottom of the harbor. Even if Ivanov managed to jump clear of the hull, he would be sucked into the vortex and drowned. Surely he was aware of that. Did he care if he died so long as he killed Kaganovich? Carter was banking on it. That's why he no longer needed me as a fall guy. The determined set of Ivanov's shoulders told me everything I needed to know: he was David, and the ship, Goliath. Ivanov figured he could do the impossible.

I looked around, hoping to spot Miller with reinforcements, but there was no one. The phone call to his office had been a waste of precious time. It was all up to me.

Running, then ducking behind the packing crates, I raced down the wharf searching for another rowboat. I found a leaky-looking tender with oars still in the locks roped to a cargo ship. Not my first choice, but beggars can't be choosers. I climbed in and quickly untied the bowline. I'd never rowed a boat before, so at first I kept going around in circles. But finally I got the hang of it, and with a steady pull on both oars I began to make progress. The waves were high and cold water slapped against the hull as I rowed past the freighters anchored between the wharf and the *Nordvik*. Up ahead, I could see Ivanov's broad back. My shoulder muscles burned. I tried to close the gap between us, but Ivanov was stronger and faster.

When Ivanov reached the *Nordvik*, I hung back, using the closest freighter as a shield. The *Nordvik* had appeared large from the pier. Now that I was closer, it looked like the Chrysler Building had slid off its foundations and floated steeple side down into the harbor. Up on the ship's deck, a lone figure paced. A guard perhaps? Carter mentioned once that the immigration agency required shipowners to hire their own guards, one on portside, the other on starboard. Then Ivanov raised his hand and the man flung down a rope ladder. Not a guard. An accomplice. Could it be Carter? I squinted at him, trying to make out any features, but all I could see was the vague outline of a tall man.

Ivanov fumbled for something at the bottom of his boat. A grappling hook. Then, moving cautiously, he slipped his arms under the straps of the suitcase and swiveled it around so it was on his back like a knapsack. The ladder was swinging like the pendulum on a grandfather clock, but he snagged it on his grappling hook and grabbed hold of the bottom rung. Grunting, he got both feet on the ladder. I watched helplessly as he began the long climb, swaying to and fro, banging against the side of the ship, his heavy boots making a scraping sound against the hull. The grappling hook fell with a splash into the water. At the top, his accomplice lifted the suitcase off his back and placed it on the deck. Then he gripped Ivanov by the shoulders and hauled him over the rail like a fisherman heaving a marlin into the hold.

I rowed toward the ship. There were a few lights shining through the portholes in steerage. I heard the low murmur of a radio coming from the top deck. A sportscaster announced the baseball game. I caught the words "Folks, the bases are loaded. DiMaggio is up to bat. Can he deliver?" There was the satisfying crack of wood against the leather ball and screams and cheering from the stands. The announcer's voice, loud and excited, yelled, "And he did it, fans! Out of the park! The Yankee Clipper hit a home run!"

No matter how much I craned my neck, I was now too close to the hull to see whether anyone was still on deck. For all I knew, it was crawling with guards. But somehow I didn't think so. Carter was too smart. He would have made sure all the guards were either off duty or down below, drunk as skunks, playing cards and glued to the radio.

There was no one but me to stop Ivanov, and I hadn't a clue what to do. Except the obvious. Climb the ladder. Shoot to wound him. Figure out how to deal with his accomplice. Whatever happened, I was on my own.

In the distance there was suddenly the sound of a boat's horn. Late at night in bed with the covers pulled up to my chin, I'd always loved that sound coming from the tugs on the East River. Tonight I didn't. It sounded ominously close, but the fog made it impossible to pinpoint from which direction. Worst of all, the tug couldn't see me. There were no running lights on my tiny rowboat. I could be crushed in an instant.

I turned back to the *Nordvik*. With Carter's gun tucked securely into the pocket of my pants, I rose unsteadily to my feet. When the ladder swung within reach, I took a deep breath and seized the rope with one hand, then the other. The rowboat rocked in the waves. Without the grappling hook, it was the mere strength of my body that kept my dinghy from drifting too far away. I waited for a big swell to lift me up closer to the ladder. One misstep and I stood a good chance of plunging into the black void below me and drowning—I wouldn't last five minutes in these frigid waters. My arms strained as the ladder swung in tandem with the waves. After a lot of flailing about, I got one leg up on the bottom rung. I raised my other leg but only managed to kick at open air. I clung to the ladder for all I was worth, but my arm muscles were weak from rowing.

A voice cut across the wind. I lost my grip and fell.

# Chapter 30

*New York Harbor, New York*

I landed hard in the dinghy. The boat tipped and lurched, sending icy water splashing over the gunwales. I sputtered and pulled myself up to see a launch knifing through the water toward me. Rubber fenders hung off it like a necklace of loose teeth, and on the prow, in gold lettering, were the words "US Department of Immigration." And there was Carter at the helm, a look of complete shock on his face. He steered the launch alongside me and dropped the anchor.

He was alone. I gripped the little finger of my left hand in the palm of my right and squeezed. Then as calmly as I could, I wiped the wet hair from my face and said, "Nice of you to drop by, Carter. I've been half expecting you." It was the kind of witty, urbane thing he would say.

"Giddy, what the hell are you doing here?"

I didn't know how to answer. With every wave, Carter's launch slammed against my rowboat. I was the pastrami in the sandwich between the *Nordvik* and Carter's boat. A couple of good-sized swells and I would be ground to splinters. Ivanov's tender had already drifted off to God knows where—more proof he didn't intend to make a return trip to the wharf.

"I'm here to stop Ivanov, just like I promised."

"But what made you think he'd be here?"

"The story was on the radio, a couple of hours ago. Mr. Edward

R. Murrow at CBS—the suspicion of typhus. I figured the detention order was your brainchild."

"Of course it wasn't. The chief medical officer just called me. That was the first I'd heard about any of this." Carter's voice overflowed with sincerity. "Believe me, I had no idea Ivanov would go this far."

"Cut the crap." I needed to conserve my strength. I'd lost a lot of blood since the abortion, so I didn't waste my energy screaming *Liar, liar, pants on fire* in his face.

"Listen, you have been through enough. I'll take it from here."

And by that he meant he'd ensure Ivanov's plan went through. Perhaps he intended to shoot Ivanov and be hailed as a hero. I suppose I should be grateful my role as patsy was no longer part of the script—or at least I didn't think I was still needed. But as they say, "It ain't over till it's over."

"Why are *you* here? Call off Ivanov."

"What are you talking about?"

"I know, Carter. Anya paid me a visit and I figured everything out."

"Giddy, you're letting your personal feelings intrude. I am sorry about everything. This isn't the time to apologize but—"

I sensed what was coming—mealymouthed protestations of how he had loved me, but our social worlds were too far apart, blah blah blah. May he topple overboard. "Don't pretend you care for me. I know you're a fascist. I know all about your buddies in England, Carter. I've heard Mosley's speeches on the newsreels, seen him marching through London, through the Jewish neighborhoods. Mosley should be arrested for treason. So should you."

"I am a loyal American. My family has been in this country since—"

"You hired Ivanov. I found Risdon's letter in your briefcase."

Even in the shadowy light I could see the surprise on his face. "What a clever little spy you have turned out to be. I was right about you from the start."

This remark I did believe. He'd been sizing me up since that first visit to his office on Ellis Island, which seemed years ago but in fact was only a few months. He was a good judge of character. Much better than me. I had to give him that.

"So you admit it."

For the first time, he spoke with honesty. "Yes, I did. But Ivanov developed delusions," he said. "Insane delusions. I could no longer trust him. He disappeared on me. I tried to find him. I even went to his squalid tenement. He would kill Kaganovich, but I also knew he would be caught, because the more demented he grew, the more reckless he became. Don't you understand? I could not permit him to implicate me."

"So that's where I came in. You wanted me to kill Ivanov. Solve your problem for you. You were too delicate—no, that isn't the word—too lily-livered to kill him yourself."

"Miller was becoming suspicious of me. I had to keep my distance from Ivanov. So when you walked into my office, yes, you were an answer to my prayers."

"Those fascist books in your library? Do you believe all that *mishegas*, that craziness?"

"Hitler has transformed Germany from a sad, dispirited country into a prosperous one. He has instilled pride in a land still struggling with their humiliating defeat in the Great War. Hitler has achieved that by culling the feeble and the sick, as well as certain minorities that weaken the fabric of his society."

"Like Jews."

"I am not ashamed of my beliefs. We need to make these same hard choices in America. How long are we going to be selective in the breeding of our pigs, chickens, and cattle, but leave the pedigrees of our children to chance?"

"You sound like a spokesman for the eugenics movement."

"Think about it, Giddy. How did this hit-and-miss system of procreation evolve in a progressive society? Sterilization of the unfit is step number one."

"That's quite a speech. How did you manage to overcome your loathing for us Jews long enough to take me to bed, and get me pregnant, and persuade me to spy for you?" Time was ticking away, but I had to ask, hating myself as soon as the words were out of my mouth. "And did you ever care for me?"

"You amused me. I had never met anyone quite like you. I admired your brashness, your resourcefulness, your willingness to take risks. Admiration is as close to love as I ever get."

His words chilled me more than the brisk wind coming off the East River. "You're a monster. You encouraged Ivanov, and now he's about to set fire to this ship and dozens of innocent people will die."

"This wasn't my plan! I had a sensible, workable scheme to assassinate Kaganovich at the embassy reception. Miller ruined it with his stringent security measures. If you analyze it properly, you must conclude that the position we find ourselves in now is Miller's fault."

"So it's Miller's fault that—"

"We've wasted enough time chatting down here. Step aside, Giddy."

There could be only one reason why he was being so frank. He intended to kill me.

In one swift motion, he launched himself into my boat. I grasped the gunwales to steady myself.

Once I got my balance, I said, "I've spoken to Miller and told him everything. He's on his way." Whose pants were on fire now? "If we stop Ivanov together, you can avoid arrest."

Carter took a pistol out of his trouser pocket and motioned to the ladder. It was a small gun, but at close range, it would do the job. "You want to stop Ivanov? Fine, start climbing."

"I intend to."

Carter wasn't as smart as he thought he was. He must have forgotten he gave me a gun. Or maybe he didn't think I would bring it with me. Or more likely, he thought he could wrestle it off me once we were up on deck. Right now, there was nothing to do but to climb.

Above me, the rope ladder swung back and forth. I managed to grab hold of the bottom rung.

"Allow me to give you a boost." Carter pocketed his gun and grabbed me around the waist, half tossing, half lifting me up. I grabbed the side ropes. "I'll be right behind you, so don't try anything cute," he warned.

I started to climb, expecting at any moment a bullet to whoosh past my head from the deck above. But either Ivanov hadn't noticed us or he was too busy turning the ship into a floating incendiary device. And so up I went. *Focus*, I told myself. *Concentrate. Stop trying to calculate who is the greater danger—Ivanov or Carter.* My hands grew stiff from the cold, and when Carter began to climb behind me, they slipped, and I nearly tumbled into the water.

"I'm not sure this old rope will hold both of us," I called down. "Wait for me to get up top before you follow."

I heard him grunt and felt the weight on the ladder lessen. He'd let go. I wasn't dumb enough to look down. I didn't have to. Below me, the blackness of the sea would swallow me in one gulp. Weakness from blood loss, hunger, or nerves, or some combination of the three, turned my knees to jelly and I froze on the ladder.

Ma's voice came to me: "You can do this, tsikele. Try a little harder." I hauled myself up hand over hand, another fifteen rungs, telling myself, *Just take the rungs one at a time, nice and easy.* I heard the sounds of clapping and foot stomping. A balalaika played an old folk tune from my childhood, "Kalinka." It came from belowdecks in steerage. Damn me, if I was going to let all those people die just because of a little pain and dizziness. And double damn me, if I was going to let Carter or Ivanov kill me.

I kept going. When I reached a porthole, I saw a woman with heavily penciled eyebrows applying lipstick in front of a mirror. I could have told her that shade of red was too harsh for her sallow complexion. A man stood behind her. From my position, I couldn't see his face in the mirror, but the porthole was slightly ajar and I could hear them speaking Russian. Not for the first time, I thanked God for the gift of acute hearing. Even so, I could make out only a few words: "Quarantine . . . can't be helped . . . typhus."

Was this Kaganovich and his wife? I hovered for a second, willing them to give me a clue. She didn't oblige, but then he turned toward the window. I drew back before he could see me, but not before I caught a glimpse of his face. It was partly covered in shaving cream, but the heavy brows and a thick head of hair matched the blurry photo I'd seen in the newspaper. This was Kaganovich, without a doubt. He was still alive. I nearly let go of the rope ladder in relief. Why hadn't Ivanov fired at him as he scaled the ladder ahead of me? Such an easy shot. Kaganovich was ten feet from the porthole. All Ivanov had to do was push it open, point, and fire. At this range, he couldn't miss. The reason, I suspected, was that a few minutes ago when Ivanov had been climbing past, he had been in the toilet, lathering his whiskers.

That such an evil man could look so banal, so ordinary, seemed incomprehensible. I considered shouting a warning at them to hide, to get off the boat in any way they could, jump into the harbor if necessary, but I had no time. I had to keep going.

I advanced past their porthole, afraid of being seen, then past the hanging lifeboats. Finally, I reached the top, stopping when I was high enough to peer over the railing. A few feet away, Ivanov was bent over the hatch cover, which was designed like a tic-tac-toe grid with ample spaces for air circulation. The cover was fastened closed with a heavy padlock, and he was tipping the spout of a fuel can through the vents. A hemp rope lay on the ground. From the smell of kerosene in the air, I suspected he had already soaked it, creating a makeshift wick to feed through the hatch cover.

As quietly as I could, I flung myself over the railing and ducked behind the ship's funnel, nearly tripping on a tall, skinny man lying face down on the deck with his head bent at an odd angle. For a panicky moment I thought it was Agent Miller, but this man was younger and more muscular, perhaps a security guard. Whoever he was, he was dead.

From the waterline below came the sound of the ladder banging rhythmically against the side of the ship as Carter began his ascent.

My sides were heaving from the climb. I took a deep breath, then called out in Russian, "Ivanov, I want to talk to you."

The splash of kerosene ceased.

"Who's there?" he said.

"It's me, Giddy."

I heard the capping of his can of kerosene and a thunk as he set it down. "What are you doing here?" His voice was coming closer.

"Anya sent me," I replied.

His footsteps stopped. I had his attention.

"Ivanov, help me to understand. All these innocent people. I understand your hatred for Kaganovich, but the other passengers? What did they ever do to you?"

"No one is innocent. Kaganovich could not have carried out his policy of extermination without their help. They're all Bolsheviks, all Stalin's toadies." His voice was high and shrill.

The music from belowdeck stopped. Someone had smelled the kerosene; there was shouting and pounding on the hatch door. I had to stall, give them time to break free, if they could.

"Anya is terrified," I said. "She has no one in the world except you. If you die, what will happen to her and Svetlana and the baby?"

"This has nothing to do with you. Go now while you can. Don't force me to shoot you."

Instinctively, I went for my gun and felt something else in my pocket, something soft and furry. I was so jittery it took me a second to realize it was Svetlana's rabbit. I pulled it out. Could a plush rabbit unraveling at the seams, stuffing falling out, save all these men, women, and children from burning to a crisp? I had only minutes to make Ivanov see reason before Carter arrived. If I didn't succeed, I had to shoot Ivanov. I stepped out from behind the funnel, holding out the rabbit, my other hand behind my back, grasping the gun. Ivanov straddled the can of kerosene, his pistol raised and pointed at my chest.

"Svetlana gave me her stuffed rabbit. She wanted me to give it to you." It was a stupid thing to say.

"Get out of here. Stop talking nonsense," Ivanov said, but his voice had lost its hard edge. "Take the rabbit back to Sveta. I won't light the rope wick until you are off the ship. I—"

"And what about you? Are you going to go down with the ship? Without you, Yuri, your family will starve." I was sweating despite the freezing air.

"Anya will have money. I have made sure of that. After my death, she will be rich."

I should shoot him while I had the chance. I released the safety catch on my gun, still holding it behind my back, trying to convince myself I could do this. "Mr. Van der Zalm has paid you?"

"If it weren't for Anya and Sveta, I wouldn't take his money. I would do this for the joy of it. He has promised to give Anya one thousand dollars after my death." He was about six feet away, close enough that I could smell the acrid scent of, what, fear? hatred? anger? wafting off him.

"Carter cannot be trusted. He will never give her a dime. He can't risk anything that would connect the two of you. A payment to Anya? Don't make me laugh. He won't even send flowers to your funeral."

Just then, a shot came from about midway up the side of the ship. It was so sharp and so quick I wasn't certain I had actually heard it. Had Carter shot Kaganovich through the porthole? A moment went by, and then more thudding against the hull.

As Ivanov rushed to the side of the ship to see what had happened, Lady Luck decided to pay me a visit. He skidded on a puddle of kerosene. He struggled to regain his footing, arms windmilling around his head, but he lost his fight with gravity and toppled with a thud to the deck. I darted forward. In the dim light I managed to pick out the metallic shine of his gun. I stomped on his wrist until his fingers opened. I kicked the gun out of his reach, then bent down and picked it up. I dropped it into my pocket along with the rabbit.

Carter swung over the railing. "Don't believe her, Ivanov. I am a man of my word, a gentleman. I will take care of Anya. You don't have to worry." Ivanov scrambled to his feet.

From steerage came voices shouting in Russian and Hungarian, muffled, angry shouts from passengers demanding to be released. There was the sound of chopping and the splintering of wood.

"How much has he given you so far, Yuri?" I shouted over the din. "A few dollars? A promise of more? What do you do if he doesn't pay? You'll be dead, and Anya and Sveta will starve. Do you want to take that chance?"

"Yuri, I've got some of your money in my wallet," Carter said. "Let me give it to you. Here, come here, take it. It's yours. You have earned it." He reached for his wallet, but I knew he was going for his gun.

"No!" I yelled as Ivanov stepped toward Carter, hand outstretched.

That was Yuri's first mistake. His second mistake was letting Carter shoot him. Ivanov went down with a scream, clutching his knee.

Carter picked up the saturated piece of hemp rope, then ran toward the hatch cover.

"Are you nuts? What are you doing?" I shrieked. "Put that down. Can't you smell the kerosene?"

Carter ignored me, threading the rope through the hatch cover. Then I saw him take out his gold cigarette lighter. I had no choice. Before he could strike it, I aimed my gun and pulled the trigger. The kick knocked me flat. Carter cried out and stumbled, grabbing his shoulder as he crashed to the deck. His gun went skidding away from me.

I yelled, "Please, somebody help me." I ran to the hatch and yanked at it. The lock held firm. Out of the corner of my eye, I saw Carter crawling along the deck trying to reach his gun.

I ran toward him and kicked his gun out of reach, then went to Ivanov's prone body. "Give me the key, you son of a bitch." When he didn't move, I bent down and thrust my hand in his trouser pocket. I grabbed a bunch of keys. I raced back to the hatch.

After a few failed attempts I found the right key and unfastened the padlock. I tossed it to one side and lifted the hatch cover. A man reeking of kerosene, with a hatchet upraised, crouched below me, about to chop me in two. I hardly recognized him. His clothes were torn, a huge bruise was forming on his forehead, his tie was stained with blood, and his fedora was missing. It was Agent Miller. Behind him were several angry passengers.

"There he is." I pointed to Carter, who was writhing in pain. "I kicked his gun over there."

Within seconds, Miller put handcuffs on Carter and Ivanov. With both men restrained, Miller returned to me.

"Good work, Giddy. I'll take over now." He gently removed the gun from my hand. Ivanov's gun was in my pocket. I gave him that one as well and told him about the dead body near the ship's funnel.

"Ivanov's accomplice or maybe a security guard," I said.

Miller directed a couple of men to stand watch over the body while, across the deck, others tended to Ivanov's and Carter's wounds.

"To say I'm startled to see you is an understatement," I said.

"That message you left at my office? The receptionist at the Secret Service building tracked me to an all-night diner where I often go when I can't sleep. I jumped in my car and raced down here, didn't even wait for backup, which was not the smartest thing I've ever done. But to my credit I did get here first, before you, Ivanov, or Mr. Van der Zalm."

So I had misjudged the nasal-voiced receptionist. She had done her job well. "But how did you get on board? Where is your boat?"

"I borrowed a skiff, or let's say I liberated one, from the wharf. It's moored on the other side of the *Nordvik*. That's why you didn't see it when you arrived. I shinnied up the pilot ladder on the port side."

"Pilot ladder?"

"All ships must have one by law. It's a ladder welded onto the side of a ship so you can board from the load line." He grinned, showing a marvelous set of white teeth.

"Wish I'd known about that handy-dandy little nautical convenience an hour ago. It would have saved me a lot of aggravation. But how did you get trapped down below?"

"I was guarding Kaganovich, positioned right outside his stateroom. All of a sudden, a man appeared, probably the poor bastard who got shot, and held a gun to my head. He frog-marched me into the hold with the other passengers."

I remembered the shot. "Is Kaganovich all right?"

"These Russkies are tough," Miller answered. "He's not only alive, he's full of complaints about the lack of security. Was that Ivanov who fired through the porthole?"

"No, Carter. He fired at Kaganovich as he climbed up the side."

"That crazy son of a bitch, pardon my French." Miller glanced at Carter, who was holding his shoulder as a couple of men loaded him onto a stretcher they'd fashioned. "We've been onto Mr. Van der Zalm for a long time. I'd just didn't have the evidence to arrest him. I'd hoped Van der Zalm would do or say something at the Lobster Bay meeting to give himself away, but he's a smooth customer. But ballistics will be able to identify his bullet, which is probably embedded in the wall of Kaganovich's stateroom. I'm going to charge Van der Zalm with conspiracy to murder, attempted murder, treason, sedition, and any other damn thing I can think of. We'll need your testimony, too."

"Just tell me when and where."

"I was hoping you'd say that, but I wasn't sure, because I know you and Mr. Van der Zalm were . . . involved. I have to admit, when we met in Lobster Bay, I figured you for part of his scheme. I apologize for that. We at the Secret Service are indebted to you, Giddy."

"Apology accepted."

"And don't worry about shooting Mr. Van der Zalm. He'll survive. It looks like just a flesh wound to the shoulder."

"I should have centered the shot better and aimed lower down."

He began to laugh, then stopped at the sight of Kaganovich emerging from the hatch, a patch of white shaving cream decorating his chin. His eyes skimmed the deck and landed on Ivanov. Someone must have told him what happened. Cursing in Russian, he marched over to Ivanov and kicked his prone body. There was the sickening crunch of Ivanov's cheekbone. Ivanov let out a cry.

Kaganovich raised his foot for another blow, but I ran over and put a hand on his arm. "That's enough. Let him be."

Miller was right beside me. "Sir, you're out of line. Do that again and I'll arrest you for assault. The Secret Service will be formally charging Ivanov, and we need him in one piece so we can interrogate him."

Kaganovich looked baffled until I translated for him.

Miller nodded at me to continue. "You're a very fortunate man, Mr. Kaganovich. This young lady saved your life."

Kaganovich extended his hand. I ignored it. He thanked me profusely.

"Tell it to the marines," I said, not bothering to translate into Russian. I didn't want his thanks. I couldn't even look at him. Instead I strode over to where Carter lay shivering on his stretcher. Beneath him, a pool of blood was spreading on the deck. I crouched down so he could hear every word.

"Miller will see to it that you are sent away for the rest of your life. And I'll be star witness for the prosecution. You'll find me anything but 'expendable.'"

Carter didn't respond. He was white with shock, but his eyes were open.

The stretcher-bearers shifted him and he screamed in pain.

Miller reappeared by my side. I felt no pity for Carter as the men lowered him over the side of the ship and onto a Secret Service launch, which had just pulled alongside the *Nordvik*.

"You should feel very proud for the work you've done for your country, Giddy," Miller said, "America might get drawn into the war in Europe, but you have delayed that day. And for that, I thank you. I've got a twenty-year-old son." He adjusted his fedora. "One of these days, I'll drop by your shop, pick up a jar of cream for the wife."

I smiled. For the first time in a long while, the weight was lifted from my shoulders. I felt at peace. I had gotten out of a jam, saved the lives of two men, dozens of passengers, a rusty old Russian freighter, and my self-respect.

Not too shabby for a night's work.

# Chapter 31

———◇———

*Giddy's Creams and Lotions, New York*

Two weeks later, I was at the cash register ringing up sales when a woman wearing a pin-striped suit and a rather rakish men's porkpie hat squeezed her way through the dozens of customers in my shop. When she reached me, she started to introduce herself, but I held up my hand to stop her. "You're Pushy McCoy." Pushy was a reporter for the *Post*. She was a career gal like me.

She laughed. "And you're the famous snoop everyone is talking about, Gitel Brodsky."

"At your service."

Pushy wasn't the first and wouldn't be the last reporter to drop in for an interview. The newspapers couldn't get enough of the capture of the "Russian secret agent," as they called Ivanov, and his collaboration with "the highfalutin Nazi" Carter Van der Zalm IV. To top it off, there were plenty of headlines about the mysterious "Gitel Brodsky, a humble yet exceedingly brave shopkeeper from the slums of the Lower East Side who brought them to justice." I didn't like my neighborhood described as a slum, nor me being described as humble. It seemed so—here was an excellent use for the word—patronizing, but complaining I wasn't. The publicity was swell for business.

Every woman in New York, even the socialites from Fifth Avenue, were dying to catch a glimpse of me. My store was jam-packed morning, noon, and night with busybodies jostling to gape at me. My cream, which I had renamed "the Secret Agent," was flying off the shelves. The new label was a sketch of me scaling the hull of the *Nordvik*. It was a famous book written by a Pole named Joseph Conrad. Sales had been fantastic.

"Can I ask you a few questions?" Pushy asked.

"Of course." I called to Hattie to relieve me on cash.

I'd needed more help, and to my surprise, Hattie had volunteered. She got bored at home during the week when she wasn't kibitzing with the spirit world at Sid's. She claimed the jazz club was no fun since I'd quit to work full-time in the store. The new cigarette girl who'd taken my place didn't have my "investigative skills." So one or two days a week, she amused herself by working here.

We'd patched up our relationship last week over a couple of drinks. Since neither of us had any loyalty to Carter, I finally pried out of her what her readings with him were all about. Turns out, one of her other customers was a "hot walker" at Aqueduct Racetrack. A hot walker, she had explained, is a stable hand who walks the thoroughbreds after a race to cool them down. Apparently barn scuttlebutt was a valuable commodity. He gave Hattie tips on promising long shots, and she passed these on to Carter and other "privileged clients."

As a salesgirl, Hattie wasn't a success, not like Ma, who had turned out to be a natural. Hattie scowled, insulted customers, and was rude to the occasional lookie-loos who never opened their pocketbooks except to dump in free samples. She had no talent for small talk or flattery whatsoever. When she was not on cash, she hobbled around the store, pickle-faced, refusing to smile. But she was good with the money, so I kept her on the register, out of harm's way.

Pushy and I settled down in the back room of the shop, where

I'd set up a kitchenette with a couple of chairs, a table, and a coffee percolator.

"Giddy, you averted an international incident and saved countless lives. I don't think it's an accident the Russian foreign minister Molotov and his German counterpart, Ribbentrop, are now a lot closer to finalizing a nonaggression pact. They say Kaganovich is recommending the idea to Stalin."

"Yes, I read that, too."

"You should be proud of yourself."

I was. The newspapers also said the arms sale didn't go through. The secretary of state sent Kaganovich whistling for his fourteen million dollars' worth of US armaments.

"I am," I said.

Pushy was scribbling down my every word on her steno pad. "There's talk of Mayor La Guardia presenting you with a medal for bravery."

"If only he knew how scared I was climbing up that old freighter."

"My advice?" Pushy put a finger to her lips. "Don't tell him."

"I suppose you're going to ask how I feel about testifying at Mr. Van der Zalm's trial," I said.

It was what all the reporters wanted to know. When he was questioned by the Secret Service, Carter claimed the best way to keep America out of the war was to isolate Russia, encourage Hitler to invade, and in that way, stamp out communism, which he saw as a greater threat than fascism. But he still pretended to be the hero, describing how he attacked Ivanov, thwarted the assassination of Kaganovich, and prevented the destruction of the *Nordvik*. He said my hatred for Ivanov was pathological because of what he did to my family in Russia and that I wanted him to burn with the ship. And as for me shooting him? His argument was "Hell hath no fury like a woman scorned." When the prosecutor and Agent Miller interviewed me, I set them straight. To my surprise, the prosecutor believed me. Me—a poor immigrant girl from the tenements—over Carter, a blue blood from Park Avenue. It helped that Miller's forensic team found Carter's bullet in Kaganovich's cabin. Carter was being charged with everything Miller promised that night on the ship. His trial was set for two months from now, to give him time to recover from his gunshot wound.

"For the record," I told Pushy, "I'm looking forward to the trial. They say he'll get a life sentence."

"Actually, I'd like to explore the human-interest angle. You and Ivanov. You're both from the same region in Russia, aren't you? Your family fled the country because of a pogrom. Was Ivanov involved? I know he was a Cossack."

Pushy was perceptive. I could see why they called her "the Bloodhound." I had to be careful with what I said. I finally knew the truth of what happened nineteen years ago, but it was a story filled with hurt and betrayal. Ivanov was already a criminal in the eyes of the law. In addition to an attempted-mass-murder charge, he had confessed to killing his accomplice—turns out the dead man I'd nearly tripped over on the deck was a "pal" from the Free Russia group who had become a liability. Right now, Anya needed to be protected.

She'd given birth early, but the baby was fine, a healthy girl. It had been hard for Anya to accept that the man she had married in good faith was a killer, but Ma and I assured her she wasn't alone. It wasn't her fault what Ivanov had done. Ma and I helped out with Svetlana and little Natasha as best we could, and I'd offered Anya some part-time work at the shop once the baby was weaned. Ma promised to look after the children when Anya attended night school classes to improve her English. Anya had signed up for a bookkeeping course in the fall. Under that lovely exterior, Anya was tough as a Siberian winter. She was well on her way to forging a new life for herself.

"I'd prefer not to talk about my life in Russia. It was a long time ago and I'm an American now."

Ma came into the kitchenette.

"Pushy, this is my ma. I owe everything to her."

Ma blushed and went over to the counter to fix me a tuna on rye.

"Nice to meet you, Mrs. Brodsky," Pushy said, then turned back to me. "Your father is here in New York, too, do I have that right?"

"My father is dead," I said. The lie felt truer now than it had before. "But I have a brother, Arnold, who was born here. He's going to City College this fall."

She jotted that down. "Do you still have family back in Russia?"

Ma and I exchanged a glance. Ma had said she'd never heard back from Bekka, but I'd sent a letter of my own, just last week. I hoped I would hear from her. To Pushy, I simply replied, "I lost contact with them years ago."

We chatted for a while longer. Pushy snapped a couple of photos of me standing in front of my shelves stacked with lovely jars and one with me and Ma. Then she exited the store with a jaunty wave, off to pound out her article. I loved this kind of attention because, as I had discovered, I was a real ham. Being famous was the best thing that had ever happened to me. The fact that it wouldn't last made it more delicious.

I headed back to the little kitchenette to eat my sandwich. I'd bought Ma a new Philco, top of the line, then brought her old one into the store. It was playing in the background as I sat down. I had taken one bite when Hattie told me there was someone here to see me. I went out front and, to my surprise, saw Morty with a thick textbook under his arm.

"Hello, Giddy," he said.

"Nice to see you," I replied. And it was. His neatly trimmed dark hair, navy wool cardigan with tortoiseshell buttons, and khaki trousers gave him an attractive bookish look.

"I was in the neighborhood, just coming from an obstetrics class at NYU. I thought I'd drop in to see how you were doing since I was so close by. Maybe I'll pick up some jars of cream for my mother and sisters."

"I'm very glad you did," I said. Such a lousy liar he was. The NYU campus was way uptown. I was pleased and touched—yes, that was the word—that he came to the store, just like I had been touched when I was dizzy in his office and he put my shoes on for me.

He smiled. "Do you have time to talk? I have something for you."

"Sure, I'm just having my lunch. Why don't you join me? I've got half a tuna on rye with your name on it."

"My favorite," he said, following me to the kitchenette.

I gestured to a chair and he sat, placing his book on the table. The title was *Diseases of the Neonate.* So he really was a doctor. I was curious what he had for me, but all I could see was white paper sticking out of his sweater pocket.

When he pushed up his black spectacles with his index finger, I realized I had underestimated him. Sure, he wasn't a looker like Carter, but he was well-built, had big brown eyes, and had a sincere smile. Plus, I suspected he had something Carter would never have—a good character and a kind heart.

"I've been reading about you in the papers," he said. "There have been so many articles. And that photograph of you posing in front of the *Nordvik?* Gorgeous. Well, you *are* gorgeous. How does it feel to be a celebrity?"

No one had ever described me as gorgeous before. "It's great for business. As you can see . . ." I pictured the shoppers lined up to get in the door. The cash register—bought secondhand—jingled.

Morty took a bite of sandwich and licked his fingers, trying to keep the mayonnaise off his tie. "You've been through a lot, but you have landed on your feet."

"I've finally got the store making money, but it's funny. I used to believe that lots of dough would make my life perfect. Now I know it doesn't. Money only saves you from doing things you don't want to do, like sewing on buttons in a sweatshop eighty hours a week, or giving Buffalo handshakes to customers at Sid's Paradise."

I shouldn't have mentioned Buffalo handshakes. I didn't want him to get the wrong impression, but nothing seemed to discombobulate Morty. He merely licked a piece of tuna off his fingers.

"You've had a rough time, but you've survived."

"Now I have to survive the surviving."

"That's a good way to put it."

Just then, *Our Gal Sunday* came on the radio. "Once again, we present *Our Gal Sunday*, the story of an orphan girl named Sunday from a small mining town of Silver Creek, Colorado, who married England's richest, most handsome lord, Lord Henry Brinthrope."

I got up and switched it off. "Such malarkey, I can't listen to it." I stacked our empty plates next to Ma's old radio.

"Not a romantic, I take it." After a pause, he continued, "This is none of my business, but do you still care for Van der Zalm?"

I made a gesture like I was throwing salt over my shoulder to ward off the evil eye. "God, no. We're *kaputski*, finished, history."

"Just checking."

"I can't decide whether I suffered a broken heart or if it was just injured pride at being used so callously."

"How do you tell the difference?"

I should have laughed at that comment but decided to be honest with Morty. "I feel disillusioned. I don't miss Carter, but I miss the idea of him, if you know what I mean. I miss believing that love exists, that I will fall in love again. But I can't take any more risks. I can't go through more heartbreak. You'd feel the same way if you'd had my experience."

I shouldn't be saying such personal things to a man I hardly knew, but I felt like I'd known him all my life.

"I've had my heart broken a few times, too, but . . ." He wiped his mouth with his hanky. "Giddy, you know what? I'm going to be a pretty good doctor. I can even fix broken hearts."

"They teach this in medical school?"

"They do. The *Journal of Recent Studies* has published an article that proves conclusively that a Broadway play, plus dinner after the show, is a surefire cure for both a broken heart and injured pride."

"That's backed up by research?"

"Trust me."

"I like you, Morty."

He smiled. "The reason I dropped in . . . is this." He took out two slips of paper from his pocket and fanned them out like playing cards. "Do you enjoy musicals?"

"Is the chief rabbi of New York Jewish?"

"I have in my hand two theater tickets for *Anything Goes* at the Alvin Theatre on Broadway for tonight. Ethel Merman? Cole Porter? He's your favorite, right? What do you say?"

He remembered. This was a kind and thoughtful man. I needed such a man. "I say yes."

Morty's face lit up. "That's settled, then. I'll pick you up here at six."

"Can't wait," I replied, and I meant it.

Morty gave a funny little bow and said goodbye, but not before buying a jar of cream for his sister. As I watched him walk out into the fall sunshine, a feeling of lightness, and the joy of a new beginning, came over me.

# Author's Note

———◈———

It's very inconvenient, but a great deal of history has played out without regard for the needs of the historical novelist. For example, as far I am aware, Lazar Kaganovich, first deputy premier of the Soviet Union, never visited the US to borrow money and arms for the defense of Russia (or for any other reason). The Molotov-Ribbentrop Pact was signed August 23, 1939. Apparently, few knew of the pact until it was formally signed. Stalin approved the agreement to buy himself time so that he could accelerate the Soviet production of tanks, planes, and artillery. And so it is unlikely that Arnold or any of the other characters would have been aware the pact was in the offing. But in the interests of plot, I have given them this information.

There is another liberty I have taken that I hope the reader will forgive. The letter from Wilfred Risdon, who was a real person, contains top-secret information regarding the Molotov-Ribbentrop Pact. Since few knew of the pact, it is highly doubtful this information would have been disclosed to Oswald Mosley.

# Sources

I have read many entertaining and informative books in the course of researching life on the Lower East Side prior to World War II. Some of the most helpful and entertaining were:

*A Woman in Berlin: Eight Weeks in the Conquered City* by Anonymous
*Walking in the Garden of Souls* by George Anderson and Andrew Barone
*The Happiest Man: The Life of Louis Borgenicht as Told to Harold Friedman* by Louis Borgenicht
*Out of the Shadow: A Russian Jewish Girlhood on the Lower East Side* by Rose Cohen
*Daughters of the Shtetl: Life and Labor in the Immigrant Generation* by Susan A. Glenn
*Jews without Money* by Michael Gold
*World of Our Fathers: The Journey of the East European Jews to America and the Life They Found and Made* by Irving Howe
*A Bintel Brief: Sixty Years of Letters from the Lower East Side to the "Jewish Daily Forward,"* edited by Isaac Metzker, with a foreword by Harry Golden
*Up in the Old Hotel, and Other Stories* by Joseph Mitchell
*A Living Lens: Photographs of Jewish Life from the Pages of the "Forward,"* edited by Alana Newhouse, with an introduction by Pete Hamill
*The Promised City: New York's Jews, 1870–1914* by Moses Rischin
*The Time That Was Then: The Lower East Side, 1900–1913—An Intimate Chronicle* by Harry Roskolenko
*Streets: A Memoir of the Lower East Side* by Bella Spewack
*Bread Givers* by Anzia Yezierska
*97 Orchard: An Edible History of Five Immigrant Families in One New York Tenement* by Jane Ziegelman

# Acknowledgments

This book would not have been possible without the support and encouragement of many friends. In particular, I wish to thank the following:

My Vancouver writer friends: Caroline Adderson, Mary Burns, Janie Chang, Claudia Casper, Leslie Howard, June Hutton, Shaena Lambert, Claire Mulligan, and Mary Novik. And a special thanks to my Mexico writer friends, Rachel McMillan, Keira Morgan, and Emerson Nagel, generous readers, and gentle critics all. To quote from *Charlotte's Web* by E. B. White, "It is not often that someone comes along who is a true friend and a good writer." And it is even rarer to have such a large group of friends who are both.

I also thank Marcia Jacobs, who gave me advice on the psychological effects of rape, and Brenda Yablon, who gave advice on Yiddish expressions.

And to Beverley Slopen, my persistent and extraordinary agent, who has been a stalwart supporter of my work for many years, always faithful, always steadfast, always encouraging.

I feel immense gratitude toward my daughter's grandparents, Lillian and Gershon Hundert, who lived the immigrant life in New York. As I wrote, their wit, humor, and dignity in the face of hardship was often in my thoughts although they have been dead for many years. May they rest in peace.

The staff at Simon & Schuster, most particularly my patient and insightful editor, Sarah St. Pierre, the Jimmy Jinx of manuscript repair. Not only can she pinpoint what's wrong with plot, prose, and character, but she knows how to fix it. What a gift.

And to Ken, the love of my life, my friend, lover, sommelier, chef, handyman, navigator, travel companion, fellow adventurer, and true-blue husband. Still crazy with you in love after all these years.

# The Jazz Club Spy

Roberta Rich

A READING GROUP GUIDE

This reading group guide for The Jazz Club Spy *includes an intro-*
*duction, discussion questions, and ideas for enhancing your book*
*club. The suggested questions are intended to help your reading group*
*find new and interesting angles and topics for your discussion. We*
*hope that these ideas will enrich your conversation and increase your*
*enjoyment of the book.*

# Introduction

In this riveting historical thriller, #1 bestselling author Roberta Rich
paints the vibrant portrait of a Jewish cigarette girl in 1930s New
York who finds the soldier who burned down her Russian village
years earlier only to be swept up in a political conspiracy on the eve
of World War II.

# Topics and Questions for Discussion

1. Discuss the friendship between Giddy and Hattie. What binds
   them together, and what comes between them?

2. Giddy would say that she has a skeptical, even cynical nature.
   Do you think that's true? What examples illustrate or contradict
   her self-assessment?

3. Giddy, Ma, and Pa are all traumatized from the pogrom. How does their trauma haunt them and shape their actions? Do you think Giddy suffers from survivor's guilt? Who else in the novel experiences trauma?

4. How does Giddy's childhood in Russia affect her life in New York? How does she describe the reality of being an immigrant, and what does she think of the American dream?

5. Giddy experiences more opportunities in America than her mother did in Russia, especially when it comes to career and romance. Compare and contrast their situations. What challenges do they both still face as women?

6. Giddy reflects, "They say that in America the children bring up the parents, but that's only half-true. The children also bring up each other" (pg. 32). Discuss the relationship between Arnold and Giddy.

7. Why do you think Giddy falls in love with Carter Van der Zalm? Do you think Carter ever had true feelings for Giddy? Were the two using each other?

8. What do you know of the Nazi movement in America? Do you see a connection between the German American Bund and present-day organizations, such as the Proud Boys and the Oath Keepers?

9. Giddy is terrified to have an abortion because she knows someone who died of a back-alley abortion. Consider the various perspectives the characters in the novel have on abortion. Why do they hold the beliefs they do? How do their opinions differ or align with current views?

10. Giddy initially believes that catching the Cossack would heal her ma and repair her broken family, but what conclusion does she ultimately come to? Discuss the idea of revenge and how it's explored through Giddy's and Yuri Ivanov's characters. Do you think revenge can be healing for a person, in this novel and in real life?

11. When Giddy learns what Pa did to Bekka, she thinks, "In my heart, I sat shiva for him" (pg. 238). In other words, she considers him dead. Do you believe that their relationship could be rebuilt in the future?

12. Consider the theme of forgiveness in the novel. Who forgives whom, and why?

13. When Giddy climbs up the side of the *Nordvik*, what do you think motivates her more—the love of her country, her hatred for the Cossack, or her anger at Carter's betrayal?

14. Do you think Giddy makes the right decision in saving Kaganovich, a man who was responsible for the murders of thousands? Or should she have let Ivanov assassinate him? What would you have done if you were her?

15. How does Giddy change over the course of the novel? Do you think she has learned from her experiences? There is a Russian expression, "The same heat that melts butter hardens steel" (pg. 7). Which do you think Giddy is—butter or steel?

16. Consider Morty's character. What does he offer Giddy that Carter doesn't? What kind of future might Giddy have with Morty?

17. Before reading the novel, how familiar were you with the politics and realities of pre–World War II America? Did you learn any new historical details?

# Enhance Your Book Club

1. For a glimpse of what life would have been like for Giddy in New York's Lower East Side working-class tenement dwellings, check out *Insider*'s guided tour of 97 Orchard Street, formerly a tenement building and now one of the sites of the Tenement Museum: https://www.youtube.com/watch?v=XZohCshF0Yg. For more information about the Tenement Museum, including access to digital exhibits and additional resources covering over one hundred years of history, visit their website here: https://www.tenement.org/.

2. Read about the rise of jazz music in America, from New Orleans to Chicago to New York's jazz scene on 52nd Street in this *Medium* article, featuring an in-depth look at Birdland, a 1950s-era jazz club: https://medium.com/@birdlandjazz/how-new-york-became-the-jazz-capital-of-america-c4495fc34c67.

3. If you're interested in learning about Ellis Island and the more than twelve million immigrants who passed through its "Golden Door" between 1892 and 1954, explore detailed time lines, discover interesting facts, and research your own history with The Statue of Liberty–Ellis Island Foundation and History.com: https://www.statueofliberty.org/ellis-island/overview-history/ and https://www.statueofliberty.org/discover/ as well as History.com. You can also view archival footage of Ellis Island in Charles Guggenheim's moving documentary *Island of Hope, Island of Tears* (1989): https://archive.org/details/gov.ntis.ava15996vnbl.